12
DRUMMERS
DRUMMING

12
DRUMMERS
DRUMMING

a novel of suspense

DIANA DEVERELL

AVON BOOKS ◆ NEW YORK

c·1

This is a work of fiction. Names, characters, places,
and incidents either are the product of the author's
imagination or are used fictitiously. Any resemblance
to actual events, locales, organizations, or persons,
living or dead, is entirely coincidental and beyond
the intent of either the author or the publisher.

AVON BOOKS, INC.
1350 Avenue of the Americas
New York, New York 10019

Copyright © 1998 by Diana Deverell
Interior design by Kellan Peck
Visit our website at **http://www.AvonBooks.com**
ISBN: 0-380-97610-2

Library of Congress Cataloging in Publication Data:

Deverell, Diana
    12 drummers drumming / Diana Deverell.
        p. cm.
    I. Title. II. Title: Twelve drummers drumming.
    PS3554.E92734A614 1998   97-44188
    813'.54—dc21   CIP

First Avon Books Printing: August 1998

AVON TRADEMARK REG. U.S. PAT. OFF. AND IN OTHER COUNTRIES, MARCA REGISTRADA,
HECHO EN U.S.A.

Printed in the U.S.A.

FIRST EDITION

QPM   10   9   8   7   6   5   4   3   2   1

FOR MOGENS PEDERSEN

ACKNOWLEDGMENTS

I am boundlessly grateful to the New Writers of the Purple Page—Lynn Daniels Anderson, Benjamin Chambers, Nancy Carol Moody, Amedee Smith, and Don Stahl. Better critics, coaches, and friends do not exist.

I am also indebted to the Warsaw Attaché Reunion for much of the Belgian and German material that found its way into this book. I particularly want to thank Cyriel and Rachel Moelans for sharing their experiences in Antwerp and Africa and for reviewing an early draft. Thanks also to John and Sheila Pugh, who guided me to Potsdam and Meissen.

A special thank-you to Zofia Rostkowska-Menasria, who helped me with my Polish.

These fine people gave me correct information. Any mistakes are mine alone.

Without the kindness and generosity of the following women this book could not have been written: Candace Berra, Molly Brann, Patricia Butenis, Marilyn Curtis, Elizabeth Engstrom, Casey Gardner, Valerie Huebner, Susan Kolander, Kathryn Marzano, Jenny Smith, and Marian Kingsley Smith.

Nancy Yost is a literary agent to die for. At Avon Books, Trish Lande Grader and Jennifer Sawyer Fisher brought the book to life. All first-time novelists should be so lucky.

AUTHOR'S NOTE

When I was a Foreign Service Officer, I always traveled by air. On my way to spend Christmas of 1988 with family in Denmark, I crossed the Atlantic one day before the Lockerbie airline disaster. I was flying east, not west, and was never in danger of being a passenger on Pan Am Flight 103. Yet I felt imperiled. The bomb wasn't on my plane—but it could have been placed there easily. I'd been lucky. Nearly a decade later, whenever I board an international flight I find myself hoping my luck will hold.

The people and terrorist incidents in this novel spring from my imagination. But underlying the fictional events are historical facts. Sad facts, some of them. Two agents of Libyan intelligence were charged with blowing up Pan Am 103. As of this writing, they haven't been brought to trial.

Preventing terrorist acts is difficult work. This story was inspired by my admiration for the people who take on that job.

—Diana Deverell
February 20, 1997

ACRONYMS, LEADERS AND ORGANIZATIONS

Abu Nidal Organization (ANO)—terrorist group headed by Abu Nidal; ANO's campaign against Western targets in the mid-1980s included massacres in Vienna and Rome airports and the LaBelle Disco bombing in West Berlin. The collapse of the Berlin Wall at the end of the decade deprived ANO of "safe" territories from which it could launch its attacks in Europe. Now based in Libya, ANO has concentrated its violent assaults on targets in Israel and moderate Palestinian organizations

CIA—U.S. Central Intelligence Agency

DDIS—Danish Defense Intelligence Service

DIA—U.S. Department of Defense, Defense Intelligence Agency

EUR—State Department's Bureau of European and Canadian Affairs

GDR—German Democratic Republic, formerly East Germany

GSG-9, Grenz Schutz Gruppe—German counterterrorism unit

HVA, Hauptverwaltung Aufklärung—the now-defunct foreign intelligence branch of the old East German Stasi

INR—State Department's Bureau of Intelligence and Research

Mossad—Israeli intelligence

NATO—North Atlantic Treaty Organization

NTSB—National Transportation and Safety Board, charged with investigation of airline disasters

PFLP-GC—Popular Front for the Liberation of Palestine—General Command, terrorist group headed by Ahmed Jibril

Colonel Muammar Qadhafi—leader of Libya; supporter of Abu Nidal and his organization

SB, Sluzba Bezpieczenstwa—intelligence service of Communist Poland

S/CT—State Department's Coordinator for Counterterrorism

Stasi—Ministry of State Security in the former East Germany

Warsaw Pact—East Bloc counterpart of NATO

12
DRUMMERS
DRUMMING

1

Only two o'clock in the afternoon, but it was the twenty-seventh of December and dusk had fallen in Denmark. The corner tower of Kronborg Castle was stark against the bruised sky. Slivers of icy wind pierced my down jacket. A strand of blond hair pulled free from my knitted cap, whipped across my eyes, forced out tears. A sob escaped me, too. The wind snatched the sound away, silencing my fear but not dulling the ache in my heart. I shoved my hair under the cap and stumbled on. I had to. Up ahead waited the only person who could tell me that Stefan Krajewski was still alive.

And he had to be! Stefan, my lover, had to be alive.

Just four months before, he'd said too many people knew that he was doing contract work for Danish intelligence. He'd spent close to twenty years in covert operations and his time was up. Soon, he'd told me at the beginning of August, he'd move inside.

And he'd move in with me. We'd been in the Allegheny Mountains when he said that. I'd saved up my annual leave, rented a cabin near Clifton Forge for the month of August. The two of us, one bed, no phone for an unheard-of thirty-one consecutive days. And I must have thought thirty-one times—at least once a day—*This is what it will be like*. Coffee-drenched mornings, sharing a newspaper. Late-afternoon beers, talking over the minutiae of daily life. Evening strolls down to the lake to see if the beavers were having a moonlight swim.

With my body and my soul, I'd loved Stefan for more than a decade, my passion for him never wavering even though we were often separated by the work he did. When we were together, we had everything we needed for happiness—except time. Finally, we'd have that, too. The urgency gone, so many hours stretching out before us, we could squander them. That was how I wanted things to be. My cherished fantasy, shattered now by reality.

Six days ago, a plane had exploded over Scotland. *Another plane over Scotland!* Global Flight 500 had departed Heathrow on December 21, bound for New York's Kennedy Airport. It came apart a half hour later over the Inner Hebrides Islands. And Stefan had disappeared.

I neared the corner of the castle and a row of ancient cannons took shape. The fortress hulked beside me, Denmark's easternmost defense for six centuries. Through the gloom I made out the tall figure of Holger Sorensen, cloaked in a Danish Army parka, standing with his back to the sea. I walked faster, scattering frozen pebbles beneath my boots.

I stopped a yard from him. He was a head taller than my five feet nine and I had to tilt my chin up to see his face. The lines along his cheekbones had deepened since our last meeting. His eyes had faded from blue to gray. And the smile was gone from them, replaced by the consoling expression of a priest prepared to mourn the dead.

I stepped past him, stared unseeing across the water toward the Swedish coastline.

Holger's gloved hand was heavy on my shoulder. In a voice weighted with sorrow, he said, "Kathryn."

I'd forgotten Holger always addressed me by my Christian name. These days my friends and colleagues called me by my initials, K.C., and I wrote it as "Casey." The only other person who still used "Kathryn" was my father. And only when he was going to give me bad news.

To stop Holger's next words, I said quickly, "I've seen the passenger list." I took a breath, pushed on. "Stefan's name wasn't on it. He knew Monday was the anniversary of Lockerbie. He wouldn't have flown an American carrier on Monday." I was breathing hard, as if I'd been running. My fingertips moved jerkily along the frost-rimed barrel of a cannon.

Holger didn't speak.

I said, "We warned everyone in the Department not to fly American carriers out of Europe last week."

Holger's voice was soft. "Did you tell Stefan that?"

"I couldn't." Anguish raised my voice still higher. I took another breath. "I didn't have a chance."

He said, "Nor did I."

The mournful cry of an air horn cut through the darkness. The ferryboat was visible a hundred yards offshore, its white hull wallowing toward the docks at Helsingør. A lone seabird rose from the stony beach below us.

Holger said, "It was some time ago you and Stefan made plans that he would join you in Washington for Christmas?"

"October." And stingy fate had doled out only eighteen hours that time.

"You made definite plans?"

"Tentative, of course. Two weeks ago, he sent word to expect him on the twenty-second."

"But you haven't spoken with him since October?"

"He never used phones."

"And when he didn't show up?" Holger asked.

"I knew his trip to the U.S. was no vacation. A lot of things might have delayed him a day. Even two days."

"So at first you didn't blame his absence on the explosion?"

"At first? No." I'd started my Christmas vacation on December 21, on leave from my job at the State Department. When the news started coming in about Global Flight 500, I was sticking bows on a gift for Stefan, a pair of cowboy boots I'd bought from a Western outfitter who sold to real ranch hands. I'd kept an eye on the TV while I struggled to wrap the matching Stetson. Polish by birth, Stefan was smitten with Western regalia.

As I waited for him to contact me, my mind slowly recorded every piece of film from the Hebrides. Long-lens shots of the motley rescue flotilla that had set out from every harbor on the island of Islay. A terse interview with an exhausted diver, his wet suit glistening like black ice. A somber view of the distillery warehouse serving as a makeshift morgue, aged oak barrels stacked against a stone wall. And above it all—again—the ash-gray sky of Scotland in December.

The explosion hadn't occurred over Scottish soil. The Boeing 747 and all two hundred and twenty-seven aboard submerged in the Firth of Lorne, one hundred and fifty miles northwest of the original disaster. But the words spoken by every newscaster were the same: Lockerbie Two.

Holger's voice prodded me. "But you got no message from Stefan and you feared the worst."

I turned, still avoiding Holger's eyes, studying Kronborg Castle. The weathered bricks were topped by a roof the color of new grass, eerily bright against the murk. I repeated the last word he'd spoken. "The worst. Yes."

On the twenty-third, I called the airline but they wouldn't release information to me. Frantic, I phoned my contact in TIP-OFF, the Department's terrorist lookout program, and she faxed me the passenger list for Global 500. Half the names were of men traveling alone. Any one of them might have been Stefan, working under cover. Too upset to face my co-workers in the office of State's Coordinator for Counterterrorism, I waited until after hours to go to the Department and log on to Intelink, the intelligence community's private Internet. I spent four hours searching electronically. I found only speculation. There was too little data to determine yet if Stefan had been on the plane. I knew I should stay by my phone, wait for his call.

I drifted around my three rooms, carefully evading the packages still sitting on my desk. Christmas Eve came. I moved Stefan's gifts to my bedroom. Then to the back of my closet, out of sight. But, awake before dawn on Christmas morning, I saw that white hat. Saw Stefan, grinning from under it, flamboyant attire no hazard in the life we should have been living.

I met Holger's gaze. "As you said. I feared the worst. I figured you and I needed to talk."

"You traveled to me."

He'd been my teacher once. I answered his unspoken question, my voice flat, parroting a lecture on evasive maneuvers. "Christmas morning I went to Dulles and got an Air France flight to Paris. Changed planes three times between Paris and Gøteborg. Rented a car, drove south and crossed to Denmark on the ferry yesterday. Went through that whole business to get you out here today."

Holger's compassionate look was gone, the sudden clarity like a tempered steel gate, clanging shut. The Major—the part of him that served as a reserve officer in the Danish Army—had pushed aside the Father—the side of Holger that made it possible for him to also serve as a Lutheran priest. He said, "Go home. There's nothing you can do here."

"I'm staying. Till we find out what's become of Stefan."

"We can't pursue this further. Stefan was checking on another development, one also related to the Lockerbie anniversary. That investigation is at a critical point. We must proceed delicately. My arrangement with Stefan required that he work autonomously. I don't know yet what identity he assumed. Nor do I know the names of his contacts, or his destination. Were it not for you, I would not be certain he had headed for the U.S."

"Maybe he suddenly went someplace else."

"Without advising you? Not likely."

I looked down, my boots a darker shade of black than the stony ground. Stefan and I had secure ways to communicate.

He knew how much I'd worry. If he were alive, he'd have found a way to tell me.

Holger gripped my upper arms. "We cannot alert anyone to the direction in which our interests lie. My people will keep their distance from the wreckage of Global Flight 500. So must you. You must return at once to Washington."

"Not until I know—"

"When was the last time you slept? The last time you ate?" His voice was harsh and he tightened his grip. "I feel only bones."

"I've always been lanky," I said.

"Slender, yes. But not this. Your face is so thin, you must have lost five kilos since I saw you last."

"So I'll eat something. I'm fine, Holger. I can help—"

"You can't. You left a trail easily read by anyone who wishes to know where you've been."

I pulled away from him, turned toward the sea. Only the whitecaps were visible. The cold enveloped me completely. I smelled nothing and didn't taste the salt coating my lips. "I had to see you—"

"And I put a great deal at risk so that you could. But it is unfortunate that your journey ends only kilometers from my own parish."

"Stefan was on his way to me. If he's dead . . ." I swallowed, tried again. "I hunt terrorists. That's my job. What I do. If they've killed Stefan . . ." I took a deep breath, made my voice hard as Holger's. "I have to stay. Have to work with you."

His face was marble. Unyielding. "You can't remain in Europe. You're not safe here." His eyes took on that steely expression again and he said, "You leave first. Drive to Kastrup and fly back to Washington."

Rage welled up in me and its heat seemed to warm the air between us. "I'll go back to D.C. But I'm not through with this. I can't be. I have to find out who did this." I started away from him, pebbles skittering under my heels.

"No, Kathryn."

If he said more, his warning was lost in the wind.

I hurried down the pathway and back around the outer wall of Kronborg Castle. The darkness outside was as complete as in the ingenious dungeon beneath my feet. It featured a shrinking cell that was reduced in size each day until any turncoat Dane who'd collaborated with the invading Swedes was crushed by his own refusal to confess.

Above me, a pennant snapped with a cracking noise. The keening wind blew in off the Øresund, the sound as haunting as the ghostly voice of Hamlet's father demanding revenge. I was running over the cobblestones. My Opel was parked in the public lot on the far side of the castle moat. Once behind the wheel, shivering, I picked my way through the seaport town of Helsingør, then out onto the motorway southbound toward Copenhagen.

I'd been driving for fifteen minutes when I saw a sign announcing that it was a thousand meters to the highway exit that would take me to Farum. The Danish Defense Intelligence Service—DDIS—had a safe house there. Stefan and I had stayed in it for six months after we fled from Poland.

Cold War Poland was where we'd met. In 1986, I was a junior officer in the U.S. Foreign Service, assigned to work at our embassy in Warsaw. Stefan Krajewski was a local hire, tutoring new arrivals like me in the Polish language. He was six and a half feet tall with well-defined chest muscles under his black turtleneck, his belly as flat as an athlete's. He wasn't handsome—his nose was too large and bony, his mouth too wide, his lips too full—but he was in far better shape than most language teachers. During duller lessons, I diverted myself by imagining him naked.

But never did I imagine that he worked for the Sluzba Bezpieczenstwa, the SB, Communist Poland's clone of the KGB. Not until he approached me with an offer of intelligence data the U.S. badly needed.

The Abu Nidal Organization had recently massacred Christmas travelers in Rome and Vienna, bombed a TWA flight over Greece and trumpeted its intention to do worse. Stefan was the liaison officer between the SB and the Abu Nidal Organization's band in Warsaw. In that role, he picked up information about the terrorists' plans. He offered to pass whatever he learned to the U.S. government, using me as the conduit.

An attractive offer. But there was a catch. Stefan needed a reason for meeting with me—one both the SB and the Abu Nidal Organization would find legitimate. It had to appear that he'd recruited me to spy for him.

Of course, I reported Stefan's approach. My security officer immediately notified the Department. In another time and place, that would have been the end of it. Jaded spy-watchers would have dismissed Stefan's offer as a sophisticated version of the honey trap and I'd have been warned against further contact.

But in 1986, we were desperate for a way to stop Abu Nidal. Washington told me to play along with Stefan to see if he'd pass me anything useful. Very likely, Stefan would tell me nothing while he tried to turn my imitation recruitment into the real thing. I was to proceed with extreme caution. My security officer was more succinct: "Don't let him get in your pants."

To protect myself, I reported every meeting I had with Stefan and got approval in advance to hand over the documents he demanded—a list of home telephone numbers of embassy staff, a floor plan of the chancery, duty rosters for the communicators. All of it innocuous stuff that the SB could get from a dozen sources.

But that's how recruitment works when it's real. Minor treason becomes major. Entrapment is a cumulative process, each compromising act leading to something more serious. No one in the Polish SB doubted that Stefan had turned me into a traitor, not until the very end.

And it wasn't until the end that I discovered that Stefan was not a loyal agent of the Polish SB. He'd joined forces with Holger Sorensen. He was working under cover for Danish intelligence. Lucky for me, because I was beyond rescue. Before I'd known Stefan a month, I was crazy in love with him. I struggled against my feelings. I made all the logical arguments. But logic wasn't worth a damn when it came to Stefan. In some primitive corner of my soul, I knew—*I knew*—I belonged with him.

That spring the U.S. bombed Libya. Terrorist groups struck back in Europe and the Middle East. Authorities were able to prevent attacks planned for London, Ankara and Paris, because of information Stefan passed to me. Enraged, Abu Nidal ordered us killed. We escaped to safety in Denmark. The Department granted me emergency leave. And I spent six precious months in the Farum safe house with Stefan.

Ahead of me, the brightly lit exit sign reflected off the mist-slick asphalt, gilding the ramp so that it beckoned like a honey-eyed road to the past. I smelled again the gunpowder on my hand, lingering from target practice at the military range. I breathed in the fragrance of healthy sweat, mine mixed with Stefan's, the odor as fresh as if we'd come from a vigorous workout. The air around me thickened with the haze of tobacco smoke. For a second I saw Stefan in the passenger seat, the burning end of his cigarette accenting the strong bones of his face.

If I exited, in another minute Stefan's left hand would find my leg. I'd feel his warmth through my jeans, the heat of his touch spreading through me as we drew closer to home. The instant I parked in our driveway, I'd bring his face to mine, feel the softness of his lips, taste again the mingled flavors of desire.

The exit sign flashed past and darkness stretched out before me. I opened the window to let in the winter air, struggling to fill my lungs before another wave of sorrow pulled me under.

At Kastrup, I managed to get on an SAS flight to Kennedy. Its departure was delayed for ninety minutes of baggage searches and the frisking of all passengers. When the beverage cart stopped beside me, the cans of Carlsberg glistened invitingly. But I needed a stronger anesthetic. My lips parted to form the initial sound in "Chivas." I was struck by a sudden memory, an image of a distillery warehouse turned into a morgue. Sheet-covered shapes on the cold floor. Was Stefan in that long line of corpses? Or did his body still drift in the icy waters? Anguish closed my throat, and I couldn't speak.

Concerned, the motherly stewardess asked again, "Cock-tail?"

My eyes on her hands, I croaked out a request for bourbon. Three Wild Turkeys formed a liquid armor between me and my pain. The agony of Stefan's loss and with it the torment of Holger's betrayal.

In Poland, Holger, Stefan and I had worked together against terror. Now, when things had turned personal, Holger was forcing me out.

When it was his help I needed most.

In 1985, the Danish Defense Intelligence Service had shunted Reserve Army Major Holger Sorensen off to a minor desk job with a limited mandate to gather information from

Danes who traveled in the Middle East. Holger's lack of experience in the Arab-speaking world was seen there as proof that the Danes weren't serious about this new effort. Plus, DDIS headquarters personnel showed no interest in Holger's reports. Holger Sorensen was dismissed as no threat to terrorist action.

But Holger's "irrelevant" experience was key to his strategy. During the first fifteen years of his military career, he had specialized in Poland and Eastern Europe. In 1978, the year he was promoted to the rank of captain, he also started a two-year stint as guest professor of Danish language and literature at the University of Warsaw. He was there at the height of the Solidarity movement and allied himself with Poles who'd lost their faith in Communism. He returned to Copenhagen, and by 1983, he was running agents into Poland, gathering data on the terrorist organizations operating freely on that side of the Berlin Wall.

Soon after he got his "minor desk job" in 1985, Holger realized that by inspiring well-placed East Bloc nationals to work covertly for him, he could track—and prevent—terrorist actions. Stefan and I gave him his first big success against the Abu Nidal Organization in Europe. By 1987, Abu Nidal had closed down his activities in Poland and established his base in Libya.

After Communism fell in Eastern Europe, Holger shifted his focus from state-sponsored terrorism to the flow of arms and technology from the private sector to radical groups. He and his people painstakingly traced illegal sales by German companies to Libya. He blew the whistle on Qadhafi's construction of a chemical weapons plant in Rabta. In an era of satellite surveillance, high-frequency eavesdropping and cybernetic data interception, Holger concentrated his assets on the ground. He stretched his limited resources to sustain a network of fiercely loyal agents in the field. It was a loyalty Holger returned tenfold.

The results were impressive, in large part because the

Father-Major's analysis of terrorist strategy was brilliant.

His analysis of me wasn't.

He'd ordered me to keep my distance from the wreckage of Global Flight 500. But I couldn't leave that investigation to others. Why didn't Holger understand that? Stefan would have. In my place, he'd have acted exactly the same.

Once, during that bleak Warsaw spring of 1986, I'd asked him if what I'd heard was true, that both his grandfather and his father had fought the Nazis. He'd made a joke and changed the subject. Not satisfied, I pressed him about his "legacy of resistance." He accused me of being romantic—a condition he claimed he'd outgrown. As a boy he'd felt cheated because he knew the Nazis would never return to Poland. So how would he discover if he could fight Fascism with unflagging courage? Endure torture? Go to his death with the names of his comrades unspoken? He'd laughed, gently mocking both me and his childhood self.

But beneath the musical banter I heard the perfect pitch of truth, and the sound resonated in me. As a girl, I'd wished for a cause to test my bravery. We were postwar children, yearning to be like our heroic fathers. We'd both grown up and into that desire—not out of it.

I was euphoric after we escaped from Poland, halfway convinced I should quit the State Department and join up with Stefan and Holger. Good idea, they both said, but don't rush into it. Stefan was being debriefed by Danish intelligence, I was on leave, we had six months to figure out what to do next. Stefan and Holger took turns teaching me basic tradecraft so I'd understand what fieldwork entailed. They both agreed I'd do well.

But not well enough, I concluded. In the long run, I'd accomplish more from behind a desk in Washington. Like the heroine of a corny movie, I left the man I loved in order to serve my cause. Probably the single most romantic notion I'd ever had. Stefan understood that. And he insisted that the Atlantic Ocean wouldn't keep us apart. For more than a decade, he'd been right.

By May of 1987, I was back in Washington, working in EUR, State's Bureau of European and Canadian Affairs. I analyzed threats against U.S. government property and personnel. In a typical case, the Admin Officer at our embassy in Stockholm might find a bootleg copy of the Ambassador's itinerary in the possession of a local employee. The employee, he'd discover, had done her university studies in Beirut and still traveled often to the Middle East. The Swedish police would interrogate the employee and staffers from Diplomatic Security would interview her co-workers.

From my windowless cubicle on the fifth floor of the State Department, I'd make huge arcs through the data. I'd pull everything that related, from press reports to satellite imagery. Talk to my contacts at Langley and DIA. Make charts, sketch diagrams, draw up lists. I'd work through the connections and outline the most likely scenario. Refine my analysis, come to a conclusion: These are incidents that have similar characteristics. These are the terrorist organizations of interest. These are the individuals you should watch.

I spotted connections other people missed. Maybe my experience in Poland was the reason. My stuff got read by the people who needed it—not everyone in the Department can say that.

I stayed in EUR until December 21, 1988—the day Pan Am 103 exploded. I was detailed to the office of State's Coordinator for Counterterrorism, S/CT, where I continued doing the same kind of analysis, but on a larger scale. The physical evidence from Lockerbie was inconclusive, the range of suspects broad. For two and a half years I tracked three hundred members of at least twenty different sects, painstakingly eliminating the individuals who could not have been involved. Tedious and time-consuming, but ultimately useful.

By then I'd run up against State's five-year limitation on

domestic assignments. They sent me to do administrative work at the consulate in Toronto—as far "overseas" as the security office would approve. I got pulled back abruptly in 1993, assigned as a staff assistant in the counterterrorism office to do follow-up after the World Trade Center bombing. My focus was terrorist groups operating in Europe, but I worked on the big cases no matter where the perpetrators came from. We all did. You see something like the Oklahoma City bombing, you feel such a terrible urgency. You can't work on anything else.

Since 1986, defeating terrorism had been the focus of my professional life. For just as long, loving Stefan had been at the heart of my emotional life. Two weeks after I left Denmark in 1987, Stefan came to me in D.C. If I needed proof he loved me, I had it then. He was doing contract work for Holger, under cover of a sales-rep job for a Danish shipping conglomerate. It was still too dangerous for me to travel openly in Europe, so he showed up every few months to spend a week, a weekend—once, only six hours. We made love, we fought, we laughed, we argued. There was never enough time. In the past few years I took three furtive trips to see him. The first time, he'd been tied up for five months in Belgium, couldn't get away. I slipped into Antwerp to be with him for a week. One Christmas after that, I made a clandestine visit to Copenhagen. Feeling safer, we conspired to steal time together the next fall at a secluded resort in Marbella. Spain was the only European country where I spoke the native language better than he did. Pretending outrage, he insisted we make a covert hydrofoil dash to Tangier so he could dazzle me with his Arabic.

All those romantic trysts, rustic or exotic—they didn't add up to four hundred days together. He would've been with me more—much more—after he quit fieldwork. A cord tightened around my heart, old longing grown so painful it would cripple me if I gave in to it. The numbing effect of the bourbon was wearing off.

The airliner video display predicted we'd land in another

fifteen minutes. I'd be back in the U.S., where Holger Sorensen had sent me. He'd banned me from the investigation. He knew my history, yet he gave me that impossible order. Terrorists had taken someone precious from me. I was a counterterrorist by profession. I had to work on this. The Lockerbie investigation had dragged on for more than two years. It ended only when a clever analyst at the CIA thought to compare a key piece of physical evidence to computer data about other bombings. By then the prime suspects were in Libya, unreachable by American and Scottish law enforcement.

I knew too much about the investigation of airliner bombings to stand aside from this one. I had to find out who'd blown up Global Flight 500. It was the only means I had to avenge Stefan's death.

I got the benefit of the time change, arriving at Kennedy only an hour later than I'd left Denmark. I was as surly with Immigration as they were with me. I caught a flight to the D.C. airport I still thought of only as "National," then took the Metro to Rosslyn. It was ten o'clock on Sunday night, December 27, when I rang the bell for Harry Martin's condo.

He buzzed me inside. When I got to the top of the staircase, he was waiting in the doorway, his sandy hair tousled as if he hadn't bothered to comb it. He was taller than me but he slouched, putting our eyes on the same level. I glimpsed my reflection in the thick lenses of his glasses. My blond hair was messy, too. For the same reason, I realized.

He stepped aside to let me in. "Aren't you supposed to be holed up in some mountain inn someplace?" he asked.

I dropped my jacket and my carry-on bag inside the door. "Didn't work out."

"You look like hell. What happened, you two have a fight?"

"He never showed."

"Stood you up? On Christmas Eve? Nice guy."

"Knock it off, Harry."

"Oh? Is the love affair of the century suddenly in the past tense?"

I didn't answer. Put my hand over my face instead.

Harry watched me for a second. Then he said, "I was thinking I could use a hot drink."

He crossed the living area to a galley kitchen. I followed and lowered myself into one of the chrome-and-rattan chairs at the glass-topped table. A few steps away from me, Harry was heating water, getting out cups, measuring whiskey, spooning brown sugar. I stared out the sliding-glass doors. A fog-shrouded Key Bridge crossed the black waters of the Potomac. Spotlights illuminated Georgetown University's classic buildings perched atop the far bank like a Jesuit beacon.

A mug clunked onto the tabletop in front of me. I inhaled coffee steam and whiskey vapors.

Harry waited until I had lifted the cup and taken a sip before saying, "Your dad called me this morning, asking about you."

"Damn. Forgot to phone and wish him a Merry Christmas." My father worried. He'd made me give him not only my work phone number but also Harry's number—someone he could call in an emergency. I raised my eyes to meet Harry's. "Anything wrong?"

"Not with him. But he said it wasn't like you to forget a holiday. Wanted me to check, see if you were all right."

I set my cup on the table. "I have to call him."

"No rush," Harry said. "We chatted. He calmed down. Invited me out for a visit. Promised to take me up in some ancient two-seater he owns with some other old codger. His words, by the way." He grinned. "Must be a great guy."

"He is." I tried to smile but my lip quivered, ruining the effect. I used both hands, got the cup back to my mouth, took another swallow.

Harry ran a hand over his hair. "Want to tell me about it?"

I wiped cream off my upper lip with the back of my hand and shook my head.

Jet-engine noise filled the silence. We watched green and red marker lights drop to our level as an airliner bound for National made its approach down the river. The glass doors vibrated.

"Then what can I do for you?" he asked.

Harry worked as special assistant to the director of intelligence policy and coordination in State's Bureau of Intelligence and Research. His job was grandly described as the nexus between the Department's consumers of intelligence and the collectors of intelligence. Translation: He did hush-hush liaison work with Langley. He'd personally handled the diplomatic fallout from the CIA's economic espionage fiasco in France.

We were both forty and single and we'd been friends since our first tour together as consular officers in San Salvador. I didn't have to pretend I'd interrupted my Christmas vacation to make a social call. I said, "Tell me what you've got on Global Flight 500."

"How much do you know?"

"Not much more than I've read in the newspapers."

"So you don't know we lost Billy Nu?"

"Billy Nu?" I shoved hair off my forehead with the heel of my hand. "I didn't see his name on the passenger list."

"You probably didn't recognize it." Harry pushed his glasses higher on the bridge of his nose. "Only his mother is Vietnamese. He's named for his father. Williamson Neuminster Junior. Boarded in London."

"Damn." Williamson Neuminster, Billy Nu, was a State Department investigator who followed up on threats against U.S. diplomats assigned abroad. "I can't believe—"

Harry cut me off. "Plus a LegAtt out of Brussels."

LegAtt was shorthand for Legal Attaché, the diplomatic title for FBI agents assigned overseas.

"You're saying they ignored the warning." My brain kicked

into gear as if I'd gotten a hit of caffeine. Four U.S. intelligence agents had died when Pan Am 103 blew up on exactly the same date in 1988. No one ever explained satisfactorily why they'd ignored a similar warning not to fly an American carrier. Both Billy and his companion had known the risk when they boarded Global 500 out of Heathrow on December 21. I felt a familiar ache between my shoulder blades, like a silent alarm.

Harry put my thoughts into words. "Maybe something drew them to that particular plane."

Drawn by the same thing that Stefan was after? I looked down at my cup. I didn't try to pick it up. My shaking hand would have slopped coffee across the table. I said, "What else have you got?"

"The NTSB says there was explosive decompression."

"I read that." All three of the plane's radios and both transponders had gone dead at the same second. There were only three possible causes for instantaneous and total loss of power to the cockpit: midair collision, massive structural failure or a bomb.

"Had to be a bomb," Harry said. "They won't go public without evidence of high-speed particle penetration. But the same date, virtually the same flight, so close to the other site— everyone knows it was a bomb. Very cleverly designed, to get past all the detection systems at Heathrow. Triggering device must have been state-of-the art." He shook his head. "We figure they could have put it right down on Lockerbie again. Guess they didn't want to make it easy for us to recover their handiwork."

I'd seen pictures of the crater Pan Am 103 had gouged in the quiet Scottish neighborhood of Sherwood Crescent. Eleven people on the ground had died that time, crushed when the cockpit tore through their homes. The terrorists had gotten so skillful, they could repeat that horror whenever they chose. Despite the warmth of the mug, the tips of my fingers were cold and the chill was spreading up my arms, toward the ache at the back of my neck.

"What's the theory on motive?" I asked.

"We see it primarily as a demonstration of what they can do."

My shoulder twitched, an involuntary shudder. "But nobody's claiming credit?"

Harry shook his head. "Nobody's inviting U.S. retaliation for this one."

"So what do *you* think of the theory?"

"Logical in a big-picture way. If they want to frighten us, they accomplished that. But you know me, Casey. I'm little-picture. Personal reasons always have more explanatory value for me."

"Somebody had a personal motive for blowing up two hundred and twenty-seven people?"

Harry shook his head again. "For blowing up one person. The other two hundred twenty-six were for free."

I went over to stand in front of the sliding door. The glass was cool against my forehead. While I stood there, another airliner swooped from the sky and roared down the river toward National.

Harry stood beside me, not touching. When he spoke, his voice was scarcely audible. "He was on it, wasn't he?"

"Seems pretty likely." My throat was closing and my words came out thick.

"I'm sorry." When he spoke again, the consoling tone was gone from his voice. "If he was the target," Harry said, "they'll be coming after you next."

3

Something cold twisted in my stomach. "After me?" I said. My voice was pitched too high, my fear too plain. I breathed deeply, tried again. "They wouldn't come here."

"Can't rule that out," Harry said. "If Stefan Krajewski was the goal, we've got a different soccer game. One where you're a player."

The cold knot in my stomach was coming undone, twisting and undulating, sending bitter liquid up my throat. Harry was trying to scare me. He was succeeding. I sat back down. "You don't know killing Stefan was their objective."

Harry took the chair beside me. The light from the overhead fixture glinted off the metal frames of his glasses. "Right now, we don't know much of anything. The FBI and half of Interpol are working on it. Until they identify the culprit, you'd be wise to lie low."

"Lie low?" I made a disgusted noise. "Don't you start in on me."

"Somebody better," he said. "You're still not cleared to work anywhere overseas."

I started to protest and he raised a hand to stop me.

"Canada doesn't count," he said. "You told me what Diplomatic Security said the last time they reviewed your clearance." He squinted slightly, as if trying to make his words perfect before he threw them at me. "Assigning you to a European embassy would be like setting up a shooting gallery."

"Billy Nu said that." I swallowed. "He was a sharp guy. But he overstated the case. I'd almost talked him out of it. All this time's gone by and nobody's bothered with me."

"But if they took out Stefan . . ." He brushed the back of my hand with his fingertips.

His touch was like a warm breeze of solace. I felt my throat closing. Not here. I clutched the mug tighter, willed away my grief.

Harry kept watching me. "They know that you worked with Stefan in Warsaw. And then there's the night you fled Poland. You, Stefan, the killer Abu Nidal sent after you—all three of you got on that ferryboat to Denmark. But the killer wasn't on board when it docked on the other side of the Baltic. Some nasty people said they'd pay you both back. Maybe they're getting started."

"Right," I said, staring at the muddy liquid in my cup.

His voice became more earnest. "And then the stuff you did after Pan Am 103 exploded." He paused, looked at me hard. He knew I wouldn't deny that I'd done work good enough to call attention to myself. "Now this bombing. We keep finding parallels. Don't you see how it could be meant as a threat directly against you?"

"You're stretching," I said.

"I don't think so. You have to stay out of sight for a while, till we figure out what's going on." Then his tone sharpened. "What have you done so far?"

I didn't answer.

His eyes went to my carry-on bag. A band of white tape crisscrossed the openings, unbroken since the pre-boarding search at Kastrup. The lettering spelled out AIRPORT SECURITY in royal blue. Harry glared at me. "What did you think you were doing?"

"I had to find out—"

"Why don't you paint a bull's-eye on your brain stem?"

The chromed legs of my chair rasped against the carpeting as I stood. "I don't need this—"

"Calm down. This is your old pal Harry. I'm worried about you."

I made a conciliatory gesture. "Guess I've gotten too much of that advice. 'Lie low. Play it safe. Take it easy.' "

"You have to wait for the dust to settle—"

"Not dust. Body parts."

He was standing, too. "Look, you can't start acting crazy. I know he was important to you. But—"

" 'Important'?" I was at the door by then. "Stefan wasn't *important* to me. I loved him." I shoved my arms into my jacket sleeves and grabbed my bag. "Losing him is tearing me apart. If you don't understand that, anything I do is going to look crazy to you."

Harry was at the door. "Casey, I didn't mean—"

"I appreciate your telling me as much as you did," I said. "But don't tell me how to handle this."

He kept on as though he hadn't heard me. "Go home. Get some sleep. Come and see me tomorrow. Let's put together a plan."

"Sure," I called from the foyer. The tired look on his face told me he knew I didn't mean it.

The frozen cement rang hollowly under my boots. Three cabs idled in the stand next to the Hyatt Hotel, their exhaust milky in the cold air, throbbing engines the only sound echoing off Rosslyn's concrete high-rises. I got into the car at the head of the line. The black skin on the back of the driver's shaved head glistened under the hotel security lights as he U-turned and headed downhill. Harry was right: I had enemies in Libya and in the Abu Nidal Organization. Good idea to be watchful. I was relieved I'd found one of the few cabdrivers in northern Virginia who hadn't been born in the Middle East.

The cracked vinyl of the rear seat was slippery as ice beneath me, the air stuffy with the smell of the exhaust. As we crossed Key Bridge, another inbound flight roared over us. The driver got off Rock Creek Parkway at the National Zoo exit and dropped me farther up Connecticut Avenue, in front of the brownstone where I owned the rear half of the second floor.

I paused outside my door, fumbling with my keys. There was nothing but lonely emptiness on the other side of that door. And two gaily wrapped packages, lying in ambush for me in the back of my closet. I jingled my key chain and regretted for the hundredth time that I'd never gotten another dog. No room ever felt empty when my Rhodesian Ridgeback was in it. Cecil had been only two when I was posted abroad for the first time. He'd accompanied me to San Salvador, gallantly accepting his new job in diplomatic protection. He'd prowled my walled yard every night, washed my face every morning, kept me safe as long as he could. He'd tried to stop the men who came over the wall, but got out only one piercing howl before they slit his throat. The State Department awarded me a fifteen-thousand-dollar salary bonus during my tour in San Salvador. There was a good reason for the extra compensation. I'd made a bad decision, taking Cecil to a danger-pay-post. I didn't want another dog until I was living in a safe place.

I wasn't there yet.

But Stefan could have protected me *and* a dog. A few weeks past August, I'd dreamed up that scenario, goofily singing, "Stefan and me and puppy makes three." The fleeting memory was like a cold draft, a chill reminder that I hadn't yet totaled my losses. I shivered as I shoved the door open.

The first thing I saw was the red light blinking on my answering machine. Stefan!

I dropped my bag and rushed over to push the playback button. The cassette spindle hummed, rewinding. It spun on and on, as though the messages were infinite in length. I clicked on the table lamp and flipped open the plastic lid. The top spindles were empty, the left one endlessly rewinding nothing.

My incoming message cassette was missing.

I pressed the playback button again, but the eerie spinning continued. I grabbed the handset and the spindle's motion ceased. I stared at the device. The LED readout showed the digit 3. Three messages of unknown length, from unknown person or persons, of great interest to an unknown intruder. I noticed gray finger smudges on the inside of the lid. I dropped the phone and held my hand palm-up under the pool of light. My fingers were coated with dust.

I switched on the overhead light. More evidence that I'd had visitors while I was away. Bookcases lined the walls of my living room. Mostly they held paperbacks and remainders, books of all sizes and shapes, shoved tight against the veneer backing, leaving a jagged edge of open shelf in front. Before I'd set out to meet the Father-Major, I'd carefully withdrawn and replaced a couple of volumes. I'd been gone only three days. The marks I'd intentionally left on the never-dusted shelves should have still been there. But all the exposed wood was powdered with dirt. Just like my telephone.

Someone had come looking for something. And my poor housekeeping had made his efforts too obvious. He'd covered his tracks with grit. I wondered why he'd gone to so much trouble to conceal his search—and then given himself away by removing the cassette. I didn't stop to puzzle that one out. Someone was too interested in me.

In fifteen seconds I was closing my door from the other side. Nobody in the hallway. Good. And nothing unusual outdoors either. But I kept my eyes roving as I hurried down the block. Nobody was following me and I wouldn't make it easy for anyone to pick up my trail. One more stop, and then no taxicab, no credit cards, no showing my ID to anyone.

Five minutes later I was in front of an ATM. The lights above it turned the skin on my hand greenish red. My hand shook on the first try and I nearly lost my card to a computer programmed for ultra-suspicion after midnight. I willed myself to stay calm and managed to extract five hundred dollars from my account. Then I made my way by public transportation to the southeast side of the District. I found a budget motel near the Anacostia River, registered under a false name and paid cash for a stingy room.

On Monday morning I walked the few blocks from that motel to an anonymous office building in Buzzard Point. At eight-thirty, I was looking across a desk at Mike Buchanan, his eyes watery from a winter cold. He blew his lumpy nose, jammed the handkerchief back into his pants pocket and waved me into the visitor's chair.

"Some cold." I sat down. "Taking anything for it?"

"You kidding? FBI agents don't need drugs." He sneezed and reached for the handkerchief again.

"Maybe the germs can't tell you're such a tough guy."

He snorted. He knew he didn't look the part. Too short, under six feet, with too much flesh hanging loose around his middle and under his chin. And no crew cut either—he wore his hair long, wavy and parted in the center.

But Mike was a veteran counterintelligence analyst in the FBI's National Security Division and one of its top spy-chasers. We'd traded information before in situations involving the illegal export of U.S.-made weapons—guns that linked the American traitors who smuggled them out to the foreign terrorists who paid big bucks upon receipt.

Mike put the handkerchief away and asked, "What's up?"

"I thought you might be able to get some answers for me."

The chair squealed as he tilted back. "What are the questions?"

"About the Global 500 bombing."

"Out of my area," he said.

"But your people are working on it?"

"Sure." He jerked his head to indicate the wall in back of him. "Staff's getting set up in there, all ready to convene the interagency task force, lay out everything we've got."

I knew there was a major case room on the other side of the wall. A long, rectangular cave with a threadbare carpet and air permanently stained by nicotine. I said, "Maybe you've picked up info you could share with me."

"You people have everything we've got."

"Right," I said, not bothering to dispute the tired falsehood. "I've been on leave. Figured I'd get a quicker fix on things, coming to you."

"But you're not officially part of the task force?"

"Not till I get an upgrade of my security clearance."

Bushy eyebrows rose to the midpoint of Mike's forehead. "I hear the head honcho in your shop handpicked you as the next candidate to fill State's position. Think folks would hurry up your background check to please him."

"You'd think that." Mike was surprisingly knowledgeable about my job situation. Obviously well aware that I'd been waiting three months for the bureaucracy to unclog and spit out a clearance that should have been automatic.

He tilted back his chair once more and spoke with a casualness that seemed studied. " 'Course, your case is complex. You *are* involved with an old SB agent."

In the five years I'd known Mike, he'd never mentioned Stefan. Why now? And why in a manner certain to annoy me?

"A *former* agent of a *former* enemy," I reminded him. "And even before we got a friendly government in Poland, Stefan defected to the West."

"Sure. To the Danes."

"They're an ally." I gestured at the wall behind him. "I've spent a lot of time in that room with you. You've never worried about how I handled sensitive information."

"I admit, no one's got a better handle on the issues than you do. No wonder the boss-man picked you for the task force."

I said, "You're not telling me anything."

Mike shrugged. "You say you're still not cleared—"

"Oh come on." I clipped off the words, my irritation audible. "Nobody in the Department thinks I'm a security risk."

The eyebrows seemed to rise higher. "The *Bureau* is less certain."

I stood up slowly, trying not to let my anger get in my way. "If that's how you feel, I won't waste any more of your time."

"Sit down," Mike said. There was no invitation in his tone.

I stayed on my feet.

"Sit down." This time spoken with all the authority inherited from J. Edgar Hoover.

"Why should I?" My voice cracked at the end and took the toughness out of my words. I'd seen Mike in pursuit of a traitor. He'd used that steely voice then, too.

"I've got a few questions for you," he replied. "So you might as well sit down and see if we can straighten this thing out."

"What thing?"

"Global Flight 500, for starters."

I sat.

"What's your interest in this?" he asked.

"I want to know who blew it up."

"Yeah. Well, that's the question of the hour, isn't it? Everybody would like to know that. But you came all the way out here to extract the latest information from me. I'm curious why you'd choose to do that."

There was a hook buried in that mild remark. I heard its barbed edge. *Why are you searching outside normal channels for information you're not supposed to have?* Mike was treating me like a suspect. I didn't need anyone reading me my rights to know I was better off remaining silent. I pressed my lips together and watched him.

Mike flipped open a manila folder. I recognized the passenger list for the downed flight.

He ran his finger down to the tenth name from the top.

Then he asked, "Who's Karsten Hansen?" The question was sharp.

Whatever wrongdoing Mike suspected me of, it had to involve Stefan. "Karsten Hansen?" I repeated warily. "Never heard of him."

"No one else has heard of him either. His Danish passport had a number that hasn't been issued yet. And no family member's come forward to ask about him."

My heartbeat was too fast and I wanted to gulp in air. But I knew better than to hazard guesses during what had taken on the rhythm of an official FBI investigation. "What's that got to do with me?"

"Ticket agent at Heathrow thinks she remembers the fellow. Such a fine-sounding Danish name, but he didn't have the looks to go with it. Dark hair instead of blond. Bony face instead of rounded. We showed her some pictures. She thought this Karsten Hansen looked an awful lot like your Polish friend."

"A million Slavs look like him. Especially to a Brit handling a holiday crowd."

"Maybe. But maybe you can tell us if Stefan Krajewski was on that plane."

"I don't make his travel arrangements."

"But you were expecting him. We know you booked a room for two at the Highland Inn. We're betting he was your date."

The FBI had researched my holiday plans? Alarm sent a flush of heat across my cheeks. "You guys got nothing better to do than monitor my sex life?"

"We keep track of foreign agents. And we do a better job than you seem to give us credit for. So tell me: Were you expecting the Pole?"

"Maybe you better tell me where these questions are going."

He paused, studying me. When he spoke, he'd softened his tone, added a note of apology. "We start checking out something like this, you know that one thing we're eager to learn is who else is checking things out."

New tactic, I realized. Badgering me wasn't working.

"As soon as you started searching for intell on the flight," he continued mournfully, "your name turned up on our list."

"Your *terrorist* suspect list? That's ridiculous. Why didn't you tell them to cross me off?"

"You know, that *was* my reaction. When one of the guys ran it by me, I said, 'Nah, you don't have to worry about Casey Collins.'"

"You weren't convincing," I said. "He tossed my house, didn't he?"

Mike didn't answer.

"It had to be you guys. Nobody else goes around running a Dustbuster in reverse." They'd searched my condo. For sure they'd also intercepted my phone messages. If I stayed quiet, Mike might reveal something I didn't know.

He retrieved his handkerchief, blew his nose, then continued. "My pal came back empty-handed. 'See,' I told him. 'Nothing incriminating in *her* pad.' Then this morning he shows me your itinerary for the past few days. 'Odd,' I admitted. 'But I don't see any link to Lockerbie Two.' Fifteen minutes later, you pop into my office asking questions about Global 500."

"I must have missed something there. Counterterrorism is my job. Of course I'm interested in that explosion. Run it by me again, why the Bureau is bothered by that."

"Maybe your interest isn't job-related. Maybe it has more to do with the people you know *off* the job."

"Come again?"

He held up a hand in a gesture intended to be soothing. "Let me tell you how it looks to my colleague. December twenty-first. You're sitting in D.C. waiting for Krajewski. Then *blam*. Plane blows up. You go racing off to Denmark. Like maybe you want to ask your pal over there, does he know why someone blew away your boyfriend."

"If Holger Sorensen knew anything about this, he'd tell you."

"Would he, now? I'm not so sure of that. We've picked up a few facts lately, gave us a new slant on doings in that part of the world. The bodies won't stay buried, if you catch my drift. Some funny business going on between that damn Father-Major and your Polish friend. That's why you're not on the task force, even though your boss raised a stink about the delay. Seems possible to us that anything you read could end up copied to the wrong people."

"The wrong people? Holger Sorensen's an ally, in case you've forgotten. You know he got six of our spooks out of Baghdad in 1990."

"In 1990, sure—"

I cut him off. "Stefan did the fieldwork. He convinced some Poles working in Iraq to smuggle our guys into Turkey, right after Saddam invaded Kuwait." I tapped my forefinger on the desk in front of Buchanan. "Holger doesn't get his intelligence information from me. He's cleared for Cosmic Top Secret or higher. He gets all his stuff through formal channels."

Mike abandoned his soft approach. "You're not that naive. But Holger Sorensen isn't the main problem and you know it."

I stood up. "If you want to talk to me, you'd better get a subpoena."

"My colleague is with the judge right now. We should be ready to serve you by tonight. Might as well wait for us in your apartment. Save us the trouble of going back for an arrest warrant."

"Arrest warrant? What's the charge?"

"You figure it out." He gave me a withering look. "Don't try to leave the country. This time your passport won't get you past the ticket counter."

"I can't believe I'm hearing this!"

"There's only one reason why you went racing off to Denmark when loverboy didn't show up. You think they know something about this bombing. If you're smart, you'll act like a loyal American. You'll tell us where you got that idea."

"But the attention—"

"Somebody blew up another planeload of people. It's too damn bad if you don't like the way we're handling the investigation. You talk to us. Or you go to jail. Simple as that."

"You guys belong at Buzzard Point," I said. "So apt, given the way you do your jobs. Feeding on dead flesh."

Mike didn't raise an eyebrow. "Right. We go wherever we smell something rotten. Brought us straight to you."

"It was you, wasn't it? You blocked the upgrade of my clearance. You decided I couldn't be trusted."

His laugh was short. "Don't have to be a rocket scientist to figure out you've had a major conflict of interest all down the line."

"You're wrong," I said, reaching for the doorknob.

He jerked his head toward the adjoining case room. "See you in there. You can tell me all about it."

I pulled the door shut with a defiant click. Nobody tried to speak to me as I left the building. Probably afraid of getting punched in the nose. My fury had to be obvious, from the tight line of my lips to the rough scrape of my boots against the carpet. Once outside, I strode over dirty gray concrete for ten indistinguishable blocks, until my legs ached and I was winded. Still mad, but no longer steaming. Cooled off enough to realize I was feeling more than anger.

Surprise. Definitely. Kathryn Collins, an exemplary career Foreign Service Officer, is implicated in a terrorist bombing? A charge so ludicrous I'd have laughed if Buchanan's misjudgment of me hadn't cut such a deep wound. It felt like betrayal.

I took a back booth in a hole-in-the-wall sandwich shop and hunched over a mug of evil-smelling coffee. I was the only customer, the cramped space silent except for a droning television set.

I thought back to June when I'd last worked a case with Buchanan. I'd gotten no hint then he viewed my romance with Stefan Krajewski as a security issue. Something must have happened during the last six months to trigger FBI interest in me.

Stefan's SB past and his current work for "that damn Father-Major" were two matters bothering Buchanan. Those concerns plus his mysterious "new slant on doings in that part of the world" had prompted him to block my promotion to the task force. Somehow, the FBI had obtained authority to snoop electronically in my phone and credit card records. That explained how they knew my Christmas plans and unearthed the details of my travel so quickly.

I picked up the coffee cup, set it down again without drinking.

So far, Buchanan wanted only to question me about the bombing. But I couldn't talk to him. What I knew about Global Flight 500, I knew from Holger Sorensen. If I submitted to Buchanan's inquisition, I might jeopardize Holger's investigation. And I had less confidence in the FBI than I did in Holger.

A chill started at the base of my neck, slithered down my spine. *You talk to us. Or you go to jail.* The first time he'd said "arrest," I'd scoffed. All I'd done was make some inquiries, fly to Denmark, and visit an FBI agent. Nothing in that merited incarceration.

But I hadn't thought it through. Someone had granted a search warrant for my condo. For reasons I couldn't fathom, a federal judge was letting the FBI treat me as a potential criminal. I couldn't explain Buchanan's interest in me but I had to take it seriously. I'd seen the Bureau mistakenly pursue an innocent security guard after the 1996 Atlanta bombing. I shivered. I had to admit it. I was frightened.

I'd made a big mistake returning to the U.S. I had to go back to Europe. Tonight, before the FBI served me with its subpoena. A rash action, fleeing the country when I had no grasp on Buchanan's case against me. Yet if I remained here, I risked spending the next month of my life struggling to stay out of prison.

I shoved the cup to the other side of the table.

No way. I wasn't going to waste more time. I had a job to do. I tracked down terrorists. And the terrorist who'd engineered Stefan's death was the one I wanted. I had to get to Holger. Once I explained the problem, he'd help me soothe the Feds. I felt a twinge of doubt. I ignored it. Holger had been wrong to send me away. This time I'd listen to my heart.

So how was I going to get out of the U.S.A. without showing my passport to an airline ticket agent?

I recovered my coffee and took a sip. Cold. I craned my neck, looking for the counterman. The TV screen caught my eye, hooking me with the standard shot of the State Department's C Street lobby. In front of the row of foreign flags was a face I recognized. I rose in my seat to get a better view. I saw the diminutive figure of Lura Dumont, reporting for United Network News. Lura. She could get me out of the country.

Lura and I came from the same rural area of Oregon. Our elementary school's tendency to arrange students in alphabetical order had guaranteed that Collins and Dumont would be seatmates. We decided on our own to be "best friends." As girls, we raced our bikes down country lanes, pretending we were riding ponies bareback. Progressed from there to games with Ken and Barbie that got kinkier as we matured. I still remembered the day Lura got her first period. I'd walked a half step behind her all the way home to hide the stain on the back of her skirt.

At age fourteen, I suddenly shot up to my adult height, a

skinny blonde destined to play center on the girls' basketball team. Except that year my mother's mental health problem worsened and she clamped down on my life like a vise. If I wasn't in the house by three-thirty in the afternoon, she got hysterical. "I only want you to be safe," she'd sob. "I only want to take care of you." I struggled, but I had to give in. By then she feared strangers indoors, too. Trembling, unable to speak, that panicky look in her eyes—I couldn't bear to see her like that. I stopped inviting other kids over.

Except for Lura. My mother was used to her. Lura was head cheerleader, wildly busy with school activities, no shortage of people wanting to be her friend. But still she came to my house every afternoon from five to six o'clock and we did our home-work together. Looking back, I sometimes wonder if I would have survived those four years without Lura.

My tutoring improved her grades from a C-plus average to an A-minus. One reason, certainly, that she kept busting in on my miserable loneliness. She'd always had an unchildlike un-derstanding of the increased payoff from long-term invest-ments. Hard to sort one motive from another when it came to Lura. When I was eighteen, my father helped me escape to col-lege. I lost touch with Lura.

I ran into her one week into my first assignment in the For-eign Service. I was trying to make sense of what was happening around me in San Salvador. Lura was there, ostensibly to do "local color" for National Public Radio. Her real assignment was an exposé on civilian massacres by U.S.-trained Salvadoran troops. She was a struggling media wannabe. I had the access that goes with diplomatic status. And I stayed on in-country after death threats forced her out. It was inevitable that she'd use me. I'd been lucky to lose only my dog.

I forgave her in less than a year. Her trenchant reporting helped put Salvador's bloodstained Atlacatl Battalion out of business. She spoke for terror's victims and I was glad I'd given her the words. Lura liked to claim that she'd shown me my mission in life. But I heard the irony in her voice. She knew she'd risked my life—not hers—to get her story. I'd forgiven her for that. But I liked her less and I didn't confide in her anymore.

Her San Sal work won her the job with UNN. She'd been based in their Washington office for the past year. My girlhood chum worked for a network with its own fleet of planes.

I reached for my cell phone. Stopped. I didn't want this call monitored. I spotted a pay phone on the wall beside the coffee-shop door. My fingers touched a quarter in my jacket pocket. At last, a good omen.

The UNN receptionist told me that Miss Dumont was in conference.

Damn. I didn't have time for telephone tag. "Tell her Casey's trying to reach her," I said. "It's urgent. I'll call back in twenty minutes."

I paid for my coffee with a five-dollar bill and asked for my change in coins. I headed up the street on foot. It was clear in Washington, the sky a washed-out blue. Office workers on er-rands pushed by; early-morning shoppers moved briskly around me. I stopped now and then to examine shop windows. And to identify anyone else strolling at my leisurely pace. Any FBI tail would become obvious fast.

What had happened to my life, that I was using my trade-craft to evade the FBI? I had to get out of this mess. I located a secluded phone booth in a hotel lobby and made myself com-fortable. This time, the receptionist connected me to Lura at once.

Lura's tone was apologetic. "She was supposed to put you through the first time."

Puzzled, I said, "You were expecting to hear from me?"

"I'd given up hope. Okay, what do you say we plan for a long sit-down? Set things up where we have two or three hours?" She made a pondering noise through closed lips, then said, "Wednesday afternoon's good for me. If you're free then—"

"Lura," I interrupted.

But she kept going. "We could do lunch—"

"Lura." I waited for her to stop. "You've lost me. I didn't call about lunch. I have something to ask you."

"But I left a message—"

"I must've missed it. Listen, I need to hitch a ride with you to Europe."

"That might be possible." I heard her flipping pages in her appointment book. "The latter part of next week I might go to Rome. I'll know something in a couple of days. Can I tell you for sure when we get together Wednesday?"

"Too late," I said. "I want to leave today."

"Not possible," she said. "There's no way I'm getting out of town this week."

"You don't have to come," I told her. "Just get *me* on a plane."

She laughed. "What am I, your travel agent?"

I shoved at my hair. Lura was making this too difficult. "I'm asking for a favor, that's all."

"And I'd love to do you one." Her voice grew cajoling. "But what's your rush? You meet me Wednesday, we can talk—"

"Lura," I interrupted again. "I have to go today." I said it slowly, punching each syllable the way newscasters do at the end of a story. Making my meaning clear without saying the words: *You owe me.*

Fifteen seconds of silence, a prohibitive amount of dead air for Lura. "Let me check what's going out today." Her voice was flat. I spent another minute on hold, listening to elevator music. She came back, all business. UNN had a backup crew leaving for Hamburg at three that afternoon from Dulles. There was room for me. Her admin people insisted that she ask—was my passport current?

The question was a good sign. It meant no one from UNN

would be checking documents at Dulles. I told her my papers were all in order and she said she'd get my name added to the passenger list. She hung up while I was saying thanks.

I piled my coins in front of me. Harry had said my father was looking for me. I had to let him know I was all right. Cancer had claimed my mother four years before, and I was his only family now. He was seventy-five and he worried about me. Safe enough to call him. I doubted the FBI was tapping his line yet. And even if Mike Buchanan were that thorough, a quick hello wouldn't give my flight plan away.

I got a busy signal.

I traveled by bus to Metro Center, then spent the next hour going in and out of hotels and stores, getting rid of any FBI tail I hadn't spotted. I made my way to Western Union's downtown office, where I paid cash to send my message to a cutout in Roskilde, Denmark, giving my travel plans and adding the pseudonym that signaled I was on the run. When we'd set up the code, I'd assumed my pursuers would be coming out of the Middle East—not from Buzzard Point. No matter. Holger would get the message. He'd know what to do.

I tried my father again. Still busy. Off the hook? Probably. Twice during my last visit, I'd discovered the handset dangling from its cord, as if he'd stepped away from the phone to answer the door and forgotten to return. Getting older wasn't helping his memory.

Back on the street again, I made a mental list of things I needed to buy: toothpaste and a toothbrush, shampoo, deodorant, a three-pack of cotton panties. What does the successful fugitive require? There had to be some practical necessities, but all that came to mind were the elimination of body odor and a supply of clean underwear.

In the lingerie section of Woody's, I passed two women pawing through a table of sale-priced nightgowns. A hot-eyed blonde held a midnight-blue negligee in front of her and gave her stout companion a sultry look.

The second woman said, "*Bardzo ladny.*" Very pretty.

I tuned in to the sound of Stefan's native language, yearning for more, but the blonde ran one hand across her breasts and lowered her voice, so I caught only the suggestive tone and not the words.

The second one laughed, old-world music rich with sexual innuendo. "*Oczywiscie!*" Absolutely.

My heart lifted in my chest, as if answering a call from the man who had so often murmured that word to me. I heard it repeating in my head, this time in Stefan's husky voice. *Oczywiscie.* One of the promises he made to me in the languorous moments after our passion was spent. *Absolutely. Completely. Always.*

No equivocation, no half measures, no holding back. Not with his love for me, not with the work that he did. I felt my loss then, a pain so terrible, I covered my mouth to muffle my torment. I bit my finger, tasted salt, then the copper flavor of my blood.

An anxious clerk touched my shoulder. When I looked up, she took the crushed package of underwear from my hand. Did I want to pay for it now? She accepted my twenty and counted out the change, all the time treating me with the wary courtesy we use to avoid triggering a reaction from the mentally unstable. By the time I'd finished, the Polish shoppers had disappeared, leaving behind a tableful of tangled nylon glistening like a new bruise.

Outside, the sunlight was sharp-edged and without warmth. I pulled my coat tighter, but still I was cold. I tried calling my father from the Capitol Hilton. I sat there, phone to my ear, waiting for my father's "Howdy." I hung up after fifteen rings, wishing he'd connected the answering machine I'd sent him for Christmas.

I was running out of time. In the gift shop, I bought a greeting card with a three-color drawing of Snoopy in cap and goggles, his bullet-riddled doghouse hurtling downward after an unsuccessful encounter with the Red Baron. Sitting on an over-stuffed chair at one side of the bustling lobby, I crossed out the birthday message and addressed the envelope to my father. "Your favorite appears to be going down in flames," I wrote to him. "But we all know we'll soon be toasting success with root beer. In my case, real beer. Hope to see you soon."

I shoved hair off my forehead. Too cryptic? But if I spelled out why he might be worried about me, he'd seize on it, worry like crazy. Better to bury my reassurance where he'd be likely to find it only if he needed it. I added a "Happy New Year" wish, a string of X's and O's, then my nickname the way he wrote it: K.C. I hiked back outside to find a mailbox instead of using the informal drop box offered by the hotel.

I tried a few more maneuvers to expose anyone following me, but turned up nothing. Sale signs were posted in all the store windows, reminding me of a December day when my mother had taken me shopping, in search of an after-Christmas bargain on a girl's winter coat, size 6X. I remembered our jerky progress along the city sidewalk as she yanked me first in one direction, then in another, threatened by cars passing twenty feet away. By the time we reached the J.C. Penney store, her terror had infected me. We huddled against the building, my mother crouched over me, both of us sobbing. Someone eventually figured out my father's name and called him to come and get us.

No matter how scared you are, you have to keep moving. I absorbed that lesson, living with my mother.

At two o'clock, I took the airport shuttle out to Dulles. I paid for my bus ticket in quarters, no need any longer to hoard coins for the phone. I hiked from the main terminal to one of the smaller fields abutting Dulles and waited in a secluded spot with a view of the UNN hangar.

A Boeing 707 jet was outside the hangar, and a service crew was getting it ready. At two-thirty, three men arrived with a vanload of equipment. They had the unkempt look of behind-the-camera TV people and I let myself relax. During the next fifteen minutes, friends or spouses dropped off two women— one blonde, one redhead—and a balding man, all weighted down with luggage and grocery bags. Still no sign of the FBI. When the pilot and the co-pilot appeared, I followed them on board.

The jet was the size and vintage of the old Air Force Two still used by the Secretary when I first started with the State Department. The section directly behind the cockpit was taken up by the same high-speed communications equipment that was mandatory on planes carrying top officials. But that was the end of the resemblance. Instead of the plush forward accommodations, there were aged economy-class airliner seats. Four were grouped around a scratched table; the rest were scattered in pairs along both walls of the plane. The cargo area had been given over to extra fuel tanks, and every bare piece of floor in the passenger area was taken up by tied-down electronic equipment, luggage and other paraphernalia I didn't recognize.

The six other travelers appeared to be veterans of the unglamorous side of all-news programming. The three early arrivals had claimed the table and started a poker game. The bald man was reclining with his eyes closed. And the two women had taken a pair of seats together. The redhead was in the process of lighting a Tiparillo. She exhaled a cloud of smoke and asked me in an abraded voice, "You Casey?"

"That's me," I said. I gestured toward the empty seats. "Make any difference where I sit?"

"Don't take the one next to George," the redhead said. "He snores. Besides, Lura'll probably want to sit with you."

"Lura?" I headed for an empty double in the rear. "She said she wasn't traveling today."

The redhead coughed, a pre-emphysema wheeze that left her breathless. The frizzy blonde beside her said, "Lura'll be here. You can count on it."

The redhead elbowed her. "But not early. Never early. You know Lura."

I dropped into the seat, hoped my alarm didn't show. Lura's sudden change of plans made me uneasy.

I was buckling my seat belt when she arrived, her cherry-red pumps clicking up the stairs like castanets. In spike heels, she wasn't five feet tall. She dropped into the seat beside mine. "You all set?" she asked.

"All set. And surprised to see you."

"*You're* surprised? Can you believe my producer is making me spend my New Year's Eve in Germany?"

"Why's that?" I asked.

Lura shrugged. We'd taxied out to the end of the runway. The pilot revved up for takeoff and the engine noise was deafening. She asked loudly, "So how come you needed a ride so bad? Some reason you couldn't buy a plane ticket like an ordinary person?"

I leaned closer. "I'm meeting an old friend. It'd be better for me if I could keep that quiet."

She gave me a knowing look. "The spy?"

Shocked, I looked at her hard. When I talked to Lura about my personal life, I left out a lot of details. She'd never heard the word "spy" from me. Now we were airborne; no way to escape. I made a show of settling comfortably into my seat and tried to sound as if I were talking about a man who was alive. "That was in Poland, years ago," I said. "He works for a Danish business now."

"Let me guess. Could his employer be Universal Export?"

James Bond's original cover job. Cute. I gestured impatiently. "A shipping company."

She snickered. "So what's the problem?"

"My security clearance is under review. I don't want to slow things down."

"Going to Europe to get laid—that'll slow things down?"

I shrugged. "You know how they are. Can't handle a woman who's got a sex life."

"A sex life with an ex-Commie spy, you mean. You should stay away from him. Or maybe you don't give a damn about your job?" She was quiet for a few seconds. When she spoke again, her voice was softer, more conspiratorial, and her sentence didn't end in a rising inflection. "I know about your security problem."

5

Startled, I said, "State Department Security interviewed you?"

"Why not? Who knows you better?" She was smiling and the perfect evenness of her teeth reminded me of a fox's incisors. "But the guy wasn't from State. Would you believe FBI?"

"FBI." I couldn't keep the shock out of my voice.

"You don't think I'd tell them anything they didn't already know? But you don't want the FeeBees to find out you're zipping over to Europe to meet the Pole, am I right?"

I said, "You're right."

"Must be really hung up on this guy. He invite you home to meet his mom yet?"

"Both his parents are dead."

"An orphan? That's a problem. You know these old-world types can't marry without the family's approval. Maybe he's got a big brother or something?"

"No such luck," I said. "There was a half brother, but he died before I ever met him."

She pursed her lips, made a worried sound. "Doesn't look like there's much chance this Pole will make an honest woman of you." Then she laughed. "Or is that his main appeal?"

"Could be right about that, too," I said.

"Well, I'm always glad to help a horny friend." She studied

her nails. "Fair's fair. You did me a favor down in San Sal. Now I've done you a favor. So we're even?"

Something was off. I'd called in my biggest marker to get on this plane. I might as well have stamped "URGENT" on my forehead. But Lura was pretending our whole transaction was routine. I tapped my fingers on the armrest, then forced myself to stop. "We're even," I said.

"Tell me again," Lura said. "How was it you got mixed up with this guy?"

"We worked on a project together."

"Right. A project." She paused as if she were letting an old conversation come back to her. "And the two of you really pissed off some people. So now there are some Arabs out there, want to blow you away?"

I hadn't told her that. And the FBI wouldn't have mentioned it. Where was Lura getting her information?

My laugh sounded genuine. "Nobody'd bother with me. My role was peripheral."

The expression on her face told me she didn't believe a word. My shirt was wet under both arms and I could feel more sweat along my hairline.

She asked, "Spoken to your dad lately?"

Warily, I said, "Thanksgiving. I flew out to spend a few days with him."

"You know how much he loves you?"

"Where'd that come from?"

"Oregon, actually," she said. "I visited my mom over Christmas. Your dad joined us for dinner one night. He tell you we had a nice chat?"

"Sure didn't mention your mother and love in the same sentence."

Lura laughed. "Not fated, I agree. No, your dad wanted to know, could he talk freely to me about you?"

And she'd said yes, of course. So I said, "You know fathers. They tend to embellish the facts."

"Your dad never stretched the truth in his life. Remember, when we were kids, you started telling everybody he'd been some hot-dog fighter pilot in the war? And he marched you around, practically door-to-door, doing a retraction? 'Dive bombers, not fighters.' 'Purple Heart, not a Silver Star.' " She laughed again. "You're not saying that Victor Collins has started making up stories?"

" 'Embellish' was the word I used."

"Why would he do that?"

"He treats my career as his hobby." My turn to laugh. "Like his collection of airplane memorabilia. Always adding another piece. Some more authentic than others."

"What he told me about you sounded authentic enough. Then I thought about my sit-down with that fat guy from the FeeBees. Didn't make much sense to me at the time. Him so earnest and concerned about your loyalty and patriotism. I couldn't understand why he was making such a big deal out of you and the Polish guy. Then your dad fills me in. Wow, Casey, it knocked my socks off."

Lura leaned closer, her hand on my arm. "That's why I called you, soon as I got back to D.C. The thing's so damn sexy. Nice American girl saves the free world. Her reward? Death threats from the Abu Nidal Organization, FBI harassment and a career shot down in flames. Make a great news story. You'll tell me the whole thing?"

I shifted in my seat, freeing my arm. "Old news. Not even good background. You'd never get on the air with it."

"FBI interest in you is *old*?"

"A routine check," I said. "No story there."

"Maybe you could give me a zippy angle?"

"Wish I could." I forced a smile. "But there isn't one."

"You sure about that?" she asked.

"So that's why you came along. Hoped I'd give you some

hot story of international intrigue." I managed a chuckle. "Sorry to disappoint you, Lura, but I'm my same old boring self."

"You certainly are that," she agreed. But her tone was off.

I faked a yawn and leaned back, shutting my eyes. Lura was making me nervous. The less conversation we had, the better. I wanted to kick myself for giving in to the impulse to trade war stories with my father. Talking about things that had happened to me years ago didn't constitute a breach of national security. But I'd told him anecdotes that I didn't ever want to read in the newspapers. I'd asked him not to repeat what I'd said, and I'd figured there was no risk he'd do that. I hadn't figured on Lura.

My dad never claimed to be a certified war hero, but he was an ace to me. I hungered to be one for him.

My weakness. It had made me act as if I were ten years old again. If I knew Lura, that lapse was going to cost me.

I tried to lose myself in the vibration of the seat beneath me, the steady throb of the engines, the musty odor of old fabric. The diesel-like rumbling transported me into an old nightmare where my fear never lessened, though I'd suffered through it ever since the night Stefan and I fled from Poland. I smelled the ocean, tasted the salt of the Baltic, shivered under its cold spray. The ferry lurched and I clutched the railing, legs apart, braced to stay upright on the deck. Somewhere beyond me in the midnight darkness was a gun. Somewhere out there was the gunman who had pursued us from Warsaw. Nazer al-Nemer, a murderous member of the Abu Nidal Organization. Had he killed Stefan? I heard an Arabic curse. A scratching, scraping noise. Saw the darker shape of a man crawling. The glint of metal that was the missing gun. The clawlike fingers closing around the pistol grip.

My body paralyzed, except for my right leg. Moving like a thing apart. Booted foot settling gently at the base of the man's skull. The brittle sound as the boot pressed against the delicate bones. Crushed the cervical discs. Ground the particles of bone into dust. I looked down, expecting to see Nazer al-Nemer. But this time I saw Stefan, his face in an agony of death, mouthing words I couldn't hear.

I woke up shaking, my neck stiff, my throat dry and my cheeks damp. Loving Stefan had brought violence back into my life. And that violence had taken him from me.

Beyond the few unblocked windows, the blackness had faded to navy blue. Lura was asleep next to me, her features relaxed into innocence, an expression I never saw when she was awake.

I fumbled my way into the toilet and splashed water on my face. The paper-towel dispenser was empty. I used my sleeve.

The poker game was still going. The bald man had a stack of newspapers next to his right hand and a sack of fruit by his left. I begged a *Washington Post* and a banana and settled myself in a vacant seat.

The jet was slow, weighed down by the extra fuel. A commercial airliner would make the trip in six hours; we'd be lucky to get there in nine. But I couldn't complain. I'd gotten away, thanks to Lura.

Lura. She'd phoned me. And my father had tried to reach me, so worried he'd gotten out his emergency-contact number and called Harry. He must've also left a message on my machine. But who'd left the third one? And who'd removed the cassette? Not the FBI. They'd surely taped every incoming call. Their man wouldn't have removed my cassette. Not after he'd been so careful to cover his tracks.

I must have had a second visitor. Someone who came in after the Feds had been there. Someone who hadn't bothered to rewind and replay the cassette first. If he had, the digital readout would have disappeared. Someone who wanted the recording itself. And didn't care if I knew it.

The FASTEN SEAT BELTS sign came on and the plane shuddered its way into a cloudbank. Lura stumbled to the rest room, carrying a makeup case. Someone passed me a paper cup of lukewarm coffee. Lura reappeared after fifteen minutes, her hair artfully arranged in a smooth cap, her skin glowing with moisturizer and her eyes carefully lined and mascaraed.

The plane slid out of the clouds into drizzle, the raindrops glistening like slug tracks across the Plexiglas window. We bumped onto the Hamburg runway soon after that and taxied to a parking area.

We left the plane via a set of portable stairs. An airport bus idled at the bottom, streaking the slick tarmac with amber and red reflections from its lights. The wet air was sticky with the fumes of jet and diesel exhaust.

Lura sat primly on the rear seat of the bus. Her hair and makeup were perfect. Only a patch of silken calf and her red shoes protruded from beneath her coat. The pilot and the co-pilot and the rest of the United Network News people sprawled on the bench seats filling the bus's midsection, surrounded by their piles of carry-on luggage. An emaciated cameraman with a graying ponytail sat by the rear exit door, holding a camcorder.

I stayed on my feet, clutching one of the center poles. The driver snapped the doors shut, then eased the bus forward. The engine was so silent, I heard only the squeal and thud of the wipers clearing the windshield. There was one passenger on the bus who had not been with us on the plane. The seat behind the driver was filled by a broad-shouldered man in a business suit. He'd been making notes on a clipboard and hadn't looked up when I passed him. From the rear, I saw only dark hair so close-cropped it exaggerated the bullet shape of his head and neck. His shirt lay in a thin white stripe at the base of his skull, like the crimp on a cartridge, the only indication of where his neck began.

We were headed toward the terminal building. I was edgy. I didn't expect trouble with Passport Control, not in Hamburg. Buchanan would have red-flagged my name and passport number in the computer system used by the airline counter people—

the ones who ask international travelers for their documents along with their tickets. At any airport in North America, I'd have been stopped at check-in. Buchanan hadn't had time or justification to do more. It was only midnight back in D.C. The FBI should be trying to serve me with their subpoena.

Still, I was uneasy. I tried to calm myself. Buchanan might alert Immigration at Heathrow or Kastrup, but he wouldn't bother the people in Hamburg. If I'd flown commercial, I couldn't get here without first stopping at a major hub. No, I reassured myself, I needn't worry. No drowsy border guard coming off the night shift in Hamburg was going to notice Casey Collins. But it took all my self-control not to shift my weight from my right foot to my left, let everyone see how nervous I was.

The driver turned, following a grid layout that would bring us around three sides of a rectangle to park parallel to the curb in front of the terminal. Seat springs complained on my right as Ponytail shifted his position. He raised the camcorder and stared through the lens, making adjustments. I let go of the pole and stepped closer to the rear door. I rubbed condensation off the window and peered out at the building.

A quartet of uniformed policemen stood in front of a television crew, its members dressed as haphazardly as my companions. They were watching our bus approach.

Something clicked. The red light lit up on the camcorder. It was aimed at me. I jerked back from the doorway and faced Lura. She was staring at the terminal, her mouth open. I said, "Some favor you're doing me."

"You should have told me." Lura's voice was shrill. "I'd never have let this happen."

"Let what happen?"

"I pitched my idea about you to my producer. She smelled a bigger story."

From the corner of my eye I saw Ponytail rise, angling for

a better shot. I turned and slammed my open palms against the camcorder. It crashed to the floor of the bus.

Ponytail bellowed.

"A bigger story?" I yelled at Lura. "That's why you're here!" I looked for a button that would open the door in front of me.

"I'm your friend." Lura was on her feet. "That's why I'm here. My producer said, 'What if Casey's in trouble? What if she's on the run? The network can't aid and abet a fugitive.'"

"Why didn't she call Buchanan, she thought I was a wanted woman?"

"I told her you weren't," Lura said. "You couldn't be."

"And she believed you, right?" I spotted no convenient button promising to open the door in front of me. I ran to the front of the bus, searching for a device that would do the trick. I didn't spot a lever. I threw my body against the door. A jarring pain shot from my shoulder to my sternum. The door didn't flex.

The stocky man seated behind the driver tossed aside his clipboard. He stood and said something terse in German. Instead of turning right toward the terminal, the driver held the wheel steady and accelerated through the intersection.

"Hey, buddy," the pilot said. "What's going on?"

The suited man held up a badge case and flashed a gold-embossed credential. "We're making a detour for reasons of security." His accent was hard to place—not German, not French, with a peculiar richness that wasn't Scandinavian either. "After I remove the woman, the driver will deliver you to the terminal."

Lura was standing in the aisle. "I never thought this would happen," she said to me. "My producer was going to call the FBI after we took off, to cover the network."

"You set it up so you could film my arrest." I made a disgusted noise. "You're the reporter on the scene."

"But I didn't want that. I wanted you to be innocent."

She'd *wanted*. Past tense. She'd abandoned that desire. Decided I was guilty of something. Moral dilemma neatly resolved. She'd done her civic duty and now she'd get her ninety seconds on prime time.

I pressed my back against the door and shoved harder. My heart was pounding. I looked wildly around. Maybe I could grab something heavy enough to break glass.

Ponytail appeared behind Lura, holding the camcorder.

"No film," said the plainclothes policeman.

The bus driver made a wide turn that took us around the far side of the terminal. He braked there, slowing us gently to a stop opposite an unmarked door.

The arresting officer stood at the head of the aisle, blocking my retreat toward the rear. He was no more than three inches taller than me, but his body was much thicker. His closely cut hair receded at the temples, and the overlarge forehead glistened like the deadly nose of a dum-dum round.

Ponytail ran his hands over the camcorder, as if checking for damage. Then the red light came on. He pushed past Lura to crouch in the center of the bus, aiming at me again.

The cop stepped forward on his right foot. Then his left leg came up and his foot smashed the camcorder against Ponytail's face. There was a popping noise, like twigs snapping. Again the camera crashed to the floor. The cameraman was curled beside it, clutching his nose, blood running between his fingers and into his mouth.

The policeman picked up the shattered device and twisted out the film cartridge. He stuffed it into his pocket and said, "Here we do not appreciate the media circus." He tossed the broken camcorder on a seat as he came toward me. He grabbed my left bicep and barked again at the driver. The door flew open and the cop pushed me through it. I stumbled, but his grip was so strong, I couldn't fall. As soon as we were both on the ground, the door slammed shut and the bus rumbled away.

With his free hand, the cop jerked open the door in front of us and shoved me inside the building. I found myself in a corridor lit by a single fluorescent tube on the ceiling. I smelled old dust. The corridor went straight for a hundred feet, then turned left at a ninety-degree angle. Somewhere out of sight, machinery clattered. My heart was beating fast. Adrenaline had my nerves tuned tight. I gathered my muscles and got ready.

The cop let go of my arm. "Run if you prefer." He gestured down the corridor. "That path will take you to the working side of the baggage-claim area. Perhaps you can slip out that way."

His bluish lips curled in a way that made his expression as snide as his tone. He knew I couldn't saunter unnoticed through a crowd of baggage handlers. And my odds were no better if I went alone back out onto the tarmac. Which left me with this man and his strange accent. "You're not German," I said.

"Obviously not." He removed a satchel from a niche beside the door and pulled out a pair of blue coveralls. He tossed them to me. Then he started jamming himself into a matching set.

There was a change in the din coming from the far end of the corridor. People talking more loudly. A shrill whistle. A dog's bark. A man's bellow. I didn't understand the German, but I recognized the abruptness of a command. The dog barked again and the footfall of heavy boots echoed down the corridor.

6

I snatched the coveralls and yanked them over my legs. They smelled of engine grease. My companion clapped hard hats on both our heads, grabbed the satchel and opened the door to the outside. Minutes later, we were in the front seat of an electric cart, pulling three linked wagons loaded with suitcases.

The cart grumbled around the terminal building, heading toward the array of planes parked beyond Passport Control. The rain was still falling, a cold drizzle that made streaks of darker blue on the coveralls, then quickly moistened all the fabric to the same damp shade. The rumpled collar grew clammy against my neck. My skin itched with the rashy feel of things out of control.

The sky was still navy blue, the winter night unaffected by the scraps of daylight on the horizon. Rain blurred the outlines of everything more than fifty feet in the distance. Closer to us, the bus idled at the terminal building. A crowd milled around it, cameramen with belts and shoulder packs, a technician juggling a padded microphone on a boom, uniformed policemen, including one with a leashed dog, prowling over the scene of my rescue. If it was a rescue.

Lura stood to one side, microphone in hand, speaking earnestly toward one of the cameras. She didn't look away from the lens. I hunched my shoulders and tried to become nothing more than a blue unisex body topped by a canary-yellow hat.

We took a meandering route through the parked planes, ending up on the far side near a collection of buildings. We stopped beside a door marked as a men's toilet. My blue-suited companion set the brake and jumped down, leaving the cart idling. I followed him around the building to what must have been the employee parking lot. He led me to a Volkswagen Jetta, dark brown, not new and spattered with mud. Two pairs of skis were racked on top. The country decal showed a capital "CH," the designation for Switzerland. I eyed my companion. Definitely not Swiss. Not a man accustomed to neutrality.

He popped open the trunk, tossed in the satchel and his hard hat and began stripping off his coveralls. I did the same. He held out a plastic bag. "Empty your pockets into this." When I hesitated, he shook the bag. "Anything that identifies you. In here—now." Reluctantly, I pulled my passport and wallet from the zippered pocket inside my jacket and dropped them in. Then I added a handful of coins.

He closed the bag and shoved it into the tire well beneath the spare. Then he slammed the trunk and motioned me toward the passenger door. He slid behind the wheel and handed me a knitted cap patterned in red and blue and sporting a fluffy pom-pom. He'd donned a watch cap that outlined his ovoid skull. He looked more like an underwater demolition expert than a skier. I put on my hat and tucked my hair inside.

The man studied me, then reached across and pulled the wool lower on my forehead until it covered my eyebrows. His fingers smelled like harsh laundry soap. He grunted. "Slide down in the seat and close your eyes as though you are resting." He backed out of the parking space. "With luck, no one will mistake you for an American fugitive. That is, if you can refrain from smiling and waving at the passersby."

My companion drove out of the lot with arrogant confidence, his right hand on the wheel, his left dangling out of sight beside his seat. We left the airport behind and joined the rush of commuter traffic. I sat up straight and my hand went automatically to the door handle. My German was rudimentary, but *Nord* and *Süd* are pretty easy to figure out. We were driving south, away from the Jutland Peninsula. Away from Denmark and the Father-Major. "Okay," I said to my driver. "You got me out of there. Thanks. I can take it from here."

"You?" He made a disparaging noise as he cut into the left-hand lane and accelerated. "If it weren't for me, your arrest would now be on worldwide television."

"A miscalculation. I can manage now."

"Manage? Oh, yes, I'm sure you can. Manage to get yourself locked up and interrogated."

"Listen—"

"No." His voice was like a club. "You listen. You should have stayed in Washington."

"I had to get out of the U.S. If I hadn't—"

"You would be someone else's problem. Not mine."

"*Yours*? Who the hell are *you*?"

"At this moment, the only person who can keep you out of prison."

The flat certainty in his voice defied me to protest. I didn't have a good one to make. Instead I asked, "But who, specifically, are you?"

His voice slid into an oily imitation of courtesy. "You must forgive my poor manners. I was somewhat preoccupied." He tipped his head down in a mocking nod. "Major Hans van Hoof, at your service."

The name was Flemish. The peculiar accent came from the mishmash of Dutch, French and German spoken by Belgians. I let my shoulders drop. Major Hans van Hoof was a Belgian soldier. And Belgium was part of NATO. The Father-Major had never mentioned any Belgian connections, but maybe Hans van Hoof was a new recruit. I said, "Holger Sorensen sent you."

"No. No one *sent* me."

"Then why did you come?"

"I was made aware of a problem. I am resolving it."

So I'd been labeled "a problem." I wasn't going to like his solution. I asked, "Where are we going?"

"Brussels."

"No way," I said. "You go to Brussels. Drop me at the next train station. I have to straighten things out with Holger."

"You can't go to Denmark."

"Has the FBI got Holger under surveillance?"

"The FBI *and* Denmark's Politi. Perhaps Scotland Yard, too. All the police hounds have your scent, Casey Collins."

"What *can* I do?"

"I'll hide you tonight."

"And then?"

"You'll get out of the way."

"What does that mean?"

His tone got harsher. "Isn't it obvious? You must take your demented activity away. You must go someplace where no one has any interest in you."

"No interest? Then I can't go back to D.C."

"No. But you can't remain here either. I've made arrangements to send you south."

"You think I'd be less noticeable in the Mediterranean?"

"Farther south."

I tried to make a joke. "Where, the Belgian Congo?"

"Whatever they are calling themselves these days. Perfect, I think. Conditions there are so chaotic, no one will notice your arrival. I know a nice, safe spot on the coast where you can take a long vacation."

"Not a chance. I'm not leaving Europe. Not until I find out who blew up Global Flight 500."

"How ridiculously American you sound."

I swallowed my angry retort. I needed to be clever now, to provoke this man into revealing his connection to Holger. "How cynically European you sound. Somebody killed your colleague. But for you, Stefan's loss is a setback, nothing more."

"I am disappointed. I expected I would be dealing with a rational person—not a hysterical infant."

Bingo. No reaction to the word "colleague." Or to the name Stefan. Instead, an abrupt conversational shift that brought me back to the edge of my seat. "Won't work, Hans. I know the tactic. Why don't you want to talk about Stefan?"

He turned his head slightly to meet my gaze. Something flickered in his eyes. Perhaps loathing. Perhaps empathy. It was gone before I could put a name to it. He said, "I will allow nothing to interfere with our plans."

Then he quit replying to my questions. After being rebuffed three times in thirty seconds, I stopped talking, too. The car took on the sour scents of damp wool and my wet, unwashed hair. The defroster put out paltry heat and a strong smell of burned dust. I was cold and the noxious odors unsettled my stomach. Van Hoof wasn't a cop, as I'd first thought. But I was his prisoner all the same. He'd helped me escape incarceration in a federal penitentiary. But he wanted to ship me to his private penal colony in Africa.

My elbow banged against the door, my muscles jerky with panic. I hugged myself, overpowering my fear. Could van Hoof do what he wished with me?

Without moving my head, I glanced at him. His watch cap grazed the ceiling and his shoulders were broader than the seat-back. He gazed intently at the road ahead, but he'd relaxed into the driver's seat, legs spread wide. My thigh was only inches from his and I saw the difference. Legs twice as thick and probably twice as powerful as mine.

I loosened my grip on myself, flexed my fingers. I was smaller and weaker, but maybe I was smarter. Maybe he couldn't control my life as easily as he thought. He'd said he'd allow nothing to interfere with his plans.

I had plans of my own. Get to Holger. Find out who had killed Stefan. And now one more: Get away from van Hoof. I stared out the window as we drove through the drizzle toward the Low Countries of Europe. This wasn't the direction in which I wanted to go. But then again, it wasn't the direction my pursuers would expect me to take. I'd let van Hoof take me where no one knew me. Where no one was looking for me. Once we'd evaded the FBI, I'd ditch him.

The prospect of action cheered me, yet I didn't relax. I needed to stay alert. And there was no way I'd permit my slender leg to brush against the massive one beside it.

We crossed from Germany into the Netherlands. Near Apeldoorn, van Hoof pulled into a service area. He watched me through the rear window as he pumped fuel. When the tank was full, he walked over to the cashier to pay. I spotted the gold-embossed cover of a foreign passport tucked into the driver-side door pocket. I leaned across his seat and found not one but two Swiss passports, kept close at hand as if van Hoof expected to encounter a roadblock where he'd need to produce identity documents in a hurry. The top one revealed a grainy photo of a generic brunette. Younger than I was, shorter, but with help from Clairol, I could pass for Fräulein Keck. Not bad on short notice. I flipped open the second passport, expecting to see van Hoof's fleshy features. But only the hairstyle matched. The face belonged to Stefan.

I was so startled, the other booklet slipped out of my hand and slid off the edge of the seat. A precious false identity. I couldn't let it get away. I jammed my right hand into the crack between the seat and the door, my fingers scrabbling. But instead of a sharp cardboard edge, my hand brushed checkered wood. I ran my fingers over it and felt the familiar handgrip of a Browning nine-millimeter semiautomatic pistol. It was the same handgun I'd trained with in Denmark, years ago. For an instant I smelled gunpowder again, felt my palm tingle the way it did after I'd fired a round. I heard Stefan's voice, softly gloating over the skill he'd coaxed from me. *Dobrze, moj skarbie. Bardzo dobrze.* Good, my treasure. Very good.

My hand closed around the grip. Exactly what I needed to make van Hoof take me where *I* wanted to go.

Metal screeched and the car door jerked open. Van Hoof's boot pinned my wrist against the frame. He grabbed the passports and shoved them into his pants pocket. His boot didn't move and I lay with my cheek flat against the driver's seat, the upholstery still warm from his body. When he bent down to retrieve the pistol, I saw sweat glistening under his eyes, and his breathing was heavy. He leaned closer and another fifty pounds of force crushed onto my wrist. I groaned.

"Kolwezi," he hissed into my ear. "At the bottom of a copper pit. That's the place for you." He stepped back from the car.

I sat up and brushed grit off my wrist. My fingers smelled of gun oil. "What are you doing with Stefan's passport?"

"Saving you from yourself."

I watched him walk around the car and lock the weapon in the trunk. As soon as he was back behind the wheel, I said, "You know what he was working on."

He got us back on the highway before he answered. "I can tell you one thing. There is nothing—*nothing*—more important than his mission. I will finish it. And you won't get in my way." His eyes were hard.

I didn't prompt him to say more. I recalled van Hoof's dangling left hand as we left the Hamburg airport. Had his fingertips been resting on the weapon? Had he planned to shoot his way past the press and the police? Or might he have found it less complicated to shoot me?

Goose bumps rose along my arms. I'd underestimated van Hoof. He'd stopped me with brutal finality. I shivered, chilled by new understanding. If I tried to take control again, I had to succeed. Van Hoof wouldn't give me a third chance.

We continued west toward Utrecht, passing canals and earthen dikes, the gray sky blending with the washed-out colors of the ground and the stone buildings to blur the horizon. The dismal landscape matched my mood. The last time I'd found myself at such a miserable disadvantage, I'd been in Poland. It was during that awful week in April of 1986, following the U.S. air attack on Tripoli. Stefan had vanished and I'd been threatened with death by Abu Nidal's hired guns.

Frightened, I fled to the lake region northeast of Warsaw to hide. I evaded my pursuers but Stefan turned up after twenty-four hours. He insisted he was there to guard me. I thought it more likely he'd come to seduce me but I was too scared to refuse protection from a former member of the *czerwony berety*, Poland's elite Red Beret commandos. I promised myself I'd be strong. I wouldn't sleep with a man I still believed to be an enemy agent.

The place I'd chosen to hide was near Wolf's Lair, the spot where Hitler's officers had tried to kill him in 1944. Stefan told me that Lieutenant Colonel Claus von Stauffenberg placed a briefcase containing an explosive charge beneath the table in the conference barracks. Then the colonel found an excuse to leave the meeting. Unfortunately, someone moved the briefcase behind an oak table leg. The room was destroyed but Hitler survived.

I knew what happened to the conspirators and I stopped Stefan before he got to the part about the meat hooks.

He paused and said, "I have always had a great fondness for Colonel von Stauffenberg."

I knew he was speaking his heart's truth to me. And with fewer than a dozen words, he wiped out my power to resist him. We became lovers that night. We'd been lovers ever since. Until now.

The muscles in my stomach cramped. The pain dragged me back to my dreary present. Beside me in the car, something squeaked. Van Hoof had shifted in his seat. I glanced his way, caught him staring at me.

Had I moaned? I might have. I cleared my throat, stared straight ahead. The wipers slapped rhythmically across the windshield. The drizzle had grown into a shower. And I felt more alone than I had ever felt in my life before that moment. Stefan was gone. Nothing I did would bring him back. I tried to console myself with van Hoof's words, that there was nothing more important than Stefan's mission. It was how he'd have chosen to die—working toward something that mattered. True, but it gave me no comfort.

Traffic got heavier as we turned south past the exits for Rotterdam and Antwerp. By midafternoon, we'd parked in a lot behind a building in downtown Brussels. Van Hoof pulled the ski cap down over my eyebrows again, then hurried me through a side entrance into a deserted lobby. A huge arrangement of cut flowers gave off a funereal odor. I thought suddenly of my mother. She'd been haunted by imaginary peril for most of her adult life. Four years ago, she'd missed the lump in her breast.

Van Hoof snatched a newspaper from the half dozen neatly piled on an end table. He glanced at it as he hurried me up a set of fire stairs to the top floor and along a door-lined corridor. He unlocked the final door and urged me inside what appeared to be a hotel room.

He tossed the paper at me. Below the fold, my stern-faced passport photo topped a two-inch story. I recognized only two words: "Kathryn Collins," right under the picture.

"Afternoon paper?" I asked van Hoof.

He grunted an affirmative. "You're a celebrity."

"In Brussels? That makes no sense. It's not like I'm some *international* criminal."

"Might as well be, now you got UNN involved. They've turned you into such a big story, the wire services can't ignore you." He tapped his finger on the picture. "You're in a hotel for Belgian military officers. If you come out of this room, one of them will recognize you. You must not open the door. I've left some cheese and fruit for you. I'll start making arrangements. Eight o'clock tomorrow morning, you're heading south."

"Forget it," I said. "I'm not going to Africa."

"What else can you do? What are your languages—Spanish, Polish, Danish? You can't talk your way out of Belgium. And I'm holding your money. You can't buy your way out. Your passport is locked in my car. It's useless to you anyway." He patted the pants pocket where he'd placed the two Swiss passports. "Unfortunately, you have no other papers. I think you must go where I send you."

"You could loan me that woman's passport. Give me money."

"Yes. If I wanted you here." He reached for the doorknob. "But I want you far, far away." And then he was gone.

Far, far away meant war-torn, AIDS-ravaged Africa. A terrifying future. But something else scared me more. I didn't know if van Hoof would let me live long enough to get there.

My stomach muscles clenched. What reason did he have *not* to kill me?

He was so hostile, rejecting everything I proposed, frustrating every move I made. I slammed my fist against the wall. I wished I'd hit van Hoof's face. He scared me, yes. He made me mad, too. And anger was a far more useful emotion.

I strode over to the door. Stopped. Turned around and hiked back to the exterior wall. Stalked along the bed to the adjoining wall. Hiked back. The room was only eight feet wide and half again as long, with a ceiling that rose to the underside of the attic roof. The clerestory windows were set in dormers, the bottom sills so high above me I couldn't see out. There were no pictures on the walls, no decorations of any kind, not even a mirror. My accommodations weren't plush enough for a colonel or a general. Van Hoof wanted to avoid anyone who outranked him. He'd put me in a garret room sparsely furnished to meet the basic needs of a noncommissioned officer. After fewer than three minutes, I was bouncing off the walls.

A stream of overheated air poured from the radiator and flowed twenty feet upward to the roof. The hot draft made my skin feel scaly. I checked out the wall unit, but there was no way to turn off the blast. The room was as hot as the Congo. Maybe old Belgian soldiers never got over their colonial service. Spent the rest of their days dreaming of the African sun. I ripped off my jacket and dropped it on the desk. Tossed my sweater on top. I kept going until I wore only my underpants.

I threw myself down on the single bed and stared at the distant ceiling. The room was silent except for the hissing of the radiator and clicks from the mini-bar as the coolant cycled on, then off.

By now Holger would know about Karsten Hansen, the unknown man with the Danish passport who'd boarded Global 500 in Heathrow. He'd know about the two U.S. government agents who'd died on the plane. Holger had told me to stay away from him. But my situation had changed. Once I explained, he'd realize that I had no alternative. I had to get to the Father-Major. We could put it all together. Give enough to the FBI to get them off my back. And then I'd help him track down the ones who'd done the bombing.

I hopped up and found a hotel brochure in the night stand. The Flemish words were close enough to Danish so that I could figure out I was situated in the heart of Brussels, near the Royal Palace, the Market Square and—most important—the Central Railway Station. The quickest way out of town. I'd wait until all the Belgian soldiers were fast asleep. Then I'd go to the station. Panhandle ticket money if I had to. Make my way to Holger.

I clicked on the television for company. From the shots of politicians meeting en masse, I guessed the announcer was reading a news story about some activity that day in the local parliament. I was halfway to the shower when the voice-over changed from a man to a woman and my picture flashed on the screen. Then shots of the Hamburg airport. The newscaster made a lengthy report in Flemish. I caught my name, along with "Global" and "Lockerbie Two." My name in the same sentence that referred to a terrorist bombing. I wanted to throw up. But I couldn't take my eyes off the screen.

First a State Department Public Information Officer: "Subject of a security investigation." Then a spokesman for the Royal Danish Army—words I understood. "Briefly under our protection in 1986. All ties now severed." Last, a quick shot of my father's back as he disappeared inside his house.

My father! They'd staked out my father. I could imagine how he was taking this. Outraged by the press. In a panic to help me. He kept his passport current so he could do so. "If you ever need me, Casey, girl," he said at least once every time I visited, "give me a call, I'll come running." And he was powerless to do anything for me.

I clicked the TV off and opened the mini-bar. In front of the canned beverages was a bunch of green grapes and a red-wrapped wheel of cheese. I shut the door. I wanted something warm. Despite the heat in the room, I yearned for a cup of hot cocoa and a piece of toast. Cinnamon toast, the way my mother used to make it, putting the pieces under the broiler until the sugar caramelized and crusted on top. Cinnamon toast was my favorite afternoon snack when I was in elementary school. I was luckier than my friend Lura, whose mother worked. My mother was at home waiting to feed me and listen to my stories. I knew other people found it odd that she refused to leave the house. But I liked that she was there without fail, my personal adoring audience. It was enough when I was ten.

I sighed. I wanted to curl up on the bed and pray I'd wake up from this nightmare. But I wasn't a child anymore. I was a grown woman sweating herself to dehydration in an over-heated room. Time to act like an adult.

I yanked open the mini-bar, pushed aside the food and grabbed a Jupiler. When I popped the cap, the scent was pungent with yeast, redolent of hops. I took a swallow. It tasted as good as it smelled. Too good for the mess I was in. My face had been on television. I couldn't leave this room tonight. I'd be recognized for sure. I held the cool aluminum against my burning cheek.

Could I trust van Hoof? No way. He knew more about Stefan's fate than he was telling. The Swiss passport with Stefan's picture proved it. Van Hoof must've been in Brussels last night—Monday night—when he'd been tapped to meet me. He said he'd gotten to Hamburg at four this morning—in time to see the cops form their welcoming committee. He couldn't have gotten the Jetta and the Swiss passports on such short notice. Those things required days of preparation, not hours. The car and the passports were intended for Stefan and the mysterious Fräulein Keck. Had she disappeared along with him? Van Hoof was keeping too many secrets from me. I wasn't going to let that man direct the next part of my life.

I went into the bathroom. The showerhead was ten feet

above the tiled floor of the stall, as though the soldiers who routinely used it were all giants. Hot water soaked my hair and streamed down my face. The water smelled faintly of hard-boiled eggs, like the hot springs I used to visit with my father. I shut my eyes and let the torrent slide over me.

If I couldn't trust van Hoof, then what could I do? Go to the American Embassy and turn myself in? Let the FBI send me home again. Fight it out with Buchanan. Do some time if I had to. At least when I got out of the Big House, no one would be chasing me. I moved my head back from under the stream and squeezed water from my hair. *Do some time. The Big House.* As if pretending I was in a Jimmy Cagney movie would make a prison term conceivable. I'd driven past the correctional facility in Lorton. Inside a place like that, I'd suffer in ways I hated to imagine.

I turned off the water and grabbed a towel. The steam-filled room had the damp-soil odor of a well-fertilized indoor garden. There was no mirror in here either. How did the Belgian Army expect its officers to shave?

I wrapped the second towel around myself and started in on the grapes. I wasn't going to jail, not voluntarily. And I wasn't going into hiding in Africa. No, I wouldn't let van Hoof bury my number one priority under his.

I needed cash and ID and a changed appearance and transportation. Everything van Hoof could give me, but wouldn't.

I spent the next hour considering the best way to take them from him. I was younger and in good shape, but van Hoof had the well-tuned body of a former commando. I couldn't overpower him. I had to take him by surprise, get him down and incapacitate him. I knew the technique, though I'd never been able to make it work against Stefan. It was impossible to surprise the man who'd trained me. Every time, I landed on the mat with the wind knocked out of me, my body pinned under his. I remembered the slickness of his skin against mine, the musky odor of his sweat, the throaty way he whispered, "*Dobrze*," even though I'd lost once again.

But then, he didn't expect me to defeat him. He wasn't trying to make a sparring partner out of me. We were in a dangerous profession. He loved me and he wanted to keep me alive. He was a tough teacher because of that. And he taught me some good moves.

They were moves that could take down a big man who wasn't expecting an attack. And van Hoof wouldn't be. The key to success, though, was getting into position on the other side of my door well before van Hoof arrived at eight o'clock tomorrow morning. I'd sleep until four. Then I'd take my place in the hallway.

But at midnight, a noise jerked me awake. I was on my feet before I heard it again. Metal scraping against the other side of my doorknob. Then the ticking slide of steel going into the lock. The click as it turned and drew back the latch. The oiled sigh of the hinge as the door opened. An exit sign in the outside hallway cast green light onto the floor of my room. A shoe scuffed against the rug.

Van Hoof had come early. He wasn't waiting until morning to send me south. He was going to get rid of me now.

I crouched, muscles tensing, right hand fisting, gauging where to strike. Before the door had clicked shut, I threw myself up and at him, putting all my weight behind that single blow to his throat.

The man I struck was at least six inches taller than van Hoof. I hit too low, my fist smashing hard into his sternum. He gripped my right arm in his and drove his left into my midsection. I went down hard on the bed, on my back, unable to breathe. The sequence reminded me exactly of my training. Right down to the acrid scent of French tobacco.

An electric prickle raced over my skin. Along with it came such a wave of elation that if I'd had air in my lungs, I'd have cried out. My wrist burned and my guts ached. The pain was real. This was no dream. Stefan was here.

He shifted his weight to his knees and let go of my wrist.

I inhaled a long, shuddering breath. My arms went around his neck then, my mouth found his and I tasted him, the smoky flavor I knew better than my own. I slid my hands under his jacket, felt his warmth through his shirt, held him so tightly against me I vibrated with his heartbeat. Not a dream! Stefan with me, in the flesh.

I was weak with joy.

I was incoherent with rage.

I moved my hands to his shoulders and pushed until I could see his face, the eyes black pools sunken above the angular cheekbones. I sputtered, fumbling over the first word. Tried again until I could voice that "You!" Then blurted out the rest:

"You better have a damn good reason for putting me through this."

The full lips curved up in that knowing grin. "What, no hello-how-are-you?"

"You're fine. I got proof enough of that." I ran my hand down his chest to his belt buckle. "Solid proof." I slapped his belly. "You're alive and well. So why didn't you let me know?"

"I did."

The wool blanket was hot beneath me. I shifted and said, "No, you didn't. I was right there in D.C., waiting."

"Someone else had to make the call. And that took time to arrange."

I kept my right hand on his chest. With my left I switched on the bedside lamp. His eyes went from black to hazel, flecked with gold. His hair was the color of strong coffee. He'd cut it as short as van Hoof's and his hairline receded in the same way at the temples. He looked older. More distinguished. Better. The scent of tobacco blended with his musky smell. I said, "Someone phoned me?"

"The day after Christmas."

"Five days after the explosion? You let me wait five days?"

He moved off me until he was sitting on the edge of the bed. The temperature in the room had to be ninety degrees. Perspiration beaded his hairline and dampened the dark smudges beneath each eye. He rubbed a hand across his forehead, then pulled off his jacket. He said, "I had to go slow. For your protection."

"That's bullshit." I stood next to the bed, glaring down at him. "You weren't thinking of me. You want people to believe you're dead. You wouldn't risk the contact. No matter what your silence cost me."

He reached for my hand. His touch sent an electric charge zinging through me. "I was concerned about you—"

I backed away from him. "Keeping me in the dark was supposed to be safer for me? You know me better than that. It didn't work. It couldn't work."

He made a snorting noise. "Whose fault was that?"

"Yours," I said. "You weren't thinking about me."

"Not true—"

I pushed on. "Two days after Christmas—when I saw Holger—did he know you were alive?"

"Not then. It wasn't until the next day that I was able to get word to Holger. They were watching him too closely."

" 'They'?"

"Some of Jibril's people dropped by his parish."

Ahmed Jibril headed a group that called itself the Popular Front for the Liberation of Palestine—General Command. They were a violent bunch, but in recent years they hadn't attacked American targets. Surprised, I asked, "Did Jibril's group place the bomb?"

"Can't be sure yet. Maybe them. More likely the Abu Nidal Organization. This was a joint action, coordinated out of Tripoli."

I felt a jangle of alarm. After his frenzied bloodletting in the mid-1980s, Abu Nidal had moved his organization out of Europe and made his main business extortion and protection rackets and terrorist operations against Yasser Arafat. His people had killed more PLO members than they had Americans.

"You think they've gone back to their old tactics?" I asked.

He shook his head. "Only an educated guess. Based on increased activity in and out of Libya. Rumors I've heard. And, of course, they've got plenty of plastic explosive down there."

The former Czech regime had exported enough Semtex to Libya to make bombs for the next one hundred fifty years. I said, "If you knew they were so active, why'd you fly out of Heathrow on the anniversary of Lockerbie? Why'd you risk it?"

"I was following somebody. A young Libyan who was supposed to have critical information about a future terrorist action. He'd made reservations a month ago on the Global flight. A colleague tracked him to Berlin on December eighteenth. Then, on the twenty-first, he boarded a connecting flight from Tegel. I was going to pick him up from Heathrow. Create an opportunity to interrogate him." He stood. "Damn, it's hot in here." He began pulling off his shirt. When he raised his arms above his head, I could count his ribs. He'd gotten thinner and the scar on his lower belly crawled like a gray worm across the pale skin.

I wanted to trace that line with my fingers, follow it down and under his belt. Instead, I moved over to the mini-bar and took out two beers. He accepted one from me and swallowed greedily. "Taking that flight was a calculated risk," he acknowledged. "The Libyan was well connected. Unlikely they'd blow up a plane with one of their own on board. But on the way to my seat, I spotted the FBI guy from Brussels. With that friend of yours, the one who looks Vietnamese."

"Billy Nu. Neither of them noticed you?"

"I managed to avoid them. But I couldn't stay on board, take a chance they'd see me, say something that would blow my approach to the Libyan. I figured I'd be better off if I got someone else to meet him in New York, hold him for me. I disembarked, planning to catch a later flight."

"Your seat turning up empty at the last minute—that didn't set off an alarm?"

"No, unfortunately. I took precautions. Apparently they worked." His voice was level, but pain thickened every word.

If the crew had noted his departure, they'd have held up the flight, searched the plane again for explosives. Maybe they'd have found the bomb. I sank onto the single chair. Despite the beer I'd drunk, my mouth had gone dry. "To make you board that particular flight, the terrorists used live bait."

"Dead now."

"You want them to think you're dead, too. Like Billy Nu and the guy from Brussels."

"So I couldn't phone you up and say, 'Hey, Casey, I'm fine.' I had to have someone else use the signal."

His eyes were sincere over the top of his beer. But I wasn't ready to give in. "You knew I didn't get the message. You knew as soon as you talked to Holger."

"I assumed you'd find out when you got home and played back your messages."

"Except all my phone messages disappeared. The tape was stolen."

He swallowed the rest of his beer. "Intercepted. They're watching you, too. Bad enough they have one example of our signaling system. Good I didn't try again and give them any more."

The golden light from the lamp lit half of his face, sharpening the strong bone of his nose, thickening the lips. I wanted to stroke that face, kiss those lips. But I wasn't satisfied with his story. Not yet. I made myself look away. "Okay," I said, "I'll buy that part of it. But what was this business with van Hoof? Why couldn't he tell me?"

"Hans wants you to think I'm dead. Says your behavior is more convincing that way."

"Using me."

"Yes." Stefan put his elbows on his knees and leaned toward me. The skin on his chest glistened with sweat. "He doesn't debate ends and means. The only thing that concerns Hans is the most effective way to put the terrorists out of business."

"He's as fanatic as they are."

"He has reason. His daughter was in the check-in line with her luggage in Vienna in 1985 when Abu Nidal's hired guns opened fire on the crowd. She survived, but she's been in a coma ever since. The doctors want to disconnect the machines, but Hans refuses. And while he waits for a miracle, he hunts."

"He wants revenge for the Vienna airport massacre?"

"That's the connection that brought him into our plans."

Stefan paused. "We'll have to make some alterations now."

"Because you're supposed to be dead?"

"Right. And Hans made a strong argument that your continued ignorance of my survival would be in my interest."

"But you talked him out of it."

"I couldn't convince him I was right." The bedsprings squeaked and Stefan stood. He took a step toward me. "Hans won't be pleased to learn I came here."

He hadn't told me everything.

I wanted the complete story.

I wanted him more.

I was on my feet before he'd closed the distance between us. I traced his new hairline. I let my fingers continue through his hair until my hand rested on the back of his neck. His left arm went around me. I drew his face to mine.

His lips were soft, his tongue wet. I tasted his beer and the rough hint of tobacco. And something more. Primal and urgent, the salty tang that comes when too much death makes you fierce for life. Nature's antidote to wasteful murder, that hot desire to breed. I tasted it in him and in myself. I gave in, gave in completely to it. My head fell back as his mouth crushed down on mine. My fingertips pressed tight against the hot skin of his back.

He pulled his mouth away from mine. "*Moj skarbie,*" he whispered. My treasure.

"*Moj skarbie,*" I breathed back.

He slid his free hand between us until his fingers covered my breast. A tingling charge radiated outward until the nerve ends in my fingertips vibrated. Blood was pulsing through every artery, surging into the capillaries, roaring into my brain with a noise like rushing water.

Heat was coming off him, a fiery warmth. I inhaled the scent of male sweat. I rubbed against him, skin on skin. The room grew dimmer, then brighter. His hand was slick against my breast, stroking, massaging, squeezing. The roaring sound in my brain grew louder. Sensation receded from my fingertips, flowed back toward my center. I gasped for air. The wall behind him was breathing, too, rubbery, moving in and out and growing rosy in color. A fuzzy halo formed around the lamp and then began to pulse and wiggle.

We fell onto the bed. I couldn't feel the wool beneath me now. All sensation was concentrating in my center; all the blood was flowing that way. I was wet, wet and eager.

Stefan slid away from me. I heard tapping, the sound of a single knuckle against the door. In seconds he was across the room, peering through the fisheye. "Cover up," he said. "We've got company."

Breathing hard, I yanked a sheet off the bed, wrapped it around me.

Stefan opened the door and Hans van Hoof marched in. The air in the room seemed to grow warmer and the oxygen thinner, as though a small inferno were burning in its center. He made a noise of disgust and glared at Stefan. "When Erika called and said you'd gone out, I knew you'd come here."

As the door whispered across the carpet, a woman moved into the light and stood beside van Hoof. She was dressed in leather—skintight, chocolate-colored pants and a darker suede jacket over a lacy camisole, an outfit that showed her lithe body. She was a few inches shorter than me, at least ten years younger. Dark curly hair, and a face that matched the one in Fräulein Keck's Swiss passport. Well, the features matched. The photo hadn't captured the vivid blue of her eyes or her attitude. Even next to van Hoof's vibrating fury, she was a presence.

The door clicked shut.

Stefan came to stand beside me and said, "She has to know the truth."

Van Hoof disagreed. "She has to go."

"Believe me," I said, "I don't want to stick around." I put my hand on Stefan's arm. "Stefan and I will both go."

The woman said, "She thinks you're leaving with her?" Her

voice was low-pitched, as though only she and Stefan were in the room.

Before Stefan could answer, I told him, "I saw the two passports. You were supposed to work with her. But you're dead now. They'll have to find her a new skiing buddy."

"Casey," Stefan said softly, "I'm not finished here."

"You know a bomb brought down Global 500. And you've traced it to Libya and the terrorists holed up there. I'll give that to the FBI. We can work on it with them, back in the U.S. The FBI has the resources to nail the bad guys."

Van Hoof's voice was like a pistol shot. "Oh, yes, let the Americans handle it. We've heard that argument before. The conflict is between the terrorists and the great world power. Leave the solution to the U.S.A."

I said, "There's some logic there."

"Gunslinger logic," returned van Hoof. "You American cowboys are so happy to have all your shoot-outs on European soil. And what happens? Viennese bystanders gunned down in their airport and Berliners dead in their disco and Scottish villagers crushed by pieces of a plane."

"You're talking 1988 and earlier," I said. "Nothing like that's happened in Europe lately."

"Because the terrorists avoided American targets here," van Hoof said. "But now we have Global Flight 500. The cycle of attack and retaliation will resume, if we allow it. No, I think we will root out this evil on our own."

"I agree," the woman told van Hoof. "We must dispose of this distraction and get on with it."

Was I imagining it, or had she moved closer to Stefan? Given him a seductive look? Had they been lovers once? Were they still? I asked her, "Who are you?"

She bent down over Stefan's jacket. Without looking at me, she extracted his cigarette pack and removed one. She rose and tossed the pack to Stefan. He caught it easily, as though the two of them had been practicing. She pulled out a matchbook, lit her cigarette and inhaled.

"This is Erika Berger," Stefan said. "She works for a private arms trader in Antwerp. Her job affords her a number of useful contacts."

Business in Antwerp had once kept Stefan away from me for so long, I'd recklessly gone to Belgium to find him. And Erika Berger was a gunrunner in Antwerp. How damnably glamorous. Had he known her then? Adolescent jealousy was twisting inside me. Forty years old, and I felt as needy as I had at fourteen. I hated that feeling. I said, "Taking this to the FBI solves a lot of problems for me. Convince me you people can do a better job."

Van Hoof raised an eyebrow at Stefan.

Stefan spoke directly to me. "You know about the secret meeting in Tripoli."

A disparate group of terrorists had met clandestinely at Libyan intelligence headquarters in September. "You think that was when they coordinated their plans for this bombing?" I asked.

"And for future actions," he said. "All using explosives cached in Libya and manpower from the terrorist organizations. All targeting American carriers flying out of Western Europe."

"Libyan intelligence agents, members of the Abu Nidal Organization and PFLP-GC, people like that—they get the explosive devices onto the planes," I said.

"Different teams of terrorists," Stefan told me. "Capturing the perpetrators of the Global bombing isn't enough. The next incident will use different manpower. We have to find out where and when they'll strike."

I said, "Granted, nobody in the U.S. government has shown any talent for penetrating Middle Eastern terrorist networks. But what makes you think a crew of lily-white Europeans can do any better?"

"Obviously, none of us would attempt such foolishness."

Van Hoof's eyes glittered. "Far better to direct our energies toward the single intellect organizing these events."

Not a Middle Eastern intellect, then. He had to mean someone who looked and thought like he did. Stefan had told me the Libyan had come to Heathrow from Berlin. Holger had been instrumental in exposing the German companies behind Libyan construction of a chemical weapons plant in Rabta. The U.S. halted that project but couldn't plug the German pipeline to Colonel Qadhafi. A German company sold him tunnel-digging machinery and he drilled under a mountain at Tarhuna and began again, his gas-mixing equipment courtesy of Siemens.

"You think a German planned this bombing," I said. "You're trying to get information from him or from someone close to him."

Erika held up her cigarette like a stop sign. "She knows more than she should—"

I looked at Stefan. "*You* can't approach him. You're too well known in Germany. You want people to think you're dead, you have to stay out of this. Better you stay with me in the U.S."

Van Hoof appeared ready to spit at me. "Being around you is equally deadly for him. Stefan should never have come to you. We don't know who may have tracked you here. Many clever hunters are seeking the reward for his death."

My stomach lurched. I took a deep breath before I said to Stefan, "There was a price on your head?"

He stared at the cigarette pack, then extracted one. He set the near-empty pack on the night stand. As he drew the lighter from his jeans pocket, he said, "Five hundred thousand."

"Then the danger is past," I said. "No one has any reason to believe you survived that explosion. Your killers have been paid off."

Van Hoof said, "No one's been paid. The contract is still open."

"Open? Who put out this contract?" I asked.

Van Hoof and Erika exchanged a look I couldn't interpret. Neither spoke.

"Who wants to make sure I've been eliminated?" Stefan blew out a cloud of pungent smoke. "An otherwise unexceptional German businessman. In the one news photo we've got, he's standing at the fringes of a company party in Brussels. A picture from earlier in the year. It only surfaced last month when police began looking for the Belgian owner of that same company because he'd shipped embargoed computer equipment to Qadhafi."

"I read about that," I said.

"Yes, we all read that story with interest. And I spotted our man. Few people would have recognized him or made the connection, his new identity is so artfully documented. Now he calls himself Gunter Storch. But I knew him rather well before, when he was Major Reinhardt Krüger."

"Major?" I asked. "You mean—"

"Yes," Stefan said. "Major Krüger was in the Stasi. He worked with terrorist groups. Few of his colleagues realized how intimately he was involved. Wisely, he disappeared right after reunification, before the extent of his collusion was revealed. Apparently he slid quietly into his new identity of international trader. But that's only a front. His primary activity is as a behind-the-scenes deal-maker between Libya and Western business. Given his background, we are certain he planned the bombing of Global 500."

"You say he's got a contract out on you. Yet you're trying to contact an informant who's got access to him. What, are you suicidal?"

"We know that more bombings will follow this one. Krüger is the mastermind behind them. I much preferred extracting the information we need in a quiet chat with the Libyan, somewhere in the U.S." He shrugged. "Unfortunately, my only alternate source is one of Krüger's German associates. A man who wants money badly enough to talk to me."

"Why not leave it to the German police? Let them pick up Krüger and interrogate him."

Stefan shook his head tiredly. "The police are hampered by rules of evidence. They couldn't detain Major Krüger long enough to get anything useful from him."

Van Hoof said to me, "You understand now? This isn't a problem that can be solved by apprehending one group of terrorists. We can't turn this over to your FBI. They may be good at catching bad guys like the ones who planted this last bomb. But we want to discover what a different bunch of bad guys will be sent to do next. And that requires delicacy."

Stefan said, "We can't help you go home, not yet. We can't give your people what we've got on Global Flight 500. Hans knows a place where you'll be safe till we can."

My safety again. Stefan claimed to be so concerned about me. But I felt pushed aside. Told to put my life on hold, while he risked everything to make contact with a shadowy informant. The matching Swiss passports and the Jetta with Swiss registration were leftovers from an earlier fallback plan. One that had Stefan and Erika posing as a couple. They'd have to rewrite the script if they wanted to bolster the fiction that Stefan was dead. But they'd still be working together.

I wondered how Stefan had missed the obvious. I could give him precisely the help he needed now. It was as clear to me as if I were watching myself on a video.

"Enough of this," Erika told van Hoof. "Let's not waste any more time."

She was so eager to get rid of me. I wished I could let her have her way. I wished I could leave. But I didn't trust her to protect Stefan. Not the way I could.

Ego. My own worst enemy.

"You'll waste less time if you let me in on this," I said. "Was Major Reinhardt Krüger part of HVA?" I used the shorthand for the Hauptverwaltung Aufklärung, the now-defunct foreign intelligence service of the former East Germany.

Interest flared in Erika's eyes. "Yes."

"I thought he must be," I said. "Then I can give Stefan a better shot at meeting safely with his informant. I have a way to distract Major Krüger."

"You?" The glimmer of interest was gone. "You're a fugitive. Discredited by your own State Department. Pursued by the FBI."

"Exactly," I said. "I'm in big trouble. If I went back to the U.S., I'd be thrown in jail. Unless I brought home a big prize. Something the FBI wants badly. Like an answer to the question that's been bugging them: How far did HVA penetrate into U.S. intelligence during the Cold War? The FBI wants to know who spied for HVA and what the East Germans got from them. The FBI would trade a lot to get all the facts. I can act as if I want to broker that deal. As if I wanted to swap what Krüger knows for my freedom from prosecution plus safe haven for him in America."

"No." Stefan's eyes were hazel ice. "You cannot deal with Reinhardt Krüger. He would destroy you."

I said, "I wouldn't go through with it. But I can make the proposition. Get his attention long enough for you to make contact with his associate. Find out where they're going to plant the next bomb."

"You think your proposal would get Krüger's attention?" Erika's tone was too dismissive. "He has no interest in going into hiding in the U.S."

"Of course he does. He knows his cover won't hold up much longer. If you spotted him in November, others did, too. And when the German authorities catch up with him, they *will* arrest him. Only the old East German spy managers are exempt from prosecution. They won't go easy on anyone as involved with the terrorists as you claim Krüger was. If he has any survival instinct at all, he's looking for a bolt-hole. He'll be eager to enroll in our Witness Protection Program."

Erika asked, "Why would Krüger believe *you* could make a deal like that?"

"The media's inflated my reputation," I replied. "I'm an important international criminal. One who's had mysterious dealings with the FBI and the CIA. Now I need to save myself. What could be more credible to a slimeball? Mutual self-interest: We don't have to trust each other. He'll go for it."

Van Hoof said, "Her situation can be turned to our advantage."

"No," Stefan said. "I won't allow her to do it."

"She won't actually confront Krüger," van Hoof countered. "She'll put out the word that she's got something he wants. That alone will be sufficient to provide the diversion you require."

"Visibility like that is too dangerous," Stefan said. "She'll be an instant target."

"Too dangerous," Erika echoed. But her voice lacked conviction. And she was no longer looking at Stefan.

I said, "Stefan will be in greater danger if I don't help him. Nobody will be foolish enough to kill me before that contract is paid. Not while there's a chance I'll draw Stefan to me. Besides, Krüger will want to hear more about my offer. He'll order them to leave me alone. I'll be bulletproof."

"The al-Nemers won't be deterred," Stefan said.

When he spoke the family name of the assassin who'd pursued us out of Poland, I heard a worried undertone in his voice that set off an echoing tremor in my stomach. But I had to do this. I pushed my fear aside. "No reason to think they're still interested in me. I've had the Department keep a lookout for them. No al-Nemers have left the Shuf Mountains in the past year."

"You must try to be objective," van Hoof said to Stefan. "We've been all through this. Your informant knows where Krüger has told the terrorists to strike next. But he's deathly afraid he'll be seen with you. The high price he's asking for that information reflects how dangerous it is for him. He'll meet you once only, at the time and place he's named. But you can't go there with all of Krüger's gunmen searching for you."

Van Hoof's voice took on greater urgency and he leaned toward Stefan. "If Casey creates a flurry of activity at another location, your chances of success are much improved. And if she seizes Krüger's attention as well, all the better."

"I agree." Erika's voice had an undertone of pleading when she spoke to Stefan. "Hans is right."

Stefan said, "The danger to Casey outweighs the potential value."

"Be objective." Van Hoof banged out the word like a hammer on hardwood. "Not pigheaded. Without her help, you'll be dead. And we'll have no way of finding out that date and flight number. This is no time for heroics."

Stefan's face went blank. As though he'd been sucker punched.

No one said anything for the next fifteen seconds.

Van Hoof broke the silence. "It's settled, then. Casey will take the initiative."

I said, "So I'll work with Stefan—"

Van Hoof shook his head. "Stefan must operate independently. Absolutely no communication between the two of you."

"We have to communicate," I insisted. "To coordinate this thing."

"No," van Hoof said. "Erika will be the liaison between you. You'll deal only with her."

Not the outcome I wanted. I said quickly, "I'm not going to be credible if Krüger sees me working so closely with someone from the Father-Major's network."

"Neither Erika nor Hans has ties to Holger," Stefan said. "I contacted Erika on my own. And she introduced me to Hans."

He'd contacted Erika? Suddenly, I was so tired I had difficulty moving my lips. "Fine," I told him, my voice weary. "I'll work with Erika. But only until you've gotten what you can from that informant. Once you have that specific piece of information, I'm going home. I'll need something to give to the FBI. And I've got to be free to answer their questions about Global 500."

"Do this for us," van Hoof said. "Clearing your name will be no problem after Stefan talks to his man."

Too glib.

But Erika spoke before I could. "I'll get to work on her. She has to *look* more like a fugitive."

"Change her appearance," van Hoof said. "Then set her up with Ebertus Wouters."

"No," Erika said. "I'll put her with one of my people in Antwerp."

Antwerp again. The town where Erika worked for a private arms trader. Erika and van Hoof were moving so fast, it was obvious they'd been over this ground before. Probably had considered and rejected an approach to Krüger through someone in Antwerp.

"We can't put her with any of your associates," van Hoof told Erika. "There has to be more distance between you two.

She'll fit right in at Bert's. Plus, his loyalty to me is not common knowledge. I'll let him know she's coming."

"At Bert's, then." Moodily, Erika lifted the crumpled pack from the night stand and tugged the last cigarette from it. "I'll work with her on her legend."

"Nothing too elaborate," I said. "I was abducted from Hamburg by a man posing as a cop. I thought he'd been sent by the same people who set Stefan up to be killed. That he'd kill me, too. I escaped."

"We can flesh that out." Erika removed the matchbook from her coat pocket. "A trucker picked her up on the E19, gave her a lift as far as the port. I'll drive her to the spot where he dropped her off, walk her from there to Bert's so she'll have the details right."

"Good." Van Hoof bent down, picked up Stefan's shirt and jacket and tossed them to him. "You have anything to add?" van Hoof asked.

"I don't want her doing this." Stefan's voice was tight.

"We don't have a better option," van Hoof said.

"I disagree." He pulled on his shirt. "But I appear to be outvoted."

Van Hoof said to Erika, "You have to move quickly. Thursday night, Stefan must attempt contact. By then all the attention must be focused on her."

Thursday night. New Year's Eve. Fewer than forty-eight hours away. "Too soon," I said. "Good idea, using a go-between to make the first contact. But I can't put the offer of safe haven in a message. That has to be done face-to-face. All I can do by Thursday is get word to Krüger that I want to deal. That may not be enough to do the trick."

"Make it dramatic," van Hoof said. "Stefan's informant will see him only during the height of the festivities, between ten P.M. and two A.M. on New Year's Eve. That gives him only a four-hour time frame in which to work. After two o'clock on

Friday morning, his window of opportunity will be locked tight." He was urging Stefan toward the door.

One more minute and Stefan would disappear again. I had to stop him. I had to know if he still wanted a life with me. "Stefan," I said.

He turned toward me, his expression unreadable.

I didn't look at Erika or van Hoof, but I felt them watching us. I opened my mouth, but I couldn't say the words. I couldn't ask if he loved me, not in front of them. Instead, I said, "This is a one-time thing I'm doing. When it's over, I'm going home. Tell me that'll be possible. That you'll help me clear my name."

"No time now," van Hoof said, reaching for the knob.

"Wait," I said.

The door clicked shut.

Erika took the half-smoked cigarette from her mouth and stabbed the burning ember into the ashtray. The inch-long cylinder folded in half, then flattened against the thick glass, the lipsticked end crushed like a blood-filled mosquito. Her gaze ran over me. Then she smiled. "First, the hair. The hair has to go."

10

By six o'clock the following morning—Wednesday—I was standing with Erika in front of a waterfront dive. Garbage overflowed from the can at the sidewalk's edge. I smelled vegetable peelings, their rotting odor blending with the briny scent of the Scheldt River.

Less than a kilometer to the north, Antwerp's gigantic port operated day and night. But at the edge of downtown on the next-to-the-last day of the year, people were still sleeping. All I heard was the lap of water in the canal and the murmur of a pigeon nested nearby.

Erika rapped twice on the glass of the entry door. The sound echoed off the cobblestones; then both sound and echo disappeared into the early-morning mist.

Someone was moving in the murky darkness on the other side of the door. A white-clad torso topped by a stubbled male face appeared behind the glass. The dead bolt snapped back, the knob rattled and the door opened. I followed Erika into a meager room, half of it given up to a scarred wooden bar backed by an assortment of bottles. I caught a whiff of the universal pre-opening smell of a workingman's saloon: pine-scented disinfectant atop stale cigarette smoke, old grease and sweat.

The man pushed the door shut behind us and walked back

toward the bar. His bare feet slapped on the linoleum. He was close to sixty years old, his sleeveless undershirt stretched tight across a large belly, his stained wool pants hooked at the waistband but unzipped. He yawned, then asked Erika a question in Flemish.

"Let's do this in English," I said. I was carrying a worn knapsack and it made a soft thud when I dropped it to the floor.

"I'll handle it," Erika said. "Bert won't rent to anyone he doesn't know."

"And not to every little shit I do know," Bert said.

I looked at him more closely. His face was mapped with the broken veins of a serious drinker and the skin sagged into furrows as though still sodden with sleep. But his blue eyes were as clear as those of a Siamese cat and as startling in his ruined face. Deep-set in pouches of flesh, they had the crystalline clarity of a pair of ice cubes. There was a chilly disdain in them when he spoke again to Erika. "This the one the major called about?" he asked.

Erika nodded.

Bert's eyes probed mine, his gaze sharp despite the liquor clouding his breath.

I started to rub the heel of my hand across my forehead. Old habit, shoving at my hair when I was uncomfortable. I stopped. All that remained of my collar-length blond tresses was a one-eighth-inch razor cut darkened to sable. I'd argued hard against going bald, but Erika had prevailed. She was so pleased by the results, I was sure she'd made me ugly as sin.

But Bert didn't appear repulsed. As he ran his gaze over a pair of pants that fit me like skin, his smile actually grew approving, maybe appreciative. I wondered if he was trying to emphasize his hostility toward Erika. I was sure of it when he spoke in a tone that was unexpectedly playful. "You want my usual arrangement?"

"Depends," I said, matching my voice to his, the way you do when you're hanging out in the neighborhood bar. I needed an ally and Bert was the best candidate who'd come along. "Does it include plenty of beer?"

He barked out a laugh. "I'm going to like you, I can tell." He pulled a skeleton key from under the bar. It clunked heavily against the wood as he set it before me. "You conduct your business elsewhere. When you're here, I'll see you're left alone. *That's* the arrangement. We can negotiate about the beer later." And then he winked.

"Fine." I put my hand over the key. "I'm set," I said to Erika. "You can take off."

Erika looked from Bert to me and back to Bert.

Bert farted.

She shrugged, then spoke to me. "Remember what I told you. Afternoon, between four and six, is your best shot. I'll get things started on my end. Let the right people know you've turned up." Then she left.

Bert bolted the door behind her. He turned and gestured toward a curtained opening. "Through there, then up the stairs."

"You go first," I said, sliding the key toward him.

"No need for that," he said.

"Humor me."

He started to chuckle, but it came out a raspy wheeze. He palmed the key and turned away from the bar. "Okay, since you're new," he said over his shoulder as he shoved aside the curtain.

Knapsack in hand, I followed him up the wooden staircase.

He unlocked the door and pushed it open. "Take it or leave it."

I saw a boxy room, one corner partitioned off for a toilet. A scratched table and two mismatched chairs sat in the center and a cot was shoved against the far wall, positioned to do double duty as a couch. The air smelled like someone had been boiling cabbage in that room forever.

Bert handed me the key. "See?" he said. "Empty. You're all

alone up here." I stepped around him. Stale liquor fumes clung to him as though they were coming out of his pores. He added, "Get some sleep. I'll look after things." Then he winked again.

I shut the door and leaned against it, listening to the slap of his bare soles as he went back downstairs.

Empty, he'd said. "Barren" was the word I'd have chosen. I felt a twinge under my breastbone, a pang of longing for my condo in D.C. Foolish me, I hadn't known then how lonely I could feel.

I dropped my knapsack and rubbed the back of my neck with both hands, trying to massage away the aching tiredness. I went to the window in the east wall and drew aside the dusty curtain. The horizon was turning a lighter gray, the rooftops zigzagging in darker outline below it. A wide alley ran alongside the building, ending in a parking lot. Beyond the alley lay an inlet named Willemdok, a fingerlike extension from the port zone north of me. A red-and-white harbor tour boat was moored there, gently rocking on the swells from the Scheldt. A sign advertised the next event in four languages. The English-language letters were so boldly drawn that I could read GALA NEW YEAR'S EVE LUNCHEON CRUISE. I could have wept, it sounded so festive. And so far removed from the life I was leading now.

I stumbled to the cot and dragged it across the room, out of the line of fire of anyone shooting through the wooden door. Clumps of dust huddled against the wall where the cot had been. I shoved the table toward the door. The legs marked a trail through the grit on the floor. If I examined the shadowy corners, I'd see cobwebs draped from ceiling to floor.

I positioned the table in front of the door. Maybe at this moment Erika was letting the "right people" know where I was. I understood the logic. Reinhardt Krüger still had a contract out on Stefan. His gunmen had been told to watch me, in case Stefan had somehow survived and was trying to make contact with me. I'd dropped out of sight in Hamburg early on

Tuesday morning. No doubt they'd spent the past twenty-four hours searching frantically for me. Not good. Who knew what they might discover? I had to surface again. Become visible, at least to Krüger's minions.

Was I crazy?

More dust puffed from the cot when I sat on it. I looked at the table. Not much of a barrier, but it'd slow down anyone who got past Bert.

Was there any terrorist so feeble he couldn't get past Bert?

I lay down on the cot, too tense to sleep. But as the minutes ticked by, my fear began to ebb. Slowly, in its place, came a sense of anticipation. I felt the way I had years ago, the night after I crashed my bike and broke my wrist. My mother had been hysterical when my father and I returned from the doctor's office, my left arm in a sling. I was a few inches taller than she was, but I felt puny before her uncontrolled frenzy. She calmed down only when my father swore he wouldn't replace the damaged front wheel, wouldn't allow me back on a bicycle. My father didn't lie. I knew I'd lost the last of my freedom. I took my wounded body to my room. My father came in later to sign my cast. He ran a hand through his hair and grinned. Then he smoothed his cowlick back down carefully, the way he always did, and told me to cheer up. He leaned close and whispered. As soon as my wrist mended, we'd start those driving lessons. But I was not to mention our plan to my mother.

Against the laws of Oregon, letting a fourteen-year-old behind the wheel of his precious Mustang. After he tiptoed from my room, I lay on my bed, pain forgotten, my heart filled with the same perilous excitement that I felt now. Outside the law, recklessly imprudent, the amphetamine rush of risk embraced. Pilots thrive on it.

I dozed off close to eight, momentarily soothed by the clatter of cars on the cobblestone street to the north. I slept too lightly, strange sounds jerking me awake suddenly, with my heart pounding. About one o'clock, I heard a murmur of voices from below, accompanied by the clink of cutlery against pottery. My dreams filled with images of steamed potatoes and fried onions. The smells grew as the crowd noises subsided. By two o'clock, I was too hungry to sleep.

And too keyed up, thinking of what lay ahead. Today, I'd start my approach to Krüger. According to Erika, the best place to begin was with a Hungarian who made his money from the sale of Soviet-standard equipment to embargoed states. Working with a local shipping agent and the gun dealer who employed Erika, the Hungarian had recently gotten a load of Bulgarian-made mortars past Antwerp customs. His fake end-user certificate gave the destination as Bolivia, but the real buyers were sitting in Tripoli. And the deal-maker reaping a fat commission from the illegal sale was one Gunter Storch, the identity carefully prepared long ago by the former Stasi major, Reinhardt Krüger.

There were others in Antwerp involved in the black market in armaments. But Erika said the Hungarian was more eager than most to do business for questionable clients. I'd call on him at the bar he owned downtown. I'd ask him to broker a deal between me and his German colleague. After that, I'd have all the attention I wanted from Krüger.

Simple enough. If I could believe Erika.

But my qualms didn't interfere with my appetite. When the rooms below me grew quiet again, I went downstairs in search of whatever smelled so good.

Bert was sitting at one of the two tables crowded up beside the bar. When he heard my boots on the linoleum, he looked up from the earthenware bowl in front of him. The slow-moving jaws were clean-shaven now and he was wearing a blue wool sweater. But the yellowed cotton visible in the V neck of the sweater looked like the same undershirt I'd seen that morning, and I was betting his pants bore stains in identical spots. Then I smelled food again. Downstairs, the pungent odor of well-cooked fish overpowered the vegetables. I felt a sharp pang in my stomach. My hunger must have shown on my face.

"More in the pot on the stove," Bert said, bending back over his bowl. "Help yourself."

I found the kitchen beyond the stairway. A gleaming stock pot sat on an immaculate gas range. Spotless utensils hung on the wall behind it, lined up precisely from largest to smallest. Recently washed bowls and spoons made an equally orderly array in the drying rack. I had doubts about Bert's personal hygiene, but his kitchen would have passed inspection in any barracks. I took the lid off the pot and the vapors hitting my face were rich enough to make a meal. The soup was so thick, heat bubbles erupted like volcanoes, plopping back into viscous craters. I ladled a bowl full and carried it into the front room. I draped my jacket over the back of a chair, sat down across from Bert and spent the next five minutes enjoying *waterzooi* made the old way with fish instead of chicken. I quickly emptied one bowlful, along with a *bolleke* of DeKoninck. I'd drunk it before, with Stefan. I stared idly at the singular ball-ended glass, found myself wondering if Erika also liked the Flemish brew.

Then I forced Erika out of my mind. I wasn't going to let her poison Antwerp's best beer.

No one came in while I ate. Bert emptied the glass in front of him and refilled it. He extended the bottle toward me. The label read "Oude Antwerpsche." That was the source of his foul breath: not gin but geneva, a near-eighty-proof spirit flavored with juniper and swilled by inhabitants of the Low Countries with the same single-minded devotion they gave to maintaining their dikes. I shook my head and asked instead for another beer.

As I ate, I studied the wall behind the bar. It was covered with a collage of posters, photographs, postcards and beer ads— the usual barroom decor. Discreetly centered above the cognac bottle was a familiar red-and-blue pictograph. The same picture of the lion beneath the crown graced the brochure for the Brussels military hotel—insignia of the regiment of Grenadiers. I looked at Bert. "You were in the army," I said.

He grunted assent.

"That where you met Major van Hoof?"

"Second lieutenant when I met him," Bert corrected me. "Came south straight from the academy." He sipped the geneva. "So green he'd never have survived that first tour without me."

"You were an old Congo hand?"

"Not so old. But a man learns fast if his first time into Africa he gets kicked out of a plane over Stanleyville."

I asked, "In '64?"

Bert nodded.

The paratroop drop into Stanleyville in 1964 was a counterterrorist legend. Bert must have been one of the Belgians sent in when leftist Congolese rebels threatened to massacre their white hostages. The Belgian paratroopers moved so swiftly that most of the two thousand foreigners were rescued. I felt my tension ease a notch. Bert was in the same business as I was. Fighting the bad guys for more than thirty years. Maybe a better ally than I realized. "But you're not in the army anymore?" I said.

Bert picked up my beer glass and stepped behind the bar to refill it. His voice was muffled. "Me and the army parted company some time ago. I have my own business now."

I glanced around. The glass door was covered with faded gold script that had been invisible the night before. Now, from the inside, I could read "Café Ebertus."

Bert put the beer in front of me and sat. He inclined his head toward the door. "See that van on the other side of the drawbridge?"

A tan Ford with smoked windows was parked a hundred yards from the café entrance. My fingertips grew cold, the familiar chill creeping toward my wrists. "You think someone in there is watching this place?"

He leaned toward me. "Not some *one.*"

"You can't see inside the van. How do you know there's anyone in it?"

"Van's been there since midmorning. Figured it was empty. Then, around noon, I spotted exhaust fumes."

"Whoever's in there got cold, ran the heater. Sounds pretty innocent to me. No professional would give himself away like that."

"Figured the same," Bert said. "But had me a new customer for lunch. Foreigner."

"From where?"

He said, "Raghead."

I rephrased it: "Middle Eastern type?"

He snorted. "Not exactly. But the same-type Allah lover. And let me tell you, I don't get many of them in here."

"Can't imagine why not," I said, hoping the joke would cover the sound of lunch roiling in my stomach.

"Maybe they don't like my cooking. Anyway, this one picked at his stew while he eye-fucked the place. Then disappeared up the street. Pretty damn sure he got into the van." He gave me a long look. "You got at least two of them watching you."

"I was expecting them." I tried to make my voice as cool as my words, but my pitch was too high to pull it off. I tried again. "But not this soon."

"They can move plenty fast," Bert said. "Their kind runs things in this neighborhood."

"Their kind? You called him a raghead."

"You been reading them damn tour guides, I bet. About how the Russian mafia controls this section of Antwerp."

"No one ever told me that Islamic fundamentalists had taken charge."

" 'Russian mafia' is a general term for the scum doing it. They speak Russian. But they're Chechens, most of them."

"Chechens," I said, suddenly recalling the most significant fact about Chechnya. "Muslims."

"Right. The ragheads stick together. Some camel driver wants you watched, he gets a local pair to park down the road. Maybe without any experience doing surveillance, but willing to help out until the pros arrive."

I asked, "You think the pros are coming?"

"I'm not stupid." He leaned closer and sour geneva vapors filled the air between us. "I *know* they're coming."

"What do you mean, *know*?"

"I mean, I know what's going on."

"Do you?"

"The major's using you to set a trap."

"Why would I let him do that?"

"I'm thinking probably he didn't give you much choice. I read the papers. American woman with a terrorist connection evades arrest in Hamburg. Next day the major sends me an American woman who needs somebody to watch her back." He gave me a sly grin. "You don't look much like your picture now, but you're the one the cops are looking for. And to keep them from finding you, you'll do what the major wants."

"And you think he wants to set a trap."

"For the ones who did his daughter. That's who he wants. Pretty obvious from what *she* said to you. 'Let the right people know.' The major's set a trap, all right. When the 'right people' get here, he'll take out the lot of them." Bert's eyes gleamed, blue sapphires. "I told you. I'm not stupid."

"No," I said. "You're not."

But maybe I was. I hadn't volunteered to draw terrorists so van Hoof could kill them. Yet if van Hoof wanted to create a dramatic diversion, what would be more effective?

I asked, "You think the major would use your place for a battleground without warning you?"

"He'll do more than warn me. He'll make sure I get in on

the shooting." This time his wink seemed less flirtatious than bloodthirsty.

"You're living in your dreams," I said. "Nobody's going to assassinate anyone. I'm more worried about what I'll run into downtown than I am about those guys in the van." I stood up and lifted the leather jacket off the back of my chair.

Bert said, "If you're going downtown, you better work on your act a bit more."

"What?"

"You dress the part fine. But it still shows. You like men, probably more than you should."

I opened my mouth to protest.

Bert cut me off. "You want to keep the horny sailors away, you got to change that. Look at the girls, not at the boys. Let people see you enjoy the same pleasures as a man."

I gave him a glance filled with loathing. "Go piss up a rope," I said.

He wheezed out another laugh. "Better." Then his face got serious again. "You're sure nobody's going to blow you away soon as you go out that door?"

I pulled on black leather gloves and made my voice as tough as I could. "There won't be any shoot-out in your front yard." Sure or not, I had to get moving. It was four o'clock— according to Erika, the best time to contact Sándor Biczó, the Hungarian arms trader/bar owner we'd picked to act as the go-between in my dealings with Krüger. I shrugged the jacket on over my bulky sweater and patted the pockets to reassure myself that I had my cap, pencil and paper and Belgian currency— supplies I might need if Biczó didn't show up. "You watch," I said. "They'll be tagging along with me."

Bert stood up. "To be on the safe side, I'll keep you covered from upstairs."

Bert knew van Hoof better than I did. If he'd figured things correctly, my going outside would ignite a war. I hoped that van Hoof was better disciplined. That the plan we'd discussed was the plan we'd follow.

My boots thumped loudly on the floor and the snaps and zippers on my jacket rattled tinnily. My fingertips had gotten colder and my hand shook as I reached for the doorknob. I pulled the door open and stepped outside.

It clanked shut behind me. The afternoon sky was charcoal gray, the wintry light fading toward dusk. Moist air dropped like a veil on my bare head and the smell of the sea was strong. I took several deep breaths and stepped out onto the sidewalk. Before I turned right, into the alley beneath my window, I glanced casually toward the drawbridge and the street beyond.

The tan Ford shuddered on its suspension, as though its passenger had jerked into alertness.

Then my back was to the van. My cheeks tingled and the skin over my skull tightened against the cold. All my muscles were pulled tight, too, from fear as well as the cold. I didn't look up at my window. But I imagined Bert kneeling there, behind the lacy scrim. Hopefully with a powerful rifle in his hands.

My thick-soled boots scraped over the damp cobblestones as I crossed the bridge toward downtown Antwerp. A car door slammed. Eager footsteps sounded behind me like an echo.

As the seconds stretched into a minute and no shots were fired, a wave of relief flowed over me. And with the relief came an exhilaration I hadn't been expecting. Yet it felt familiar. Slowly I realized why. I'd felt this same giddy excitement the night I bound myself to a man I believed to be a Communist agent. Stefan. Warsaw. 1986. It had been a long time since I'd gone out looking for trouble. Long enough to forget the thrill when I started to make my own.

After I passed the street called Godefriduskaai, I turned right and then left again, moving steadily into that part of Antwerp most hospitable to men employed in Europe's second-largest port. Off-duty seamen were trolling the streets. I pushed between pea coats and uniforms, jostling men who muttered at me in Russian, Spanish and something atonally Asian. No one looked at me for longer than a second. They were all more interested in the glass-doored closets lining the streets. The men controlling Antwerp's prostitution trade rented out the stalls in eight-hour shifts. The women working that late-Wednesday afternoon were paying prime-time rates.

I stepped into the indented doorway of a ship chandlery. The odor of urine was so strong my eyes watered. Beyond the glass were the shadowy outlines of sailors' necessities, made from brass and hemp.

I saw myself in the darkened window. My reflection was appalling, a blend of my bald mother after chemotherapy and the haunted look of a World War II collaborator being punished by the French Resistance. Beneath my shorn skull, my eyes burned darkly, the skin around them bruised-looking. Below the bulk of jacket and sweater, Erika's pants outlined a frame worn gaunt over the past few days.

I turned and lounged against the door, bracing the sole of my right boot against the wooden frame, my leather-encased arms folded across my chest to display all the zippers to best advantage. I kept my face turned toward the hookers across the street, as though I were in the market for love. But my eyes were busy searching the sidewalks.

I spotted a man with the angular body that comes from an ill-fed boyhood in the Caucasus Mountains. He became suddenly engrossed by a tattered handbill on a kiosk a hundred feet away. I shoved myself upright as though making a decision. Directly across the street, sandwiched between a stall occupied by a fleshy blue-black woman and one housing a near-albino blonde, was a solid wooden door. The neon glowing above it read "The 21 Club."

All I had to do was go into The 21 Club, order a beer and nurse it while I waited for Sándor Biczó to make his customary late-afternoon visit to his bar. I'd identify myself to him as the notorious Casey Collins. I'd let the Hungarian know I had something to sell to his most important German contact. If his reputation was accurate, the Hungarian would move quickly to alert Reinhardt Krüger that a deal was in the works.

My eyes went back to the man tailing me. I hadn't counted on performing for an audience. The surveillance had kicked in ahead of schedule. But it might prove helpful if the man watching me reported my visit. If Sándor Biczó didn't think my offer worthy enough to pass on to Krüger, a report on my movements might spur Krüger into demanding to know what I'd been doing in the Hungarian's bar.

I rubbed the heel of my hand across my forehead. All these assumptions, any of which might be wrong. Nothing to guarantee I'd provide the distraction that Stefan needed. But I had to create some activity. Van Hoof had said they had no better options.

A burly man elbowed me out of the doorway. His eyes had the unfocused look of the seriously drunk and he reeked of the cheapest brand of geneva. He faced the entry and shot a stream of urine onto the sidewalk between his feet. I jumped sideways to avoid the splash and stumbled into three uniformed Japanese sailors. The exchange of polite apologies didn't take ten seconds, but it placed me ten feet farther down the sidewalk. I moved into another malodorous doorway and checked for my tail. I'd led him so carefully to this point. I didn't want him to miss my entrance into The 21 Club.

A late-model BMW idled across from me, two men huddled inside. I squinted, thought I saw one pass something to the other. Probably a drug deal going down. I looked quickly away, spotted my tail on the same side of the street as I was, standing near five or six men who'd clustered behind a British sailor. The Brit had opened one of the doors to negotiate with the thin Asian woman inside. My tail was scanning the street.

I took a step toward the curb. A Vespa buzzed past from the left, carrying a pair of women. The driver had a bleached-blond ducktail and wore a long-sleeved jersey tie-dyed in shades of purple. Her passenger was covered by an oil-stained mechanic's coverall that matched the dirty streaks of silver in her equally short hair. The driver swerved to avoid me and sprayed slush over a jaywalker. A male voice yelled something and one of the women responded with a Flemish expletive. The woman riding pillion grinned at me and raised her clenched fist in a salute. Looking at her, I saw the real value of my outfit. I was one more woman in the army of militant feminists visible on the radical fringe of every European political movement from the Greens to the Bader-Meinhoff gang. We were sisters. It felt strangely right. I saluted her military-style, with the ninety-degree flourish my father always added.

The Vespa buzzed away, followed so closely by a minibus that the scooter might have been acting as an escort vehicle. The van was unmarked—but not the man in the passenger seat. The butterfly bandage bridging his nose was a dead giveaway. His ponytail swished against the window and I knew I was looking at my favorite television cameraman.

I jumped back and pressed myself against the door behind me.

Both Ponytail and the driver were staring at the other side of the street. As I watched, the driver pulled into a loading zone in front of the ship chandlery. He shut off the engine and the lights. And then both men disappeared from view, into the back of the van. Perfectly positioned to film anyone going into or out of The 21 Club.

Somebody had tipped off the press that Casey Collins was planning to visit Sándor Biczó.

I scanned the sidewalks in both directions. A leftover hippie type lingered near a vendor's cart. Was he taking too long to eat those Belgian fries? Might he be a cop, under cover? My gaze went back to the BMW. Maybe the men inside were a pair of FBI agents.

I stayed in that doorway for another five minutes. The BMW left. The hippie stumbled past, eyes glazed from whatever he'd drunk before he stopped to dine on potatoes. The crowd shifted, eddied, changed faces. Only me, my tail, and the news van remained stationary.

No police types were here yet. But one of the press people would call the cops as soon as I was spotted. Filming my arrest had to be their goal. If I was careful, I could slip past the van and into the bar. But it was likely UNN had someone waiting inside. Their man would be interested in any strange woman coming through the door. Asking for the Hungarian would be like holding up a sign with my name on it. And if Bicző was there, I couldn't stick around and talk with him.

I pulled my jacket tighter. The sheepskin collar was coarse against the back of my neck. My shoulders drew back; my arms moved away from my sides. I shoved at the jacket sleeves, pushing them higher up my arms. Felt my biceps harden. I spread my feet wider. My rib cage expanded as I inhaled. And then, under my breath, I muttered the Flemish curse I'd heard over the roar of the Vespa.

I could handle it. What was the response time for the Antwerp police force? Had to be at least three minutes. So get in and get out in under three minutes. Tight. But workable.

I stuffed my gloves into a pocket, pulled out pencil and paper. I scrawled a brief note, one I hoped would convince Biczó to keep a date with me tomorrow noon. Then I covered my new hairdo with a soiled knitted cap of mustard-colored wool, faded so that it was only a shade darker than the pale circle of my face.

I joined a group of merchant seamen rolling down the sidewalk and used them as a shield as I crossed to the other side of the street. The Chechen picked me up right away and followed. I edged in front of the men admiring the black girl and opened the heavy wooden door beneath the neon sign.

A hallway cut six feet straight back to a second door. It opened into a rectangular room, maybe thirty feet wide and as deep, the expanse of polished floor tiled in black-and-white squares. An oval bar stood in the center, stemware dangling from a wooden rack above it, a slender bartender wiping the ebony top. Scattered across the checkerboard floor were settees and armchairs upholstered in red imitation leather. I ignored the men lounging on the furniture and headed straight for the bar.

The brown eyes of the undersized bartender were almost black, as shiny as the hair slicked tight to his head. With his white shirt and black bow tie, he looked as though he'd been hired to match the decor. He gave me an inquiring glance and asked a question. His Slavic accent twisted the words into something that sounded like no language I knew.

Cool air touched the back of my head. The door behind me had opened. In the mirror above the bar I saw the reflection of the man following me. His expression was confused, as though he'd wandered too far out of his league. He edged over to an empty settee and sat.

The mirror showed movement down the bar to my right. A head turning my way. The newsie? Figure yes and move fast.

My glance went back to the bartender. He was watching the man who'd entered after me. The bartender's face was frozen into a questioning look, still waiting for an answer to his garbled what'll-you-have.

I leaned across the bar and said softly, "I have a message for Sándor Biczó."

The bartender looked as if he hadn't heard what I'd said. His right hand was sliding slowly back toward his edge of the bar.

I grabbed his right wrist with my left hand and yanked, pulling him off-balance. He had to slap his left hand on the bar to keep from hitting the counter with his nose. His face was so close I could see the delicate fringe of eyelashes along his lower lids. I leaned closer and breathed out, "Please," while with my right hand I pressed a five-hundred-franc note into the hand I'd captured. "Please," I said. "Don't ring for anyone."

He pushed himself upright, and his fingers tightened around the money. His carpal bones felt as thin and brittle as those of a bird. I released his wrist and slid my note toward him. "Give my message to Mr. Biczó."

He covered the scrap of paper with his left hand. His expression was unreadable as his right hand slid back, again automatically reaching beneath the bar. Calling the in-house thugs? Maybe they liked to screen Mr. Biczó's visitors.

I sensed movement to my right as the newsie got off his bar stool.

I turned and sprinted for the exit. From behind me came the slap of two pairs of shoe soles running over tile. The bartender yelled in Russian, staccato instructions. I heard the soft thud of bodies colliding. A curse in Arabic. A shrill "Sumbitch!" shrieked in a New Jersey accent. The all-purpose "Fuck your mother" in Russian. Sounds of blows against flesh. Scuffling shoes. Then I was through the exterior door.

I plunged across the crowded sidewalk and into the street. I tugged at my cap, pulling it lower on my forehead as I dodged around a bicycle. I was facing the news van. The rear door popped open. Ponytail yelled, "It's her!" He jumped to the ground and raised the camcorder to his shoulder.

A second man leaped out, holding a walkie-talkie. "She's here," he shouted into it. "She's right here."

A third man leaned out the driver's window. "Shut those damn doors," he ordered Ponytail. The van's engine roared. Its headlights came on and it reversed a foot.

Behind me, I felt a blast of warm air and heard an eruption of male voices.

I charged in front of the van and down an alley beside the ship chandlery. I heard more shouting behind me, running feet, the van's motor revving. As its headlights lit the passageway, I reached the other end. I shot to my left down a narrow back-street and around a corner into open space. I avoided a cluster of drunken sailors, cut past an imposing church and fled into another set of streets containing a jumble of architectural styles.

I paused at the corner of a broad avenue. My breath was ragged, my side ached and I was soaked with sweat. Across the avenue was a strip of tree-lined park, the barren branches stretching toward a gloomy castle. The forbidding battlements reminded me of the Kronborg fortress. Of that awful moment in Denmark when I had tried to accept that Stefan was dead.

I turned toward the sound of a straining engine. The news van was creeping toward me, Ponytail hanging out the passenger window.

I put my head down and ran directly at the van, and then past it up the street. I dodged to my right when I saw the marked police car bearing down on me. I shoved upstream through a crowd of office workers rank with tobacco and after-shave. I slowed at Grote Markt, trying to blend into the crowd.

Silvius Brabo towered above me, the statue greenish gray in the dusky light, arm raised to throw the severed hand of the giant Druoon Antigoon into the Scheldt. I knew it wasn't likely that "Antwerp" was derived from the Flemish *hand werpen*, hand throw. But with all my heart I wanted to believe the legend, that one truehearted fighter could dismember an enormous oppressor, liberate an entire town.

I yanked the yellow cap off my head, stuffed it into my jacket pocket and dropped both into a nearby waste bin. Then I strolled away as though Brabo had pointed the direction.

The crowds thickened, heading toward the Central Station, and I used them as cover and buffer. I moved briskly, taking streets at random, careful to head in every direction but back to Bert's. I passed Rubens's workshop, the Bourla Theater, other landmarks I didn't know, couldn't recognize, couldn't name. After a half hour, I was out of the crowds and I couldn't spot anyone behind me.

Still, I continued my zigzag maneuvers for another hour, circling northward, checking every intersection before I entered it, proceeding with the same breathless caution I'd exercised in the driver's seat of my father's Mustang.

I had the Café Ebertus in view by seven o'clock. I slipped into a pathway between two buildings a half block away. The evening sky was black, thick clouds hiding the moon. The temperature was only a few degrees above freezing and my breath was white in front of my face. The bricks around me were filmed with mist and smelled of diesel exhaust. I hunched into my sweater and kept my eyes on the street in front of Bert's.

The tan Ford had disappeared from the drawbridge. By seven-thirty, all the other parked cars were also gone from the roadway. The two remaining in the lot beside Willemdok had been there the night before—not new arrivals. A half-dozen men exited from the café between seven-thirty and eight. All were pale-skinned and dressed like workingmen. After eight, nobody went in or out. Traffic on the street was sparse by then, only a pair of nondescript sedans puttering by without showing any interest in the area.

The pursuit, the escape, the pumping rush of all that had kept me warm. Till now. The contrast made it worse. The cold from the frozen stones slowly penetrated my boot soles. My toes lost all feeling. The sweat-soaked wool sweater was clammy against my torso. But my hands and face were the worst, the damp frigidity penetrating beneath the skin, into the flesh. I blew on my hands, but my breath felt cold. I shoved them into my armpits, yet even that didn't warm them.

Five minutes past nine o'clock, I came out of my hiding place and slipped into Bert's building through the kitchen door. Bert was there, sleeves pushed up to his elbows, hands in a sudsy pan of dishwater. He finished rinsing a beer glass, then headed for the front, drying his hands on his pants as he went. I heard the dead bolt slam home. Then the interior lights in front went off.

He shuffled back through the curtain.

"You usually close about now?" I asked.

He raised his eyebrows. "You expecting somebody to stop by?"

"I sure didn't invite anyone," I said. "But I can't guarantee they won't be coming around. Better if you stick to your usual pattern."

"Closing after supper is my usual pattern," he said. "I make my money off the lunch crowd. Only stay open later when I want the company." He went back to the sink. Glassware clinked together. "And tonight I'm not interested in finding out who might walk in."

"That Ford's gone." The kitchen was warm and steamy and smelled of dish soap. My fingers itched as they started to thaw. "So what are you worried about?"

Bert turned to look at me. "Somebody's still interested in you. I saw them set up, or I'd have trouble picking them out myself. Very professional."

"Who?"

"More camel drivers."

I ran my hand over my scalp and asked, "Nobody else?"

Bert's gaze was sharper. "You *are* expecting more visitors."

"I ran into some people downtown I didn't expect to find there."

"Who?"

"Press."

"Waiting for you?"

I shrugged. "Waiting right in front of the place I was headed for."

"Like they knew." He sounded disgusted. "I told the major to be careful with her."

I asked, "Erika?"

"Of course Erika. Anyone else know where you were headed?"

"Only her."

He was still holding a soapy glass. It splashed back into the sink. "I can't figure why the major brought her into this. What reason's she got for helping him? She could be rolling around in a bin of diamonds."

"Diamonds?"

"Her father's one of the biggest traders on Hoveniersstraat. That's enough for me. I spent half my life sweating in the Congo. And why? So those bastards could get rich off the diamonds." He chewed on his lower lip, shook his head. "She's got a game of her own going."

I rubbed the heel of my hand across my forehead. "I don't know. If Erika wanted to blow my cover, it would've been quicker to give the news team this address. She couldn't be certain she'd get the same result by tipping them off to look for me downtown."

He grunted. "Really piss off the major, she blows this setup. No, she stays on the right side of him."

"But if we know she leaked the info—"

"We know." He reached above his head and pulled a bottle off the top shelf. "But the major won't believe it." He unscrewed the cap and splashed geneva into a still-damp glass.

"But why—"

"I haven't figured that one out yet." He poured the liquid down his throat, then tipped up the bottle again. "But I will."

I'd be figuring, too. I waved aside Bert's offer of geneva. I had to deal with my other problem. Tomorrow I hoped to meet with Biczó. I didn't want anyone else tagging along. I'd need Bert's help to evade the pros who were watching me. I thought over my options while he emptied a second glass and filled another. As he sipped geneva, I explained my difficulty. He said he had a way to take care of it. I stayed for a few minutes longer, waiting as he finished his drink. The light in his blue eyes slowly dimmed, as though the geneva had woven itself into a curtain between him and the world. I helped myself to some fruit from the counter, said good night and went upstairs.

I slept heavily, deadened by fatigue and enmeshed in circular, convoluted dreams. Nightmare chases through the streets of Antwerp, chases that didn't end. I was being pursued by men without faces. And then I was chasing others. Stefan, looking back over his shoulder at me, then running faster to get away. Once, my father holding hands with my mother, both laughing through a game of tag where I was always "it." Cold, tired and running, on and on.

I woke up when daylight came through the window at eight o'clock in the morning. I breakfasted on an apple, then settled myself at the window. At ten o'clock, the Flandria company crew drifted in and began setting up for the luncheon cruise through the harbor.

A caterer's truck arrived and unloaded hotel-size pans onto the red-and-white tour boat. Musicians were next, burly men in short pants hauling huge instrument cases. At ten-thirty, a man I didn't know strolled out of the Café Ebertus, wiping his mouth as if he'd enjoyed a morning beer. He opened the ticket booth and went inside, taking his time about setting up for the passengers who were starting to arrive.

At five minutes before eleven, a black Mercedes rolled up beside Willemdok. The man who emerged from the rear door was about five-eleven, his hair graying at the temples. The description fit the man for whom I waited. The shoes were the clincher. As well polished as his car, they were a pointed-toe Italian design that shouted out a price of five hundred dollars per pair. Or maybe per shoe. Nobody in the arms trade had to wear Hush Puppies.

The Mercedes drove off and Sándor Biczó stepped briskly up the gangplank and onto the boat.

A shrill warning blast came from the horn.

I headed for the door.

12

I dashed outside. Bert's early customer now manned the ticket booth. Bert had prepared him and he waved me on to the gangplank. A dockworker in blue overalls gave me the once-over, then looked quickly away when I met his eyes. As soon as I stepped onto the deck from the gangplank, he began unhitching it from the boat.

The vessel lurched. I staggered and gripped the railing as we moved toward the center of the canal. The water-level restaurant was crowded with holiday feasters, the crush in front of the bar three-deep, fists waving currency in the air, the noise of conversation and laughter as thick as the visible cloud of cigarette smoke. Then a pair of accordions wheezed, and oom-pah music boiled out over the human din.

I climbed the exterior stairway to the next level. Tables and chairs were arranged on the open-air deck, but so far I was the only one interested in outdoor seating. The glass-enclosed booth for the tour guide perched above me. Empty now, as no one below could have heard his lecture. This touring party was interested in exotic food and drink—not in collecting facts about the port of Antwerp. I stood at the railing, facing the Café Ebertus. A man in an expensive topcoat walked casually past the ticket booth, moving slowly enough to read all of the information posted there. The group that had me under surveillance now was too professional to storm after me when I left the café. They'd missed their chance to follow me on board. They would be trying to figure out how best to pick me up again. Sándor Biczó's attendance would heighten their interest. With luck— lots of luck—this move would draw attention away from Stefan and the man he could meet with only tonight.

The sea breeze was cool against my cheek and I tasted salt on my lips. On shore, the worker in blue coveralls was coiling rope. My boat cruised past the raised drawbridge, out of Willemdok and through Kattendijkdok into the busier section of the port. On the starboard side, beyond a warehouse marked "FIAT," I spotted a freighter flying the Polish flag and unloading coal into a sooty pile. Past the coal was a fruit wharf, covered by bins filled with bananas. A Vespa with two riders buzzed out from behind the bins and along the waterside roadway, briefly keeping pace with the tour boat. Then the scooter disappeared into a clutch of agricultural combines parked haphazardly in the next lot.

I stood next to the port-side railing, looking out at an oil refinery fronted by an expanse of smooth asphalt. Despite the cloudy weather, lawn chairs were scattered along the water's edge, occupied by bundled fishermen.

Leather soles slithered across the deck behind me. I kept my eyes on the fishermen. A man's voice said, "Not the water quality I would choose." The accent was that of a middle-class Brit.

I turned and noted how well the voice coordinated with the tweedy attire. But the mouth rounding those vowels was thick-lipped and surrounded by the fleshy features typical of a Slavic peasant. Sándor Biczó added, "I'm told the carp they catch are acceptable."

"Carp?" I repeated.

He waved a hand toward the fishermen. "I hear some foreigners in Antwerp will pay any price for their New Year's carp. Maybe you know someone like that."

Carp for New Year's dinner was a Warsaw tradition. "Sorry

to disappoint you," I said. "The only expatriate Pole I knew is dead now."

He leaned against the railing. From beneath us came the faint sound of yodeling, followed by the stamping of a hundred pairs of feet as the crowd joined in on the chorus of the song. When the thumping subsided, Biczó said, "Your note said you had something of value to offer my German partner. Naturally I assumed you meant Stefan Krajewski."

He trained his pale gray eyes on my face. His left eyelid was marked by a black mole so thick it kept the lid from opening fully. The drooping eyelid gave his expression an ominous asymmetry.

I forced myself to stop staring at the marked eyelid and recalled the name by which the Hungarian knew Krüger. I said, "I've heard that Gunter Storch could assist me in resolving certain difficulties. I am willing to offer something in return for that assistance."

Biczó made a dismissive gesture. "If you need help, why don't you turn to your friends in Denmark?"

"I have," I said. "But the priest no longer takes my calls. Doesn't want to deal with an international fugitive."

"I doubt I can help you either," Biczó said. "You say the Pole is dead. Then you are of no interest to Gunter Storch."

"You are mistaken. I have another valuable item I'm willing to sell to him."

"And what might that be?" he asked.

"I can explain that only to him."

"Then what do you want from me?"

"Set it up. Arrange for me to meet him."

"Why should I do you such a great favor?"

"I'm sure your partner will show his appreciation."

"I see. I came, certain that you were going to offer me the Pole. Now you say he's dead."

"Of course he's dead—"

"My partner wants proof of that. Let's begin there, say as a gesture of your good will. Start by giving me some tangible evidence that Krajewski was on board Global Flight 500."

"Evidence? What sick . . ." I began. My voice broke. Then I let anger supplant grief. "Go to hell. You think I've got a piece of him in my pocket? Some body part I can show you, prove he was blown to pieces?" I let out a furious breath. "If I did, if I had a single square inch of him, it wouldn't be for sale. Not to you. Not to anyone. Not for any price."

Sándor Biczó watched me, a faint hint of menace in his expression. Then his gaze went to something moving off to my right. Out of the corner of my eye I saw a figure in blue coveralls climbing the stairs from the deck below. I leaned on the railing and took in a deep breath of sea air, trying to regain my composure.

The tour boat was angling to port, to take us north again along Kanaaldok B1. A Russian freighter blocked the waterway to the east, its port of origin scrawled across the stern in faded Cyrillic letters. Its off-loaded shipment of Lada cars lined the edge of Churchilldok.

The blue-clad man came over to the railing to stand beside Biczó. The new arrival wasn't a native Belgian. And it wasn't likely he was part of the crew. Below his skullcap of close-cropped dark hair, his eyes were as shiny as anthracite in the smoky skin of his face.

I couldn't suppress my gasp.

His was the face of a dead man. A face that haunted my dreams.

I felt as though my heart had stopped beating.

"Ah, my friend Fouad is familiar to you," said Biczó. "He wants to invite you to visit his home. The al-Nemer family wishes to hear what you can tell them about his brother's final moments on earth."

Not a dead man. But his little brother. I knew Nazer al-Nemer's family tree. When Nazer died in 1986, Fouad was only eight years old. Now that he'd grown up, he'd come after me.

I shuddered. I didn't want to go anyplace with this vengeance-driven child of the Abu Nidal Organization. My back was against the railing. I heard the scrape of a window sliding open somewhere below me. Accordion music blared out. I caught a whiff of garlic, blended with the fishy odor of raw mussels. Then the window clicked shut, cutting off sound and scents from below. I tasted the coppery flavor of my fear.

"I've nothing much to tell," I said. "All I know is that Nazer al-Nemer disappeared in May 1986, during the ferry crossing from Warnemünde to Denmark."

Biczó blinked, the mole black against the white eyelid like the skull-and-crossbones label on a bottle of poison. "That's *all* you know?"

I said, "I'd like to be more helpful."

"And I'm sure you will be," Biczó said, "when Fouad has an opportunity to assist you with your recollections."

"I appreciate his offer of hospitality," I told Biczó, "but it would be more profitable for both of us if I first spoke with your German partner."

He laughed. "Perhaps you are right," he said, "but I prefer the al-Nemers' cash now. I have no faith in this vague future reward you speak of."

"Don't let him trick you out of your money," I said to Fouad. "I have nothing new to tell you about your brother."

"He speaks no English," Biczó said.

"Then how can he question me?"

The Hungarian's eyes glinted.

Dread pulled my muscles tight. I glanced at the stairway, gauging how best to make my break.

Biczó reached inside his jacket. When his hand came back out, he was holding a nine-millimeter Browning High Power pistol. "I don't recommend declining the al-Nemers' invitation."

Thirteen cartridges, I thought, staring at the shiny metal. An unlucky number for me. "You're bluffing," I said. "You won't shoot me. This isn't the Third World. This is Belgium. They've got cellular telephones and efficient police forces. People will hear the shot. The cops will be there to arrest you as soon as the boat docks."

"But we are docking right now," Biczó said.

We were only a few yards from the battered stern of the Russian freighter, nestled into the niche reserved for the intraport shuttle boat. Biczó gestured toward the stairway. "The pilot of our boat was happy to make this unscheduled stop."

Fouad leaped nimbly down the stairway to the lower deck. Biczó nudged me after him. I stumbled down, toward the party sounds below. Maybe I could attract attention from someone inside. Biczó jammed the pistol into the small of my back and laughed again. "My man is covering that exit. For the next five minutes, no one will be coming outside. So you see, you are leaving this boat with us. Dead or alive. That much of a choice is yours." He shoved me toward the dock. It was three feet higher than the lower deck of our vessel, even with the top railing.

My heart beat faster. Glucose pooled in my muscles, ready to provide instant energy there as more adrenaline dumped into my bloodstream. I heard buzzing.

Fouad had climbed up onto the dock and now gripped a three-stranded hemp rope that was tied to the boat's railing. He pulled on the rope, snugging the tour vessel tight against the rubber bumpers.

Biczó jabbed me again with the gun. "Go on," he said. "Climb!"

I lifted my right foot onto the bottom rail. I took hold of the top rail with my left hand. The buzzing grew louder.

A motor. Coming closer.

I put my left foot onto the railing.

"Hurry up," Biczó said.

Then I saw the Vespa racing toward us. The same pair of women I'd seen last night in front of The 21 Club, right before

UNN had arrived. In front, the driver, no helmet, bleached-blond ducktail sharpened by the wind, mouth open in a shout, teeth bared. Fouad turned his head toward the noise.

I kicked back hard with my right foot. My boot connected with Biczó's chest. He cried out in pain. I grabbed the rope with both hands and yanked Fouad off-balance. I let my momentum carry me—and Fouad—back onto the deck. I landed feet-first on the Hungarian's gut. The gun was in his right hand. I jammed my foot onto his wrist.

Fouad sprawled nearby, dazed from the impact of falling headfirst onto the steel plates. But not dazed enough. He scrambled toward the gun.

I bent over, trying to grab it first. Biczó bucked then, nearly tossing me off. Faintly, from the other side of the door, came the crashing sound of accordion chords. The deck vibrated as those inside stomped at the end of each phrase of the chorus.

Fouad cackled. His hand was on the gun. Then he sighted on a point right between my eyes. The mechanism clicked as Fouad cocked it with his thumb. The first cartridge slid into the breech with a silvery sigh.

I looked down into Fouad's eyes, pools of darkest hate.

His head snapped back. A black circle appeared on the bridge of his nose. The circle blossomed into a rose. The rose crumbled, shattered, and Fouad's face was gone. I gagged, tasting the bile as it rose from my stomach. I stumbled off Biczó's wrist.

A woman's voice spat out a command in Flemish.

Biczó rolled over, facedown, and locked his fingers behind his neck.

"You did need a little help," said the woman in the oil-streaked mechanic's coverall. "He thought you might."

He? Surely not van Hoof. Stefan?

Mechanic jumped down to the boat deck, landing with a grunt. She straddled the prone Hungarian. Then she reversed her revolver and clubbed Biczó at the base of the skull. His body went limp.

The driver revved the Vespa and grinned at me.

I asked, "Who sent—"

"A friend," said Mechanic. "We enjoy this kind of thing." She tucked the revolver into her pocket and jerked her chin toward the door to the restaurant. "There another scumbag inside?"

"Blocking the door," I said. "And this stop is supposed to last only five minutes."

As if on cue, the idling engine rumbled more loudly.

"We got rid of the ugly fellow in the Mercedes," Mechanic said. "You better leave before anyone else comes along."

I climbed up the railing and onto the dock. The vessel began easing away from its mooring and a gray-green ribbon of water appeared. I grabbed the rope to stop the boat from swinging farther out into the waterway. The coarse hemp scraped my palm. I looked down at the boat deck. Fouad al-Nemer sprawled near its edge, blood pooling beneath his cheek. My stomach cramped again. "What about him?" I asked Mechanic.

She kicked the corpse twice to push it under the deck railing. The gap between the vessel and the rubber bumpers had widened enough to allow the body to drop over the vessel's side and slip silently into the greenish water.

"Bye-bye." She hoisted herself to the top of the railing and stretched her arm toward me. I leaned out over the strip of water to take her hand and she leaped across to stand beside me.

I released the rope. The band of gray-green expanded. The tour boat edged into the mainstream.

"The other goon on board should be plenty busy," she said, "trying to figure out where that blood came from and why his boss is asleep. I'll wait here, handle anyone else who turns up in this neighborhood. You go with Danièle."

I took a step toward the Vespa. "Thanks," I began.

Mechanic made a brush-off motion with her hand.

From the rear seat of the Vespa, I looked back over my shoulder at the tour boat. Faintly, I heard another blast of oom-pah music. Thankfully, not the last sound I'd hear on earth.

The Vespa buzzed around the final Lada in the line of off-loaded cars and pulled onto the roadway. Danièle followed it south, twisting and turning her way out of the port district.

"Where are we going?" I shouted into her ear.

"No English," she said over her shoulder.

Never mind. Stefan had to be the "he" to whom her friend had referred. He'd sent these women to save me. I clutched Danièle tightly around her bony waist and pressed my body against her spine, willing my own trembling to stop. I'd come so close this time—so damn close to my own death. Then suddenly Fouad's face dissolved in front of me. I wanted to curl up in a ball and shut my eyes.

But first I had to get to Stefan. Had to tell him what had happened. Erika had sent me to Biczó in the first place. She must've sent the newspeople right after me. Maybe she'd only wanted to delay me, give Biczó time to sell me to Fouad. The result was a trail of disasters—a trail that led right back to Erika. I had to get word to Stefan. I had to warn him that Erika had set me up. And might be about to do the same to him.

I huddled closer to Danièle, trying to absorb her warmth and halt my slide into physical shock. Her hair was cut ragged against the back of her neck, the bleached ends greenish above the mouse-brown roots. She smelled of kerosene and bacon grease, but I caught the faint scent of violets beneath.

We stopped on a sidestreet at the eastern edge of Antwerp, near Schijnpoort. We were beside a dirty brown Jetta with a CH decal. The passenger door popped open. "Get in," Erika said, leaning across from the driver's side.

I didn't move off the scooter.

She slapped her hand on the seat. "You must return to Bert's at once."

I snorted. "Bert's? You want to make it easy for the al-Nemers and their friends."

"We can't have people searching for you." Her voice held a note of impatience. "Get in. We must go."

I climbed slowly off the scooter. "Prove to me Stefan knows what's going on."

"Who do you think recognized the danger to you when Fouad al-Nemer left Lebanon? Knew that Fouad wanted you dead—because you killed his brother." She paused a second for that to sink in. "Come. Soon Stefan must approach his informant. He needs you to show up at Bert's."

I couldn't argue. I had to keep the gunmen occupied while Stefan made his move. Reluctantly, I dropped onto the seat and closed the door.

Erika pulled forward out of the parking space. "Fouad al-Nemer was driven by his family's vow of revenge. He was acting alone. But the others who've come are controlled by Krüger. His instruction to them is to keep you under surveillance. No violence."

"You're so sure all of them will follow orders?"

"Their discipline is infamous." She slid around a truck double-parked for unloading. "But if there are any other lapses, we will take care of it."

"We? You mean you and Bert? Against a gang of terrorists? Good luck."

"Bert is more formidable than he appears."

"I'm not worried about Bert."

"Oh, it's me you think unequal to the task." Her laughter had a mocking undertone. "And after I sent Danièle and Hilly-Anne to save you. You don't appreciate the fact that I risked two of my best people."

"*Your* best people? They said '*he*' sent them."

" '*He*' told me you'd need help. *I* called them."

She cut back across the main artery and onto the web of streets bounded by blocks of water. She edged the car into a loading zone and pushed the engine into neutral.

I said, "I wouldn't have needed rescuing if you'd stuck with the plan."

"If *I'd* stuck with it? You changed the location for your meeting with the Hungarian."

"What choice did I have, after you tipped off UNN?"

"Me?" Erika was incredulous. "Hardly. But the coverage raised your profile. Sure to get Major Reinhardt Krüger's attention. Perhaps worth the risk."

"Raised it too much," I said. "I have to get out of Antwerp."

"So far only Krüger's team seems to know where you're hiding. But I have people on the lookout. We'll move you from Bert's before the police or the press can get to you."

I rubbed my forehead. "I didn't tell Bert I was going to The 21 Club. Only you knew that."

"*I* didn't call UNN."

"If it wasn't you—" I began.

Sudden understanding lit Erika's face. She had a good idea who'd called the television people. Before I could press her, she said, "I now have an excellent reason to contact Krüger myself. I'll report what Biczó attempted."

"You have a line to Gunter Storch—to Krüger himself?" Surprise sharpened my voice. "Then why did I have to go through Biczó to get to him?"

"It's plausible that you might have heard of the Hungarian's activities. Not so likely the State Department has any information about me. Far more logical, then, for you to try to contact Krüger via Biczó." She leaned toward me. "It's equally plausible that I would hear you'd turned up in Antwerp. Of course I passed on what I knew to people who'd be certain to inform Krüger. What better way to get his attention focused on you?"

I sat silent for thirty seconds, letting Erika's last words sink in. My cheeks got warm. I said, "I don't like the way things are going."

"You are acting your part marvelously. Van Hoof wanted

a dramatic flurry of activity. You gave it to him. Now you must keep their attention."

Her calmness irritated me. That and her total refusal to offer me any explanation for her behavior. I asked her, "Why are you in this?"

"Bert asks me the same question. I don't answer him either." She waved a hand in the direction the car was pointed. "Go to the corner and turn right. The Café Ebertus is beyond the drawbridge."

The afternoon sun did nothing to lighten the dingy exteriors. Erika expected me to walk down this gloomy street, past all the lurking dangers. Then I was supposed to march boldly into Bert's and remain there as if I hadn't a care in the world. And let the world watch me throughout.

"Go on," Erika said, leaning across me to open the door. "Nobody's going to bother you now."

Erika claimed she'd saved my life. Claimed my best move now was to sit inside the Café Ebertus like a tethered goat. Claimed doing that was the only way to help Stefan. I didn't like her. Worse, I didn't trust her. But I couldn't prove my suspicions unless I first did what she'd told me to do. Until I let her sabotage me again. I rubbed a bruise on my calf.

Erika. I seemed to be joined to her with the sailor's knot that only grows tighter as you struggle against it.

13

White light flashed like a strobe on the street outside. I smelled gunpowder. The café windows vibrated, but the thick glass muffled the sound of the explosion.

Bert slid the geneva bottle across the floor. "Happy New Year," he said.

I checked my watch. "You're two hours early." I refilled my glass. The liquor smelled as vile as the fumes seeping in under the door.

We were sitting on the floor behind the bar. The doors were locked and the lights out, except for the glow from the television mounted at one end of the bar. Bert was far less sanguine than Erika about the possibility of attack. He'd picked this drinking spot because it offered the most protection. But so far, the only assault had been on my ears, from the people outside celebrating the end of the year.

Low-volume cheering came from the television. UNN gave us a shot of the crowd in Red Square. Fireworks blossomed over the Kremlin. Ten o'clock in Antwerp. Midnight in Moscow.

Like an echo, another rocket exploded in the street outside. Bert peered at me across the rim of his glass. His chin dipped in a nod of approval. "You didn't blink," he said. He sounded like a doting father, his voice thick with geneva-enhanced affection. He emptied the bottle into his glass. "Now you're acting like a soldier."

"This stuff has paralytic effects." I stared at the bottom of my glass. Shots with beer chasers. I should've passed out hours ago. But nothing could silence the insistent pulsing in my head. RUN-RUN-RUN, my blood drummed, as gunpowder exploded all around me. But we were at the critical moment now. At the beginning of that four-hour time period on Thursday night, when Stefan's informant was willing to be approached. Only because of that was I willing to sit where all of Krüger's people could easily find me. And only because of the half liter of geneva inside me was I able to stop myself from crawling away.

Flames engulfed the television screen. A building ablaze somewhere. The camera panned the watching crowd. A mix of bundled men and near-naked women. Standing in front of a ship chandlery. Then another shot of the burning building. A neon sign that looked as if it were melting. The numbers "2" and "1" running down the bricks.

I staggered to my feet and fumbled at the volume control. I heard "Antwerp."

"What happened?" I asked Bert.

He was standing beside me, clutching the neck of the empty geneva bottle in his fingers. The camera showed an ambulance waiting beyond the fire trucks. Doors open, the gurney empty. Bert's forehead creased as he concentrated on the voice-over. He said, "Explosion inside The 21 Club."

"Lots of casualties?" I asked, my throat suddenly dry.

Bert shook his head. "Don't think so. They interviewed someone who'd been working out front. Blast mostly blew the girls out their doors. A few scrapes, nobody killed. The hooker they talked to said there were no customers inside the bar. The owner showed up around six and threw everybody out. Told the girls they couldn't use their back exit through his premises."

The rooftop flames subsided under the steady stream of water from the pumper truck. Only a thin ribbon of smoke came out the front door. A pair of masked firemen shouldered their way through the opening. The voice-over grew more somber.

I asked Bert, "What about the owner?"

"Girl thought he was having a private party in there tonight." Bert stopped and frowned again at the television. The two firemen came out and held an inaudible conference with the paramedics. Then one of the white-clad attendants slammed the rear doors of the ambulance. The camera panned back to the blackened building before cutting to an on-the-scene reporter. Lura Dumont's vulpine features filled the screen.

"The charred remains found inside are believed to include the body of reputed arms trader Sándor—"

The translator's voice cut in, the Flemish version drowning out Lura's English-language report. I heard my name. Global. Lockerbie Two. Then the news report ended. And we were back with the cheering crowds in Red Square.

I said, "She makes it sound like I had something to do with it."

"Plenty of witnesses know you were here all the time."

"You and that bunch outside will give me a great alibi when the cops show up."

"I wasn't thinking of the cops," Bert said. "But some of the Hungarian's pals are probably out there. They know you weren't downtown blowing him away." He paused, then reached up and clicked off the television.

Two down. Fouad al-Nemer first. Now Sándor Biczó. My enemies were dying like flies. New ones would hatch like maggots.

I heard nothing. But Bert must have. In a single fluid motion he set the bottle on the floor and a pistol appeared in his hand. He slid through the curtain and into the kitchen.

I flattened myself on the floor. My fingers curved around the neck of the bottle. I was too drunk to shoot straight. But I could do some damage with jagged glass.

"The major," Bert said softly.

I felt a draft of cold air, but the locks and hinges were so well oiled that there was no sound as Bert opened and closed the rear door.

Van Hoof spoke from the curtained doorway. "Upstairs," he said to me. "Harder for them to spot me up there."

I released the empty bottle and sat up.

Running footsteps slapped on the cobblestones outside. Beyond the glass of the entry door, a burning fuse sprayed sparks across the pavement. Then I heard a pop-pop-pop like small-arms fire. My body trembled as I fought the overwhelming desire to slither on my belly into the darkest corner of the room. The geneva coating my tongue took on the taste of tin. I couldn't move. The firecracker colored the air outside a smoky chartreuse, then sputtered out.

"Please," van Hoof said. "Please come now." His voice was thin. And I'd never heard the word "please" from him. I had to see his face. I had to find out what had gone wrong. By the time I got to my feet, my face was filmed with sweat and every muscle ached.

As I came through the curtain, Bert's fingers brushed my arm, a gentle pat. "I'll keep watch," he said, speaking to me like a comrade-in-arms.

I realized that was what we were now, Bert and I. The idea made me feel braver.

"Get the lights on up here," van Hoof growled from the top of the stairs. "Make it obvious you're in this room, as if you've only now awakened."

I shoved past him and through the unlocked door. "I know the drill." I went to the east wall and pressed my face to the window, counting to five as I rubbed my forehead. I reached up and tugged the curtain over the glass. Then I turned to face van Hoof, who'd seated himself on the cot, out of sight of the window. Beside him, the wooden door hung open, a wedge of staircase illuminated to old gold by the triangle of light falling through it.

I folded my arms and leaned back against the wall. "What's happened?"

Van Hoof grunted. "Stefan's informant was supposed to be on holiday, cross-country skiing in the Ardennes. Meeting Stefan under cover of a big party tonight. Stefan went yesterday. But the man never arrived." He sighed. "Seems that when you surfaced in Antwerp, Krüger insisted his associate come here."

"Here? You mean the associate is hunting Stefan?"

"No, he's not an assassin. More what you call a right-hand man. Follows Krüger's orders. Goes where he's sent."

Now it all made sense. How else could Stefan have warned Erika so quickly about Fouad al-Nemer? "Stefan's in Antwerp, isn't he? He followed this guy here. Did he make contact with him?"

Van Hoof shook his head.

Air escaped my lungs in a gusty sigh. "Just as well. Antwerp is way too hot now, for all of us. Stefan can't go near this guy while he's in this town."

Van Hoof sat hunched at the edge of the cot, elbows on his knees, eyes on the floor, a foot soldier who'd marched fifty kilometers over cobblestones. The weak light turned his cheeks a sickly yellow beneath the powdery growth of beard. "The opportunity to reach this man has passed," he said in a flat voice. "Stefan can't get anything from him anywhere."

"Then it's over."

Van Hoof raised his head. "For Stefan. Not for you."

"Me?" I wasn't interested in hearing what more he thought I could do. "I'm through. I can't guess what Erika did to ruin things for Stefan. I'm not going to let her set *me* up again."

"What are you talking about?"

"Everything—and I mean everything—has gone wrong. Can't you see? Erika's the only one who could have sabotaged me so effectively."

"No—"

I cut him off. "Maybe you should listen to Bert. He doesn't

trust her. And why should I? Look at what's happened. She brings me here on Wednesday morning. Then she's supposed to go off and let her contacts know I'm in town. She tells me she figures it'll be twelve, maybe eighteen hours before the bad guys show up. But they were in place before noon. Right from the start, I was off stride. I've been playing catch-up ever since."

"But that speedy response may have worked to our advantage—"

"You weren't out there dealing with the consequences. And then, when I got to The 21 Club, someone had tipped off UNN to look for me there."

"Erika didn't—"

"Who else could it have been?"

"Fairly obvious," van Hoof said in that weary voice. "Krüger did it."

I needed a second to absorb the suggestion. The chair creaked as I lowered myself into it. I rubbed at my forehead. "Why?"

"A test. Sensible on his part. Were you truly a fugitive?" He glanced up at me, his eyes dull. "You did well. After that performance, Krüger's interest in dealing with you increased significantly."

"Interest in dealing with me? He let the Hungarian sell me to the al-Nemers."

"Krüger didn't instigate that." Van Hoof pinched the bridge of his nose between his thumb and forefinger. "More likely, all the attention made Biczó nervous. Then Fouad al-Nemer offered to take you off his hands—and sweetened the deal with cash."

"I still think Erika—"

"No. I have thoroughly investigated Erika Berger. Her credentials are unimpeachable."

"Credentials?"

"Like me, she is seeking justice for a crime committed by the Abu Nidal Organization."

I waved my hand in a gesture of disbelief.

Van Hoof said, "You recall how active Abu Nidal's people were in Europe in 1980 and 1981?"

I recalled. I was still at the Foreign Service Institute in Rosslyn then, one of thirty brand-new junior officers preparing for a first assignment. We learned quickly that large European cities had become killing zones. Most of the hit-and-run attacks on synagogues and Jewish-owned businesses had occurred in Paris and Vienna, but no European country had escaped.

Van Hoof said, "Erika Berger was a schoolgirl in 1980, a student at a private Jewish academy in Antwerp. One July day, the teachers took their pupils on a field trip." He inhaled a deep breath. "Two grenades. Those animals threw two grenades into a busload of children. Twenty-one lived to wear the scars. The twenty-second bled to death. Erika's older sister died in her arms." Light flared in his eyes, the dullness burned away by anger. "So don't talk to me of sabotage by Erika."

A plaintive note floated through the open doorway, the noise as soft as a mouse moaning in its sleep.

"Don't miss your cue, Erika," I said loudly. "Or does the script call for you to stay out there?" Only one squeak to signal her approach. She must have known those stairs intimately.

Her head appeared, her shining hair momentarily haloed as she came silently up the last few steps into the triangle of light. I'd been ninety percent certain it was Erika. No one else heading for the major could have gotten past Bert so soundlessly.

"There's no script," she said, coming into the room to stand beside van Hoof. She put her left hand gently on his shoulder. He glanced up at her and she murmured something in a consoling tone as her grip on his shoulder tightened, then relaxed. His left hand rose to his shoulder, so that his solid fingers covered her slender ones.

The gesture made me think suddenly of my father. An inexplicable sadness welled up in me, followed swiftly by a flash of indignation so sharp, my own hand rose with the fingers together, palm out. A slap heading for Erika's smooth cheek. I stopped myself. Where had that sudden fury come from?

Erika gave me an appraising look. "I had nothing to do with the deal between Biczó and Fouad al-Nemer."

Van Hoof added, "As soon as Stefan warned her of the danger from al-Nemer, Erika put the rescue plan together."

I said, "As soon as Stefan warned her? You mean she didn't act until he told her to. If he hadn't found out . . ." I shook my head. "Nothing you say will convince me to work with her. I'm through with this operation."

"Not yet," said van Hoof. "Not when you have positioned yourself perfectly to deal with Krüger."

"I agreed to do this much only in order to distract Krüger. Give Stefan a chance to reach his informant, find out what he knows about Krüger's plans to blow up another airliner. Now he'll have to find some other way to contact him. I'm finished. All I want to do is clear my name so I can go home. How you go about extracting what you need from that informant is your problem."

"The problem has changed," said van Hoof. "That change makes it your problem, too."

"I don't think so."

Van Hoof said, "Stefan's informant has disappeared."

"He has been found." Erika stepped over to the table and dropped so gracefully into the rickety chair that it made no sound. Van Hoof and I sat silent, waiting for her to finish. She pulled out a cigarette. The flame on her lighter wavered in the air as though her hand were trembling. She inhaled deeply. "Krüger's associate was in the club with the Hungarian. Both of them were waiting for a third party who never appeared."

"Krüger set them up," I said slowly, taking the chair across from her. "Killed off his major snitch along with Biczó."

"Yes," Erika said. "Stefan says he will not find anyone else willing to talk to him. Not in time to prevent another attack."

Van Hoof shifted his gaze to me. "But *you* have a chance to get to Krüger before the next airliner blows up."

For a few seconds no one spoke. Something exploded outside. The window glass rattled and took on a greenish cast. Van Hoof's eyes stayed on me, an old cat too tired to pounce on the mouse he'd cornered.

Erika was watching me, too, her gaze sharper than van Hoof's, as though she were carefully measuring my reactions. "Krüger dealt so severely with Biczó's interference as an object lesson for the others. To demonstrate that you're under his protection. That's how eager he is to hear your offer." She inhaled deeply on her cigarette. "Krüger wants you to come to him."

"I can't do that. I've had too little training in fieldwork."

"You have an aptitude for it." Erika blew a cloud of smoke toward me, then dropped the cigarette stub to the floor and ground it beneath her shoe. "You were successful in Poland."

"That was a long time ago."

Van Hoof said, "Stefan called you a natural."

Had he? Consider the source, I reminded myself. Both van Hoof and Erika would tell any lie they had to. "Stefan was the key to any success I had. Professional planning and backup."

"You'll have that," van Hoof said.

"Oh?" I let my skepticism lengthen the syllable to two.

Van Hoof's voice was impatient. "I will direct the operation. Ebertus Wouters and Erika Berger will be the core of an excellent support team."

"Not of my team," I said. "You can't be certain that Krüger is interested in my offer. Maybe he only wants me. Maybe he's setting another trap for Stefan and wants me for bait."

"Possibly." Erika lit another cigarette. "But there is reason to believe his greater concern now is his personal safety."

"What reason?"

"He paid off on the contract." She leaned across the table. "As of a half hour ago, they've stopped watching you."

I rubbed at my forehead. "Biczó said that Krüger still wanted proof that Stefan was on board Global 500."

"Maybe your behavior was proof enough," Erika said.

I shook my head. "Not likely. Something odd about the man's change of opinion. Maybe he's trying to get Stefan to drop his guard."

"Then Stefan must be doubly careful," Erika said. "But I think Krüger has decided it's important that no one keep watch on you. That there be no witnesses for his meeting with you. In case you are bringing him an offer of safe haven." She leaned toward me. "He's ripe, Casey. Ready for picking. By you."

"I don't think so," I said.

"This was your idea," said van Hoof. "Why are you now so negative?"

"In the last two days, I've moved way up on the Most Wanted list. I can't contact anyone in D.C. to set this up. I'd be arrested before I could make a move. And I can't approach Krüger without some evidence that the U.S. will give him the deal he wants."

Erika said, "I'm sure you can find a way."

Van Hoof's voice was full of regret. "The combination of money and a safe haven in America has likely become most attractive to Krüger."

"No one else can make him the appropriate offer," Erika said. "For that, we need you."

"All I want to do is clear my name and go home," I said. "I'm not going to try to deal with Major Reinhardt Krüger. I'd go to hell first."

But, of course, hell was where I'd ended up.

14

The altar candles wavered. Cold air moved across my face, the room so vast it had its own wind currents, unrelated to any predawn breezes swirling about beyond the stone walls. Unrepentant and nonconfessing, I lurked in a side chapel of the largest Gothic church in the Low Countries, waiting to keep the bargain I'd struck with Erika and van Hoof. Waiting for Stefan to give me his reading on what was happening.

Never mind the Herculean efforts they'd both expended to keep me and Stefan apart. They were so desperate to overcome my objections, they'd decided to hazard our meeting.

Their idea, not mine. I'd told them further talk was futile. Sure, I wanted to prevent the next bombing. I wanted that information as much as van Hoof and Erika did. But I couldn't get it. I'd played the deal-maker to draw Krüger's attention away from Stefan. I'd hoped to come out of it with enough hard information to clear my name with the FBI. It hadn't worked out that way. There was nothing more I could do to help them.

But van Hoof and Erika insisted on the meet with Stefan. I didn't know why they thought he'd aid their cause. He'd been adamantly opposed to my involvement earlier. Yet Erika had huddled with van Hoof, and finally they demanded I listen to Stefan's version of events.

I didn't know how to refuse. I didn't want to see him. I'd

thought that he was dead. And then, after eight days, he reappeared, still alive. He'd carefully avoided explaining where he'd been for a week and a day. I hadn't asked. Why make him tell me he'd gone to Erika? Stefan and I never voiced promises of sexual fidelity to each other. But like a thousand foolish humans before me, I'd assumed that because I had no other lovers, neither did he.

I'd trusted him and he'd broken the faith with casual indifference. I felt like I was bleeding inside, pain threatening to overwhelm me. Seeing Stefan again could only make it worse.

But I couldn't use that excuse. Not to Erika, not to anyone. I had to go.

At five, I'd left the café and cut through the red-light district. I saw no one following me. It could be true, that Krüger had called off the surveillance.

I avoided the ruins of The 21 Club, but from three blocks away the smell of damp ashes was strong. The streets were littered with firecracker debris.

By five-thirty, I was beneath the soaring spire of Onze Lieve-Vrouwe Kerk, Church of Our Lady, the site of worshipful construction, fiery devastation, opulent restoration and furious iconoclastic plundering since 1352. It was still so dark, I had difficulty spotting the wasplike tail of a battered Vespa a hundred feet to the right of the entrance.

Indoors, I stood in the side chapel, inhaling air made oily by the combination of cool moisture and dust. Next to me was a stained-glass rendering of the Last Supper. I thought of what had followed. The thin-lipped farewell kiss, the thirty pieces of silver. Easy betrayal. As old as time. The shimmering glass became a smear of murky colors, like a blurred memory.

I turned my back on it. I couldn't let myself wallow in self-pity. Stefan was one of my passions. I was also committed to preventing horrors like the explosion of Global Flight 500. I wouldn't have been drawn to him so forcefully if we hadn't shared that passion. Whatever else Erika might be to Stefan, she'd been crucial to continuing his mission. He needed her help to stop the terrorists from blowing up a second plane. And much as I disliked her, I no longer doubted she shared that goal.

Through Erika, Stefan had found van Hoof, a man with a most personal reason for joining them. They'd defined a common interest in Reinhardt Krüger, the former major in the East German Stasi who'd put a price on Stefan's head. Krüger was our target. I had to focus on getting information out of him.

I turned to survey the room again. A rumpled figure stepped out from behind the pulpit, neck craned as though to study the ornate carving. Startled, I caught my breath. A shaft of light touched her hair then, and I saw Danièle's trademark ducktail. Good. Erika's team was in place. I checked my watch. Five forty-five. I tucked my chin into my collar and tried to look devout as I moved slowly past the choir stalls and slipped into the confessional. I leaned closer to the square opening in the partition and began, "Bless me Father—"

"*Sto lat,*" Stefan's voice interrupted. May you live a hundred years. New Year's greeting in Polish, the language he murmured when we made love.

A tremor went through me. I'd break down if I let those memories surface. I said quickly, "*Godt Nytaar.*" Happy New Year, in Danish. The language Stefan spoke on the job. Strictly business. That was the only way I'd get through this. I added, "Van Hoof wants me to go talk to Krüger."

"No. I told Hans. You have too little experience in the field. It's far too dangerous for you. But you told him the same thing."

No. I hadn't stressed danger. I'd said I had too little chance of success. But it wasn't worth debating. "How much time do we have before the next bomb?" I asked.

"I estimate no more than a week."

A week. Not enough time to get another agent in place. It had to be one of us. "So who does that leave? Van Hoof?"

Stefan muttered a negative. "He would have been the logical choice. But not now."

"Why not?"

"Too unstable."

My mind again flashed the image of Erika consoling van Hoof earlier. "Has something happened?"

"His wife died yesterday morning."

"Died? How?"

"Drug overdose."

"Suicide?"

Stefan grunted.

I rubbed my palm across my scalp, the bristles still sharp against my skin. "Did she leave a note?"

"Yes. Her daughter a withering shell. Her husband obsessed. Her life unbearable. What you might expect."

I imagined a young woman comatose, wasting away. I shuddered. "My God . . ."

"Yes. We cannot use him for this."

I stared at the opening in the partition between me and Stefan. All I could see was the rough black sleeve of a cassock. "Erika thinks Krüger is eager to hear about a safe haven."

"I'm sure he's more than eager. That news photo was published widely in November. Eventually someone else will recognize his face in it. The Germans are prosecuting several men who committed similar crimes. And besides . . ."

His voice trailed off. Another secret he didn't want to reveal?

"And besides what?" I asked. "Is there more I need to know about Krüger?"

"The Israelis have also discovered Gunter Storch's true identity. The man must find a refuge. Yesterday, the Mossad nearly caught up with him."

How had he learned so quickly what the Israelis had attempted? Easy. He'd spoken with one. Erika.

Suddenly, it was so obvious. Daughter of a diamond merchant. And Antwerp's diamond market was controlled by Jews. Recruitment of local Jewish citizens was standard practice for Israeli intelligence. They'd found Erika. She'd identified van Hoof as someone useful. Then she'd played on his feelings for his daughter, to gain his trust. I remembered van Hoof's haggard face, Erika's solicitous posture. Now I understood why that scene had made me think of my father, why it had brought back the misery of loss. I'd stood in the identical position Erika had taken with van Hoof, consoling my father after my mother's death. Somehow, Erika had replaced van Hoof's daughter in his affections. I remembered my outraged reaction when I'd seen them together. As if Erika had stolen *my* father from *me*.

So cold-blooded, using that ploy to draw van Hoof into an Israeli scheme. I let my disgust color my voice. "She told van Hoof she'd survived a terrorist attack on Jewish children. She said she lost her sister."

"She did. And as soon as she turned eighteen, she offered her services to the Israelis. They saw at once the value of grooming her to infiltrate the illegal weapons traffic in Antwerp."

"I thought you disliked cooperating with the Israelis. You told me the Mossad uses everyone and everything it can for its own purposes. I agreed with you, remember?"

He said, "You're suggesting they will use Erika to exploit us all?"

"Doesn't that seem likely?" I asked. "You told me what the Israelis call the Danish Defense Intelligence Service. *Fertsalach.* 'Little fart' in Hebrew. You help them and they mock you for being an easy mark."

"But we want them to underestimate us. Just as we want them to believe that Erika is loyal to them."

Skepticism made my tone acid. "She's not?"

"She has found that her interests coincide more closely with ours."

Did he believe that? I said, "Then why not use her? Obviously she communicates often with Krüger. She's confident of her attraction for men. Surely Krüger could be persuaded to meet with her."

"Perhaps. But Erika has no experience with interrogation. On her own, she could not extract the information we need."

On her own. Something quivered in the pit of my stomach. Whoever went after Krüger would be working alone. He'd been attacked. He'd avoid any situation which made him vulnerable. There'd be no opportunity to burst in and take him prisoner. I said, "He has to be drawn off his turf, away from his protection."

"And Erika has no credible way to do that."

"She can't offer what he's interested in—money and a safe haven in the U.S." I shook my head. "You can't use Erika. Van Hoof is sidelined. Has Holger got anyone you can use?"

"Other than me? No."

"And you can't do it. You're completely blown as far as Krüger goes." Then, the finality in his tone got through to me. "But you'll try anyway."

Beyond the opening the sleeve moved, but he said nothing. Now I knew why he'd been terse and secretive. He had his own plan and he didn't want me to challenge it. He was out of luck there. "Mr. Noble Hero going to His Death." I got louder—I couldn't help it. "What, you're so good, you can get Krüger alone, make him talk? Forget that. I can find out more about the next bombing than you can."

His retort was swift. "Don't be ridiculous."

"Offering him resettlement in the U.S. is a better plan. I can make that offer."

"You can't deceive a man like him," Stefan said.

"Deception was exactly what I did in Poland. You described me as 'a natural.' "

"You were working with me. That will not be the case this time."

"I'll have Erika and her pals. And there's Bert and van Hoof."

His silent pause stretched to thirty seconds. At last he said, "But at some point you'll be alone with Krüger and his bodyguards."

I shivered, suddenly chilled. *On my own.* I wrapped my arms around my body and willed the fear out of my voice. "Better me than you. Krüger never put a contract out on *my* life."

His voice grew more intense. "The whole thing may be only a bluff. He'll put you in danger, expecting that then I'll come to your aid."

A needy voice inside me cried out, *And would you come?* I spoke louder to drown it out. "Then how can it possibly be better for you to attempt this on your own? I have to take that chance."

He spoke without pause now. "You can't communicate with your own government. How will you convince anyone you can keep your side of the bargain?"

"I've got friends I trust. Harry Martin, for one. He's good and he's quick. We'll have to find a surreptitious way to contact him. But he'll do it. He'll make it work."

"Suddenly you have a solution for every problem." His words came out clipped. "You came here determined to do this."

He was right. I hadn't realized it. But on some subconscious level, I'd figured it out. Lousy as my odds were, they were the best odds anyone was going to get. I was the only one who could get close enough to Krüger to find out what he was planning. And I had another, more personal reason.

"I told you I wanted to go home. But you've done nothing to help me clear my name. It's all up to me." I was breathing too fast. I forced myself to slow down. "What makes my offer to Krüger so compelling is that there's so much truth in it. I *am* wanted by the FBI. My career *is* ruined—unless I can pull off something of this magnitude. If I want to stay out of jail, I have to make sure that next bomb never goes off."

"Foiling a single plot won't clear your name."

"No?"

"You must bring the man out, to people who can force from him all of the information he's got."

"Well, of course that's the plan—"

"One far too difficult for you to execute with the resources available."

"You underestimate me."

"Never. I have never underestimated you."

"Erika and van Hoof think it can be done."

He swore, a Polish curse ringing with vengeful malediction. "They don't understand what they're asking you to do."

"And you do?"

For the next few seconds it was silent in the booth. "He murdered my informant."

"His right-hand man, I take it."

"And his oldest friend since earliest childhood." Stefan's voice was so tight the words fell between us like stones. "He killed him without hesitation."

My mouth was dry. I forced myself to speak. "This is business. I'll make it work."

"Maybe you are more eager to take this monumental risk because I am so unequivocally opposed to your doing so."

"That would be childish of me."

"Perhaps you are too angry with me to hear the truth in my words."

I wasn't going to listen to what he seemed ready to admit. I understood now why Erika had sent me to Stefan. She wanted me to know that if I didn't go after Krüger, Stefan would. She'd accurately guessed how I'd react. Known me better than Stefan seemed to. *He* wanted to talk about why I was angry with him. As if telling me that he and Erika were lovers would stop me. As if then I'd refuse to save his damn life.

Standing, I said, "Being angry with you has nothing to do with my decision. Going to Krüger isn't some kind of payback. I'm the only person who can do the job." I turned to leave.

"Wait," Stefan said, his tone urgent. "There's something I must tell you. You have to know about me and—"

"No," I said, cutting him off as I moved away from the sound of his voice. "Not now. I won't hear your confession." And then I was out of the booth, hurrying toward the exit, trying to outrun my pain.

15

It took two precious days to set things up the way I wanted. Erika did her part swiftly. Within hours we knew that Reinhardt Krüger was willing to meet me on the southern outskirts of Berlin at an undisclosed location—I wouldn't learn the specifics until after I'd begun traveling toward him.

Van Hoof and Bert left Antwerp immediately so they could work out of our new headquarters in Berlin. Erika and I remained in Belgium until Friday afternoon, hammering the last crucial nail into our carefully constructed plan.

Reinhardt Krüger was no amateur. He'd situated our meeting on his turf, building in safeguards along the way that gave him all the advantage. He expected deception and he was ready to expose it. Our negotiations had to be as real as I could make them. I had to have somebody working for me Stateside.

My first choice for that role was Harry Martin. His State Department job in INR gave him all the right connections. Plus, we'd been friends ever since we first served together in San Salvador. He wouldn't automatically turn me in to the FBI— not without first hearing me out. But that had to be done in person and in Europe. I'd need to push all of Harry's hot buttons if I wanted him to imperil his career to save mine. If I couldn't convince Harry to play by our rules, we'd bench him until the game was over. I wasn't giving another of my old pals the chance to do an end run around me.

Erika knew instantly how to proceed. We'd go through Holger Sorensen, of course. She said she could communicate with him securely and we wouldn't have to waste time briefing him on our activities.

I agreed immediately, as if I weren't surprised to learn that someone in Antwerp was transmitting regular reports to Holger. I hadn't guessed that he was involved in this operation. *Heavily* involved, I realized after Erika had edited my message down to one cryptic sentence: *Bring Harry Martin to Berlin ASAP.*

According to Erika, her Mossad connections delivered my message to Holger Sorensen at noon. Within four hours we had confirmation back: *We will join you no later than 0800 on 3 January.*

Erika and I left for Berlin, driving the Jetta in shifts through the night. She didn't need a false passport for this part of the operation. The businesswoman Erika Berger could travel openly in Germany whenever she pleased. Kathryn Collins was not as fortunate, so I used Fräulein Keck's identity to register at an anonymous Novotel a block from Tegel Airport. Slept, washed and waited in my room for Holger and Harry.

Holger was as efficient as Erika. Late on New Year's Day, Harry received a telegram purporting to be from a contact he'd cultivated when based in Spain. As requested, Harry rushed to Málaga, where Holger shanghaied him onto a Danair charter returning holiday revelers to Berlin after package tours along the Costa del Sol. They checked into the hotel early Sunday morning, the third of January.

Holger conferred hurriedly with me. Then we confronted Harry in his room. I spoke first, laying out what I wanted him to do.

Midway into my speech, Harry stood, began stalking

around like a Bengal tiger in center ring. Then stopped and said, "They figure out I've been talking to you, they'll have me dressed in an orange jumpsuit and talking to my lawyer." He looked as peeved as he sounded.

I could guess what story Holger had used to win Harry's cooperation. One that had lost most of its credibility as soon as Harry found me alive and in good health, asking him to do a distasteful task. Jet-engine noise rumbled, grew louder, filled the room. I spread the miniblind with my fingers to peer out, but all I saw against the anvil-gray clouds were the red neon letters of a sign announcing that this part of Berlin was Siemens territory. I dropped the blind and turned back to Harry.

"I don't have time to argue," I said. "Nobody has to know I'm involved, at least not at first. Just go in there and find out if they're willing to deal for a former Stasi major."

"You claim this dude was a heavy hitter in the Hauptverwaltung Aufklärung. How heavy are we talking?"

"The man was in Department Nine up until he faked his suicide in 1990."

Harry stopped pacing. HVA's Department Nine had done formidable damage to American interests. Department Nine successfully induced at least a dozen American soldiers to spy for HVA at U.S. military bases in West Germany, while at the same time compromising every operative the CIA ran in East Germany. Harry froze his features into the blank nonexpression he'd perfected playing poker with the Marines in San Sal. "Give me the rest of it," he said.

Holger slid a photo from his pocket and passed it over. "Our man as he looks now."

Harry glanced indifferently at the picture, then let his hand drop to his side, his posture challenging Holger to say something to relieve his boredom.

Holger named Reinhardt Krüger, detailed his former career and briefly outlined his current business operation, including the Gunter Storch alias.

I took the photo from Harry. It showed a man's head and shoulders in sharp focus against a background of blurred leaves. Probably snapped covertly by someone working for Holger. Krüger wore his dark blond hair swept back from his broad forehead in a style that made his face appear heart-shaped. Strong nose, nice lips, a dimple no larger than a thumb-print in the pointed chin. A pleasant face, made more so by the addition of a modest pair of wire-rimmed glasses. Nothing hinted that Krüger was a man who'd orchestrate merciless acts of international terrorism.

Nothing in what Holger was saying hinted at that either. Krüger was too savvy to seek refuge in the U.S. if anyone there might blame him for the Global 500 bombing. It was important that Harry hadn't yet connected Krüger to that incident—or to any other.

But, of course, Harry caught the discrepancy. He said to me, "Your specialty is supposed to be counterterrorism. Krüger worked in counterintelligence. That's *not* the same thing." He plucked the photo out of my fingers and tucked it into his shirt pocket. "Who suggested using Krüger for this deal you want to make?"

"I selected the target." Holger spoke before I could. "I understand he has some concerns about the future business climate for him in Germany. I heard he might be susceptible to an offer of safe haven in the U.S."

Harry's eyebrows shot up. "I can guess where you heard that."

"I have a number of useful sources—"

Harry cut him off. "But there's only one in place to give you this stuff. That guy you Danes had inside the Stasi. The one you code-named Gorm. We spotted him back in action last year. Hanging around that ex-Stasi group, the one set up to help former officers in financial distress."

"Gorm has done some work for the organization you mention, the so-called Insider Committee for Rectification." Holger spoke calmly, as if he weren't surprised that Harry knew so much about his undercover agent. "Not with Krüger directly, of course, since in his role as Gunter Storch he denies any Stasi connection. But over the last couple of months Gorm has had occasion to speak to one of Krüger's associates. That one dropped some hints about his employer's state of mind. When it became clear that Kathryn needed help clearing her name, I saw how she could use Krüger to get things started."

"I bet you did." Harry's voice was tight. "But your focus is supposed to be illegal arms flows to radical groups. Why are *you* collecting information about Krüger?"

Holger dipped his head toward Harry, a gesture of respect. "I heard you were well versed on the structure of the NATO intelligence branches."

I broke in. "Holger's interested in any German who's part of Qadhafi's supply system."

"Trade with Libya?" Harry was watching us both intently. "Back to terrorism. So now Krüger's got ties to Qadhafi. What about before, when he was still in the Stasi? Are you saying that a former major in East German counterintelligence played a role in international terrorism?"

Holger said, "In the eighties Krüger did some work on the armaments side, getting East Bloc ordnance into terrorist hands, but that was mostly a sideline. I'm convinced that the radical Palestinian terrorists worked closely with someone in HVA, but we've no evidence implicating Krüger. Certainly, he'll be able to fill in some of the gaps in our information. But his specialty was counterintelligence."

No change in the timbre of Holger's voice, no verbal or physical tic, suggested that there was any duplicity in his words. I felt a chill on the back of my neck. You don't expect a Lutheran priest to be so skilled a liar.

Harry chewed on the inside of his cheek. "All right. You say Krüger is nervous about his future in Germany, looking for a soft landing in the U.S. Maybe I buy that. But spell out for me again how Casey benefits from brokering the deal."

"Isn't it obvious?" I asked. "Krüger's my ticket home. He'll have the names of any Americans who stayed on HVA's payroll after they rotated back to the U.S. The FBI wants to nail those traitors more than they want me. They'll have to back off. I'll have enough space to make things clear, prove I'm not guilty of anything."

"Not guilty of anything? What's all this crap I keep seeing on television? Hamburg, Antwerp, arms deals, burning buildings, dead bodies—you sure *look* guilty."

"If that's what you think, let's stop this right now," I said.

"Get off the tall pony," Harry said. "I wouldn't be here if I thought you were in league with terrorists. You got to admit, though, Casey, you're in one hell of a mess."

"The situation's complicated. It'll take some time to clarify things. But if I come in there with Krüger, I can demand that they pay attention while I explain."

Holger said, "And, of course, Krüger may be able to supply other information that will clarify some of the FBI theories now clouding Kathryn's future."

I blinked. *Other information?* What did that mean?

Harry didn't seem puzzled. "Back off, Sorensen," he said. "I trust Casey. I didn't say I trusted you."

"Look, Harry," I said, "I've got to go meet this guy. I won't get anywhere with him unless he's convinced I've got a line of communication open back to the U.S." I rubbed a hand over my scalp, the hair a quarter inch long now, silky against my palm, moist with nervous sweat. "Are you going to front for me in D.C. on this?"

"I need to talk to you alone first." He glared at Holger.

The Father-Major turned his right wrist to check his watch. "Five minutes," he said. "She has to leave this place in seven minutes, or the rendezvous with Krüger won't happen."

"Got it, Your Holiness," Harry said, shoving the door shut behind Holger. He hooked the safety chain, then muscled me into the bathroom. It smelled of disinfectant. He turned on the fan and the faucets in both the sink and the bath.

"I doubt anyone's listening in," I said.

"You doubt it." Harry gave me a scathing look. "Well, I'm certain that the Great Dane is doing his damnedest to hear every word." He gave me a shake and put his face inches from mine. "Now, you tell me why you're pretending you don't know who Krüger really is."

I could hardly breathe. In a strangled voice, I said, "You did a good job of acting as though you'd never heard of him."

"For *his* benefit." Harry put his hand on the back of my neck and pulled my ear toward his lips. "You know I checked out this guy back in '86. I was probably more relieved than your Danish buddy was after Major Krüger killed himself. But you obviously didn't tell Sorensen about me. So why should I mention that I'm up to speed on Krüger? Why not hear what else got left out of his story?"

Harry had checked out Krüger in 1986? He'd been relieved when Krüger died? Why? And why did he think I knew that? We were tiptoeing together through a minefield of misinformation and I didn't have a clue to what might set off an explosion. Gingerly, I asked, "Was there anything else Holger forgot to mention?"

"You noticed how he downplayed Krüger's association with the terrorists." Harry gave a dry laugh. "Trying to shift the blame to a single archfiend tucked away in the bowels of HVA."

"I thought you preferred that little-picture approach."

"Only when it's true. The Stasi was a bureaucracy, like any other. No single individual was ever responsible for anything. All of them had their asses covered. Just as well. We know Krüger's dirty, but not so dirty we can't do business with him."

I let my breath out. Harry had ended up where this interview was supposed to take him. Ready to deal for Krüger—but not to hang him. "You'll do it, then—handle things for me on the D.C. end?"

His expression clouded. "Going to this meeting—you sure he's not going to make you disappear?"

"I'll have company all the way to the spot where Krüger's leaving my instructions. There'll be another team in place to back me up from there."

"I guess it's not that risky for you."

"Not much risk at all." I tugged at his sleeve. "So it's a go on your end, then?"

"You didn't answer my question," Harry said. "If Krüger's interested in coming to us, you're the obvious choice to bring him home. So why didn't you say that?"

I let my gaze drift around the bathroom. The brown-and-tan tiled walls were spotless, the porcelain tub scrubbed to alabaster whiteness. Beneath the astringent odor of pine, the drains emitted the sweetish scent of decay. Why did Harry think I was so obvious a choice? I couldn't risk asking. I licked my lips. "Holger didn't feel he needed to spell it out."

Harry's expression was suddenly compassionate. "Sorry. Guess it's still hard for you to talk about." He squeezed my arm. "This will get their attention. Some people might think it's ghoulish so soon after Krajewski got blown apart. But it's the sort of thing that the spooks go for." He pulled the photo from his pocket and held it up so that Krüger's image faced me. "Once you know, he starts to look familiar."

I could feel the small hairs on my spine begin to stand up, one by one. The resemblance was subtle, but it was there, especially in the bone structure. A Slavic skull covered over with tightly drawn Prussian flesh. A common mix. Nothing alarming in what Harry was saying—until I put it together with what he hadn't said in the past.

Harry—my nosy, advice-dispensing pal Harry—had never asked *me* a single question about Stefan's background. He'd gone to more reliable sources to compile his dossier. Knowing

Harry, I assumed his file was complete right down to the hour of Stefan's birth and an exhaustive list of every living relative.

The man in the picture looked familiar because the man in the photo was family.

Harry flipped the photo around so he could see it. "Must've got those cheekbones from their father," he said.

The running water splashed against the basin and the ventilator hummed in the ceiling above. The fluorescent lights pinged at odd moments. And in my brain inexplicable behaviors suddenly became sensible actions, the pieces clicking into place like the solution to Rubik's Cube. Stefan Krajewski and Reinhardt Krüger had the same father.

"I thought Stefan's half brother died in a car accident." I kept my voice carefully neutral.

"*I* never had a doubt Krüger was dead," Harry said. "Masterful stroke, wasn't it? Burn a body beyond recognition in a crash fishy enough to raise a lot of questions. Leave clues so the police discover quick that the scene was rigged. They conclude it was all a setup, intended to obscure the fact that he killed himself. Of course the cops stopped there. Why not? What was he, the fifth or sixth Stasi guy to off himself that spring?" He shook his head. "What a shock when Billy Nu brought in that picture."

"What a shock," I echoed.

He tapped the photograph with his index finger. "Notice how seamless his new identity was? Few people would connect Gunter Storch to Reinhardt Krüger." He raised his eyes to my face. "Billy tell you how he got on to it?"

"Not in detail." My voice was steady. Hanging around liars, you're bound to pick up a trick or two.

"The FBI's Legal Attaché in Brussels thought there might be an American connection to that renegade Belgian company, the one doing business with Qadhafi. LegAtt's big on criminal investigation, so he enlarged that old news photo and projected it onto the wall of his office. Billy Nu was in town writing reports after a trip through the old Warsaw Pact. He'd finished updating your file, wanted to ask the FBI guy something about the next one. And boom! Krüger's mug is right there on the wall, twice as big as life, smirking at him. Said he blurted it out. 'Casey's in for it now.' "

"He got that right," I said.

Harry frowned. "Too bad Krüger stayed under the Storch cover. No reason to, after the German courts decided against prosecuting bureaucrats like him. Some people might think he was trying to conceal Stefan Krajewski's ex-Stasi connection. Makes it look bad for you."

Seriously bad for me. Quickly, I said, "He channeled Stasi funds for his future use. He wouldn't like to repay that. And I hear he has enemies."

"Sure he does," Harry said. "Otherwise, he wouldn't be so eager to come to us."

A fist banged against the door. "Our time is up," Holger said from the other side. "We must leave."

"Okay," Harry said, shutting off the faucets. "I'll go back and set up the deal. They'll jump at it. He's got information they want badly. Just remember: He has to tell them Stefan wasn't working with him. If you can't persuade him to do that, the FBI will claim Krüger could've sent more than Western technology to Qadhafi. They'll figure he passed on intelligence, too. Classified stuff he got from your lover."

And they'd suspect that my lover got at least some of those secrets from me. "I know."

Harry lowered his voice and spoke more slowly. "But you have to bring him to us. All the way home, Casey. You leave him in Denmark, like you did with Krajewski, the questions will never be answered. That bunch of Viking vigilantes will burn you all over again."

The fact that Stefan and Krüger were brothers changed everything. I no longer had any choices. I had to bring Krüger back to the U.S. Once there, I'd have help to make him reveal which airliner was scheduled to explode next. And after that, we'd force him to tell the truth about Stefan and me. Nothing less would earn my life back for me.

The pounding grew louder. I said, "I have to go."

"Like always." He grinned as he unlatched the corridor door. "Running away from me to be with another man."

I grabbed my hat and coat, donning them in the elevator as Holger, Harry and I descended silently to the ground floor. I hurried outside to the waiting taxi. The two men hovered inside the Novotel lobby, watching me through the glass-fronted double door. They both wore khaki slacks, wrinkled across the hips from hours spent sitting in airliners. On top, Harry wore a royal blue cotton sweater with a V neck; Holger had on green wool with shoulder patches, the type of sweater issued to military personnel and sold all over Europe in surplus stores. Insulated from the cold, out of the action. Tall men, inclined to stoop, they stood without speaking to each other, watching me, their approaches to the world so divergent, they might be from different planets, not just different continents.

The Mercedes taxi smelled of polish. It was warmed by a scentless heater and powered by an engine silent as death. Hans van Hoof was behind the wheel, a Tyrolean hat with a feather incongruous above his thickly muscled neck. Van Hoof playing at being German—I felt a rush of affection for him. I was in a hell of a mess, Harry had said. And like Harry, van Hoof was helping me get out of it. In his own huffy way.

"You are late," he told me.

I smoothed the maroon folds of my wool coat. When I stood, it covered me to mid-calf; when I sat, it touched the toes of my wine-red leather boots. My head was covered by a matching broad-brimmed felt hat. Elegantly bundled up, my features hidden, but my silhouette easily identified at a distance. Designed by some spy costumer fixated on Mata Hari. I replied, "I'm only two minutes behind schedule. You can make that up."

The skin on the back of van Hoof's neck turned a darker bronze. "You cannot afford to be so blasé. Krüger was specific to the last detail. You must be at the Cecilienhof at exactly ten forty-five. If you miss the tour bus—"

"But I won't. You'd never set up a schedule that depended on an American being on time."

He made a growling noise, low in his throat, but I saw his lips twitch as if he were struggling to suppress a smile. He knew I had him pegged. He was having trouble keeping up the grouchy attitude. Better be careful, or he'd find himself actually liking me.

"Is everyone in place?" I asked.

"You won't recognize anyone except Bert. But Erika's people are there. They'll stay with you to whatever rendezvous point Krüger selects."

I patted my coat pocket. A basting thread had created a false bottom. Below it was the transmitter that would make it possible to track my movements when I wasn't in sight. "And Erika's Mossad buddies—they understand this is our operation? They're covering my back, nothing else?"

Van Hoof rolled to a stop in Theodor-Heuss Platz, so close to an idling tour bus that exhaust fumes clouded our windshield. "Those are their instructions."

"They better stick to them."

"Erika has briefed them fully. Number one priority is getting you in and out unharmed. Shouldn't be a problem. If Krüger wants safe haven, he'll have the same goal."

Sure. If safe haven was what he most wanted.

The tour bus was sleek, its lower body the color of thick cream. A lanky man with two Nikons looped around his neck was helping a fur-coated woman board through the rear door. Another bundled pair came out of the lobby of the high-rise hotel, which had once provided accommodations for guests of the British Berlin Infantry Brigade. This English-language tour to Potsdam had been laid on primarily for the benefit of retired

British military officers who wanted to visit the site where Churchill, Truman and Stalin had met in July of 1945 to determine the future political structure of Europe. I could use it to travel toward Krüger in company of *my* choosing.

As I climbed out of the taxi, van Hoof said softly, "Take care." I managed a smile in reply, then slammed the door.

I joined the queue at the rear door to the bus, my breath white in the icy air, my neck chilled below the brim of my hat. I pulled my scarf higher to fill the gap and rearranged the fringed ends in front.

I spotted Bert in the rearmost seat, lips pursed, appearing to concentrate on the newspaper in front of his face. He made a show of turning the page, lowering the paper enough to make eye contact. The message in his was as clear as if he'd spoken: *Chin up, girl, I'm with you.* Heartened, I took the window seat ahead of the rear door. The floor-heater vent was working overtime. The odor of hot wax rose from my boots and my feet itched from the sudden change in temperature.

A slender man in an orange blazer and red cap bounded on board to stand in the center aisle. He began his spiel as the bus pulled away from the hotel. The cloud cover outside was so low it almost touched the curved walls of the Olympic Stadium, where in 1936 Jesse Owens gave Adolf Hitler a foretaste of the future humbling of his master race. The boulevard wound south through the leafless Grunewald, the ground beneath the trees as free of sticks as if it were swept daily.

We rolled across the forgotten border and onto rutted highways of the former German Democratic Republic. Unkempt fields stretched beyond the berm. The feeble daylight faded still more under the thick cloud cover, the sky darkening to match the soot-stained buildings of Potsdam.

A black mood settled over me, the charred emotions you feel after you've been badly burned by your lover.

For more than a decade, my security file must have shown

that Stefan had a half brother who'd worked in HVA—and I'd known nothing about it.

Harry had known. He'd carefully done his research on Stefan's half brother. And as my friend, he'd been glad when Krüger died and security could erase the question mark next to my name. Harry naturally assumed that Stefan had long ago given me the critical facts. His half brother's name. His rank. His assignment in East German intelligence. But Stefan had told me only that his father had an older son with a different mother. At some point he mentioned that his half brother had recently been killed in a car accident. And he'd never spoken of him again.

Harry also assumed that I'd learned as soon as he had that Krüger was still alive. He figured that Billy Nu would discuss that issue in the context of my background investigation. Billy Nu, who'd been protecting me for years, who knew my security file by heart—Billy Nu hadn't talked to me about Krüger. So why had Billy remained silent?

Mike Buchanan's signature stood out in bold relief. The FBI was already interested in the Belgian sale of embargoed computer equipment to Qadhafi. Buchanan must have surmised a U.S. connection. He was predisposed to detect a treacherous American. When his man in Brussels spotted Krüger in the infamous news photo, Buchanan had made the logical leap from Krüger to Stefan to me.

He would have gone immediately to my security file. According to the regulations, I had to disclose any close association I had with a foreign national. My written reports regularly included Stefan. I'd never named his half brother. When Buchanan consulted my file, that omission must have alarmed him.

He'd gotten on my case immediately. Gagging Billy. Combing through my life for evidence of clandestine meetings. Tapping my phone. Examining my financial records. Interrogating Lura.

He'd relied on the FBI's favorite counterespionage tactic. Let the suspect think she's under no suspicion, catch her in the act of treason. The longer I went without mentioning my link to Krüger, the more likely it became that our connection was criminal. Then Global 500 went down with Billy Nu and the Brussels LegAtt on board. My name turned up on the FBI list as someone who'd shown suspicious interest in the bombing. On Christmas morning, I slipped out of the country and Buchanan had immediately gotten authority to search my condo. When I returned to the U.S., he resolved not to let me escape again. Lacking sufficient evidence to arrest me then, he tried to bluff me into a voluntary confession.

The bodies won't stay buried, if you catch my drift. I hadn't. I knew nothing about Krüger then. I'd thought Buchanan was overzealous, misinterpreting spurious information that wrongly implicated me. Turned out he was much sharper than I'd guessed. *Some funny business going on between that damn Father-Major and your Polish friend.*

Very funny business indeed that had put Billy Nu and the Brussels LegAtt on Global 500. Reasonable to assume they'd been lured to their deaths to halt further damage to Reinhardt Krüger, alias Gunter Storch. No doubt Buchanan tied that back to me, too.

Buchanan had bluffed. And I'd fled. For Buchanan, flight was *prima facie* evidence of my duplicity. That rash act had guaranteed my arrest warrant.

The bus continued on through the murk, past Frederick the Great's rococo castles, which sat like ornate jewels on poisoned ground. By the time we reached Cecilienhof Palace, the clouds were spitting ice pellets.

Out of the bus, I felt the sleet sting my face. Clutching the brim of my hat to keep the wind from taking it, I hurried toward the brooding building. New by European standards—built at the beginning of this century—it looked more like an oversize hunting lodge than a castle, a retreat of wood and stone where men came after the killing to compare their trophies. We gathered inside the entrance, coats rustling, boots stomping. The camera-laden man beside me glanced around and said disparagingly to his companion, "Mock Tudor."

The museum guide appeared, professorial in a gray cardigan with elbow patches. His hair was sparse, his teeth bad, his speech in English a relic of the Communist era when he'd committed it to memory. We began in the room used by the Soviet delegation. The guide listed Comrade Stalin first in every reference he made to the three men who'd met here. Four men, really, he was careful to note. Midway through the Potsdam Conference the Brits had held an election, booted Churchill out of the Prime Minister's job and handed it over to Clement Atlee. We passed furniture, wall hangings, memorabilia—all gifts to the German people from Comrade Stalin. We reached the library used by the British delegation and I stopped listening to the guide.

My eyes automatically went to the book I'd been instructed to locate. *The bookshelves in the wall facing the door by which you enter. Fifth shelf from the bottom. Fourth volume from the left.* I forced my gaze away from it. I took two steps toward the modest desk, cordoned off by a velvet rope. I checked my watch. We'd begun the tour on time, at ten forty-five. Now it was eleven-fifteen. I was where I was supposed to be.

I furrowed my brow in an expression I hoped looked meditative and moved as I'd been directed, to stand in front of the many-paned French door. It looked out on the palace's rear lawn, a sweep of winter-brown grass sloping a hundred yards to the water. In 1945, the American president had come from Berlin by boat down the Havel River, probably mooring only a short distance from where I stood.

About a third of the way to the river, a trio of men lingered with their trench-coated backs to me, hatless, staring out across the water as though waiting still for Harry Truman. The man in the middle was shorter than the other two, older, with white hair pushed toward me by the wind. The men flanking him were thuggish security types with stocky bodies and hedgehog haircuts.

Time for me to move closer to the book holding the next part of my instructions. As I shifted my weight, I saw the center man smooth the wisps of hair with his right hand, patting the crown as though the cowlick of his youth still tormented him. That gesture—I knew it.

I froze. I couldn't take my eyes off the white-haired man.

He turned his head to peer off to his left. I saw the thickened skin drooping into jowl below his jawline. The small eye that I knew was set in a web of wrinkles. Six weeks ago, I'd pressed my lips against the soft, slack skin of his cheek and took comfort from his familiar scent, Mennen For Men, the bottle of emerald liquid a fixture beside his sink all my life.

Six weeks ago, we'd celebrated Thanksgiving in Oregon. Now I was in Potsdam. And so was my father.

17

I leaned toward the window. Pressure on the velvet cord moved the stanchion an inch across the floor, the rough squeak like a shriek in the quiet room.

The three men turned and started toward me. I saw my father's face full on. His eyes were clouded. I wasn't sure he registered the sight of the building in front of him. Let alone his daughter peering out from the security-barred French door. Then the threesome veered off to the left and I couldn't see them anymore.

I went over to the bookcase. Reached up and pulled a book out at random. My eyes wouldn't focus on the page. I couldn't read the title. My heart fluttered inside my chest, a bird trapped in an airshaft. Only by an act of will could I keep myself from gasping.

I pulled out another book. My damp fingers marked the cover. In all, I left my fingerprints on at least a half-dozen books. Finally, I held *Plutarch's Lives* in my hands. It smelled of mildew and the binding was frayed. I removed the folded onionskin inserted between the cover and the spine. Then I carefully put the book back on the shelf.

I looked at three more books before I crossed to the exit door, where our guide waited. In a loud voice, I asked for directions to the women's rest room. I didn't listen to his reply. I knew my next stop was the adjacent building, which our tour group had reserved for a catered Sunday dinner. My boot heels clicked against the cement as I crossed the space between the two buildings. The air inside was heavy with the sweet-sour smell of venison marinated overnight for sauerbraten and then left to simmer since dawn.

I latched myself into a stall in the ladies' toilet and unfolded the paper. My instructions were to find the red-brown Ford parked in the third row of the lot, key beneath the driver's seat. Use it and the map beneath the seat to get to the indicated location at ten minutes before three o'clock. Divulge my destination to no one.

That was all. No *WE HAVE YOUR FATHER*. No sentence beginning, *IF YOU WANT HIM TO LIVE*. Krüger didn't have to put his threat in writing. I knew that to keep my father safe, I had to arrive at this meeting alone, without backup.

On the other side of the partition, an aerosol can sighed. I smelled hairspray. I heard a murmur of German. Then the tinny sound of small change hitting the dish set out for tips. My wristwatch read 11:25. The minute hand seemed to spring ahead to 11:26. So far to go. So much to do. I lifted the lever and water roared into the bowl.

I slid my hand into my coat pocket. My fingertips found the basting threads and broke them. I inserted my thumb and forefinger through the false bottom. The tracking device was a centimeter in diameter. I dropped it into the sanitary-napkin receptacle. I flattened my hat and stuffed it in on top of the transmitter. A corner of winy-red felt stuck out. I tamped it down. Then I yanked off my coat. The lining of charcoal silk slid over my hands like water. I turned the coat inside out and draped it over my arm so that the gray color showed instead of maroon.

The five-mark coin I dropped into the tip dish rang against the porcelain. The attendant's head snapped toward the sound of real money. While she was scooping it into her apron pocket,

I hurried into the anteroom, dumped my coat into the waste-basket and pulled crumpled paper over it. If the attendant discovered the coat, it was hard to guess where she'd go with it. But the transmitter would keep on signaling from inside this room.

The henna-haired woman defending the cloakroom folded her arms and raised both her chins. She tried hard to make me understand that she couldn't give me a wrap unless I first produced a claim check. My flustered incomprehension won her over. Plus the German coins I kept shoving at her as though I were equally confused about their value. She let me have the ratty fur I'd last seen on my British tour companion. I shrugged into it and lifted my scarf up over my hair.

Outside, I kept my head bowed, my feet moving. A gust of wind cut my eyes like a whip and I stumbled. Bert stood watch beside the open door of the tour bus, shoulders hunched. He held a lighted cigarette. His hand moved toward his mouth as he pretended to enjoy one last smoke before going inside to eat. I walked purposefully by him, the distance between us less than fifty feet. But he kept his eyes on the buildings.

The Ford was easy to spot—a European-built, four-cylinder compact with a manual transmission. The ice on the windshield was no more than would have accumulated in fifteen minutes. The velour seat was warm and I smelled minty chewing gum.

The engine responded eagerly. I headed southwest toward Wittenberg, where Martin Luther nailed his Ninety-five Theses to the church door in 1517. Not my destination today. Krüger had summoned me to a hideaway in the Spreewald, the picturesque forest bordering the river flowing southeast from Berlin. I was heading for Wittenberg only to discover if I'd eluded my minders.

A mud-spattered Audi pulled in behind me. In my rearview mirror I saw a woman driver with a male passenger. They weren't Krüger's people. It wasn't likely that Krüger would allow anyone else to know he was considering refuge in the U.S.

Even if he *were* having my movements watched, he'd do it surreptitiously, to see who else was keeping track of me. The car behind me had to be one of Erika's teams, borrowed from the Mossad.

So Bert had spotted me. My protector, he'd scrambled to get my backup in place. He'd managed to alert at least the pair in this car. They'd be wondering what I'd done with the transmitter. They'd want to keep me in sight. I puttered along at a slow speed, driving south on a pockmarked highway. As we approached Beelitz, the Audi moved up. The car tapped my rear bumper and the horn blared. The woman took her hand off the horn and jerked her thumb to the right. The command was unmistakable. *Pull over.*

I slowed to twenty-five, scanning the side streets for a likely spot. Halfway along the town's main street, I saw an alley that cut through the middle of the block to a parallel street. I turned into the alley, downshifted into second, held in the clutch with my left foot, braked with my right. The Audi pulled in so close that the off-white paint on its hood became pink in the reflection from my brake lights. The driver's side door opened and a tall woman got out. Her blond hair was braided and coiled on top of her head in the style favored by Wagnerian opera singers. An imperious Brunhild, she slammed her door and took a step toward me.

Even the pros make mistakes.

I released the brake. I moved my foot off the clutch while at the same instant I mashed the gas pedal to the floor. The Ford shot down the alley, the perfect racing start my father had taught me, ordered me never to use on a public street. A pedestrian jumped backward out of my way. My tires squealed through the sharp left into the street. I bent over the wheel, urging the car forward. At the first cross street I turned right, heading for the countryside.

I'd gained maybe five seconds' lead over the Audi. I raced down the side road, took a curve on two wheels, fishtailed onto a gravel road and found a dirt track leading into a patch of evergreen trees stunted in their youth by the GDR's coal-poisoned air. The road split, then split again, and I took first the left fork, then the right, following narrowing tracks blanketed with red-brown needles. For the last kilometer, I was on no discernible road at all, gliding across a carpet the same shade as my car, wending my way between the scrawny trees until the gaps became too narrow to continue.

I turned off the engine and rested my forehead on the steering wheel. It was silent except for the random noises from the cooling engine. I smelled only my own sweat. I raised my head and checked my watch. Twelve thirty-three. My path had been unpredictable and far-ranging. Unless my followers were lucky, they wouldn't come near me. And if they did, from ten yards away my car was invisible, blending in with the forest floor.

I let out a sigh. The people in the Audi couldn't make the systematic search it would take to find me. No matter how well documented they might be, Israeli agents preferred not to attract attention to themselves in Germany. I was safe from them so long as I didn't move.

I forced my neck to stiffen, dragged my head upright again. I had to move. I had to go to Krüger. The rendezvous location was one hundred and fifteen kilometers away on back roads. I had little more than two hours to get there. I couldn't linger. I had to return to the road. Risk being spotted again. How big a risk? Surely the Mossad hadn't put more than two cars into this operation. Not enough to cover the three-hundred-and-sixty-degree circle around Potsdam, trying to discover which way I'd gone.

Was there any chance they knew my destination?

I had to figure no. The Mossad had made an attempt on Krüger's life. He would be careful to go only where he felt certain they wouldn't find him. My destination in the Spreewald had to fall into that category, a private place where Krüger was confident his enemies would not surprise him.

Steam coated the inside of the windshield. I rolled my window down to let cooler air inside, and into my lungs. The Israelis wouldn't cruise around for long in this rural area. Give it another ten minutes. By then they'd be on their way back to their base. They'd lost Casey, they'd report to my friends in Berlin.

My friends. Holger, Erika, van Hoof—all three of them had conspired to keep me ignorant of the blood tie between Stefan and Krüger. They'd known that Krüger had a most personal interest in Stefan. One that made him interested in me as a key to Stefan. They knew that. And yet my trusted colleagues had sent me into the field against Krüger without taking the most minimal steps to protect my father.

I saw him standing there on the bank of the Havel, the chill wind ruffling his hair. The memory of his bare head made my throat ache. He had looked so defenseless. I still thought of my father as a man who wore hats. When I was young, he never went downtown without his gray fedora. At home he kept it in a metal rack on the back of the hall-closet door. It was a serious hat, like police detectives wore in old black-and-white movies.

When I was fifteen, Lura's parents had rented an oceanfront cottage for a week. My mother had a hundred reasons why we couldn't do the same. I knew she didn't want to leave our house. I tried to entice my father into taking only me for a real vacation at the beach. "Casey, girl," he said unhappily, "you know we can't do that." Of course we couldn't leave my mother alone overnight. We had to take care of her. But, stubbornly, I asked him again, and then again. His words didn't change, just grew heavier with regret.

I was mad. My father's world was bigger than mine. He had his business to run, a ten-employee agency that leased semitrailers to freight companies. My homebound summer was hot and arid, but he was enjoying himself with colleagues and customers—I was sure of it. Like a jealous wife, I went through his wallet in search of receipts and ticket stubs to tell me where he'd gone without me. I sniffed his discarded shirts for odors of tobacco, perfume, theater popcorn—proof that he was having fun though I was not.

By the time I was old enough to understand the concept of an unfaithful husband, I'd long since stopped searching for proof of my father's infidelity. My first attempt at intelligence collection and analysis failed because of a faulty premise. There was no intelligence to collect. My compassionate father bent his rules for my benefit. For his own, never.

He'd stubbornly continued wearing his hats long after they'd gone out of fashion. If I closed my eyes, I'd see him in his gray fedora with his overcoat buttoned to the neck. My father. Clinging to old-fashioned ways, old-fashioned virtues.

Neither he nor I belonged in this half-world of deceit. I'd get us both out of it. I didn't need backup. Krüger feared for his life. Taking my father hostage was an extreme measure of self-protection, a mark of how desperate he was to reach a safe haven in America. I controlled that outcome and I could make the deal on my terms. And my terms started with releasing my father. Once he was safe and I had Krüger on U.S. soil, the FBI would force the truth from him. We'd stop him from blowing up another plane. And I'd clear my name.

A breeze moved through the trees, forcing the branches against one another. The scraping noise vibrated inside me. I felt like one of those trees. Gaunt and brittle, surviving in a poisonous atmosphere, sustained by what lay at the core of my being.

I pulled off the bulky fur and tossed it onto the backseat. Then I turned on the ignition and maneuvered the car back the way I'd come. I got lost twice, the second time forced to spend ten minutes turning the car around in a space that constricted my corrections to increments of inches. It was one-fifteen before I reached a pair of ruts I could follow.

I bumped slowly eastward for a kilometer before they grew soggy, then disappeared beneath a greenish patch of water I didn't dare to enter. When I tried to back up, my drive tires spun in the mud. I fought off panic, tried again. Got some traction, managed to reverse direction. The ruts led to gravel, and I followed it to pavement. I tried going east again, skirting the E-8 and Route 246 and all the carefully laid out east-west, north-south highways where the team in the Audi might be waiting. It was after two and I was only past Luckenwalde when a hailstorm rattled down. In seconds ice blocked the windshield, forcing me to pull over. I lost eight minutes.

At three, I was still west of Lübben. I hadn't eaten. I felt nauseated, my insides twisted tight. My destination was at least thirty minutes away, at the far end of a peninsula formed by a curve of the Spree. On the hand-drawn map, it had the shape of a drooping male organ, the road like a vein along it, ending in a wartlike X at the end.

I reached the end of the road at 3:40. Fifty minutes late.

Krüger's hideaway proved to be a weathered A-frame cabin, a fenced dog run extending from one side. No animal barked at me from beyond the ten-foot-high chain-link fence.

Flanking the front door of the cabin were windows as dark as the wintry dusk gathering outside. No vehicles in sight. No sign of habitation. No surprise. I was too late.

I tapped my finger on the steering wheel. Krüger wanted this meeting. He'd arranged it in elaborate detail and he'd surely prepared a contingency plan. I had to check the door, see if he'd left a message for me. As I climbed out into the chill, I caught a whiff of the gamy odor of the dog pen. Smelled woodsmoke. Heard music. A country tune, sung in English. I closed my eyes to listen better.

Two women in an old duet. Naomi and Wynonna Judd. Belting out a tune that Stefan loved to hear *me* sing.

18

I put a careful foot on the bottom step. Then stepped cautiously onto the porch. Hanging neatly from nails on each side of the doorframe were chains of different sizes. A set of fine links that looked like a choke collar for a dog. Beside it, a matching piece that would serve as a leash. Then three weightier lengths, strong enough to shackle a full-grown man. One six-foot strand with links so heavy-duty I could see the individual welds despite the fading light.

I pushed at the door. It swung slowly open. The Judds were louder, concert-volume, and the smoky smell was stronger, mixing with the scent of the polished pine floor. I was in a large room on the ground floor of the A-frame, the woodstove centered on bricks beneath a spiraling iron staircase. I got an impression of massive furniture on my left, a kitchen tucked into the rear on my right. Except for the glow from the burning logs, the only light came from the bulb inside the refrigerator, silhouetting a tall, thin figure.

The song ended and the tape whirred for a few seconds before clicking into silence. The refrigerator door whooshed shut. The man turned to face me, his right hand holding a bottle, his left reaching toward the wall. He flicked a switch and yellow lamplight splashed down from the suspended light fixture onto a round wooden table. Krüger's hair turned to a dark gold cap and the lenses of his glasses went opaque, shiny as the isinglass in the door of the woodstove.

"St. Pauli Girl," he said, popping the cap off the beer bottle. He set it on the table, beside a frosty mug. "I understand that's the brand you prefer."

I hadn't expected to confront a gracious host. His courtesy jarred me. My voice came out harsh, the sound of a rusted hinge. "What do you want?"

"Come in and shut the door."

Wary, I didn't move from the doorway.

He dropped into a wooden chair on the far side of the table and lifted the bottle. He filled my glass, the foam glistening above the amber. "Now, come and drink this while it's still ice-cold, the way you like it."

My music. My brand of beer. The temperature at which I liked to drink it. He was letting me know he'd made himself an expert on my personal tastes. Giving me enough hints so I'd conclude that he knew everything there was to know about me. Unsettling, but in the end, only a ploy to improve his bargaining position. I wouldn't let my uneasiness show. I pushed the door shut and forced myself to saunter toward the table.

A throaty humming came from near the stove. A large dog lay there, muzzle resting on forearms, sharp-edged ears pointed toward me. A German shepherd. To the Germans, a *schäferhund*, sheepdog. Who had named this breed? Surely creatures like the one I was looking at had never herded sheep. More likely, torn them apart.

The dog's eyes reflected the glowing coals. The rumbling thickened and grew more menacing.

Krüger said something in German. A sharp, grating phrase, heavy on the fricative. The dog noise stopped instantly.

I'd made it to the table by then. I sat casually, my gaze on Krüger. His face was as pleasant as it had appeared in his photograph. Behind the polished lenses of his glasses were eyes the color of mud. I picked up my drink and took a long swallow of beer. The flavor was traitorously perfect.

"Excellent," Krüger said. "Now, it seems best to me that I travel to the U.S. with you and your father."

Good. He wanted safe passage badly enough to ask for it. Deliberately, I put the mug down. "And how do you see us making the journey?"

"You arrange for an Air Force jet to pick us up from Templehof on Wednesday. Your father and I will meet you there, just prior to departure."

"You want to travel in style," I said.

"Style, yes. Wednesday is something of an epiphany for me. But safety is my chief concern. This particular arrangement will afford me the greatest amount of protection."

Protection from whom? Not just the Mossad, not with these precautions. I hid my alarm under a taunt. "You're that afraid of me, you need to use my father for a shield?"

"Your colleagues are not trustworthy. They've given you bad information. They've gotten you into trouble—your father will tell you that."

"You don't know anything about my father."

"Of course I do." He removed a cassette from his shirt pocket and waved it at me. "And I have this."

The tape was the same size, shape and color as the one taken from my telephone answering machine. He'd sent someone to my condo. My throat tightened. I should have realized he was behind that break-in.

Krüger reached back to the boom box sitting on the counter behind him and ejected the Judds. He shoved the other tape into the machine and pushed Play. First came a half sentence in Lura's breathless tones, ending her message. Then the voice of my father. After a querulous post-Christmas greeting, there was a long pause as though he'd hung up. Finally, "Is everything all right? I'm worried about you."

Krüger stopped the tape. "I knew you hadn't played back

that message. And that was my fault. Collecting that tape from you was a bit of overcaution on my part. When I heard your father's distress, I wanted to set his mind at ease. So I got in touch." He leaned toward me, so close I could see the comb lines in his hair. "The FBI had been there. Told him you were involved with an unreformed Communist and other unsavory characters. Your father got the idea that you might try to make a new life someplace else."

"You told my father that I'd fled from the U.S. permanently?"

"He got that idea." Krüger shrugged. "Not so unlikely, under the circumstances. You have been sleeping with an agent of the Polish SB. Of course your father worried that you'd gone into hiding."

"And you told him you knew where I was."

He made a dismissive noise. "I offered him an opportunity to communicate his concerns to you. It must give you great joy, having so devoted a father. He came all this way to persuade you to return to America and turn yourself in."

He'd made my father *his* ally. "That's tidy. You'll be his hero, then, helping him bring me home."

"And keeping you out of prison when you get there. Yes, your father will be most appreciative. And you will, too, I think." He reached across the table with a movement that was arrogantly sexual. I smelled an unfamiliar aftershave, testosteronal in its penetrating virility.

So that was it. He was making me part of the deal. He wanted to fuck his brother's woman.

Krüger's fingertips caressed the back of my hand. The flesh on my arms tightened, as though the skin might form ridges and inch away. This man must have been an invisible presence in my life for years, probing obscenely into my intimate secrets. The realization sickened me, souring the beer that coated my tongue.

It wasn't Krüger who'd invaded my condo. Yet I felt as if

he'd gone often into my bedroom and fondled my lingerie. I imagined his fingers unfolding and stroking every undergarment. Then carefully replacing them in my bureau so that I'd never guess what he'd done. When I dressed, it would be as if I were rubbing his scent on my body.

His touch felt like a trickle of icy water over my skin and I saw no heat in his umber eyes. His carnal insolence had nothing to do with lust and everything to do with intimidation. My stomach clenched and the sour taste flared again in my throat.

I tried to calm myself. This was a negotiating strategy, nothing more. Whatever his personal interest in me, his main goal was getting to safety. Once I had him in the U.S., I'd win. For now, I had to play along. Beneath his fingers, my hand lay like a dead thing.

"Where's my father?" I asked in a conversational tone.

"He's comfortable."

"Comfortable?" I recalled how my father had looked, outside the Cecilienhof. I jerked my hand away. "You drugged him."

"You're mistaken." He gave me a pitying look. "Of course, the long journey was stressful for him. I was prepared to offer medication. But sedation wasn't needed. Nature has seen to that."

He was hurting my father! I gripped the beer mug, willing myself not to panic. I had to stay calm now, concentrate on how to rescue us both.

Krüger stared at my fingers twined around the handle of the beer mug, his expression clinical. His murky eyes weren't cold, I realized. They were empty. I thought suddenly of a pathologist, dissecting knife in gloved hand, slicing the prints from the ends of my fingers. Whatever it took to keep me and my father in line. I slid my hand into my lap and forced my voice to hold steady.

"This is a fine plan," I said. "But you haven't given me anything to merit military transport out of Templehof. And so soon. You might have to settle for something less grand."

"I will settle for nothing else. I know precisely the degree of protection I need."

I kept my face impassive, steeling myself for what I knew had to be coming next.

Krüger punched the play button.

The voice on the tape was unfamiliar. "This is Debbie calling from Crown Books. It's noon on the twenty-sixth of December. That first edition of *The Secret Sharer* has turned up. Give me a call if you want to bid on it."

Krüger pushed the stop button. He withdrew a thick softcover book from behind the machine, plucked an index card from it, then slid the book across the table. THE PORTABLE CONRAD blared up at me, the title all in caps and boldface, superimposed above a color photo of a South Sea island. Krüger said, "I admit, I'm overcautious. We checked. There is a Debbie working at the Crown Books outlet nearest the State Department. And she said that you'd inquired several times about different works by that author." He palmed the card in his left hand, touched the writing on it with his left index finger. His mouth formed a word as he studied the card, but he made no sound. Then he looked up at me. "But that Debbie—*she* didn't phone you on December twenty-sixth."

"And that proves something?" I laughed. "There's more than one Crown Books in Washington."

"I can recognize the hallmarks of a code." He folded the card carefully, slid it into his shirt pocket. "You did a commendable job laying down a foundation. I'm sure you fooled the FBI. But my man was persistent. He found a copy of the story for me, in case it contained clues. I didn't have to look further than the name on the cover. I know who's read every word written by Joseph Conrad. Such a hopeless romantic, my brother." He sniffed. "*The Secret Sharer*. If he'd died, would someone have called you about *The Heart of Darkness*?"

He knew his brother was alive. He'd known when he

stopped the hunt for Stefan and paid off the assassins. That move had been part of the complex hoax that had drawn me to him. Krüger had made me his quarry and I didn't know why. I felt light-headed, dizzied by that sudden awareness. I was lost in a house of mirrors where I saw nothing clearly. To get myself and my father out, I'd have to feel my way along, step by careful step. "Is that what you want?" I asked. "Protection from Stefan?"

"My brother is obsessed. Who can guess what he might do to me next?"

Did he fear Stefan? Or was he only feigning alarm, another ploy in a Byzantine con game I had no hope of penetrating? "So if I go ahead and set things up the way you want, I get to take my father home."

"And I will help you clear your name." His mouth curved up but the deadness in his eyes turned the smile to a grimace. "We will work together."

He was too certain that he'd be the one in control. He didn't fear future interrogation by the FBI. He'd done something to insure it would never come to pass. If I took him with me to the U.S., I'd end up as his new pet. Wearing a choke collar— the kind that would enable him, with a single motion, to force me into submission.

The back of my neck quivered, my sense of danger strong enough to lift the hairs at the base of my skull. I raised my chin. "And if I refuse to do this on your terms?"

"Then I won't leave Germany. I'd enjoy a change of scenery, but it's not vital. I can have a comfortable life without going to the U.S. You, on the other hand, will have to find some other way to solve all the problems my brother has created for you."

It was a bluff. Could I afford to call it? "And my father?"

"I'll arrange for his flight home." He got up from the table, crossed to the stove. The dog raised its head, jingling the links of its collar. Krüger scratched the animal between the ears and the dog's body elongated in a blissful stretch, showing the nipples along her belly, the folds between her legs.

Krüger reached past her to pick up a piece of firewood. He opened the stove door and tossed in the stick. "Of course, I cannot guarantee your father's safety on a commercial flight."

The wood must have been dry. Immediately there was a crackle and light flared from the door. Krüger's glasses blazed with the reflection.

My eyes went to the cassette player. It was an older model, boxy with a shiny silver exterior. The brand name shimmered in the firelight: Toshiba. Same brand that had contained the bomb which blew apart Pan Am 103. Another unmistakable message for anyone who'd spent years following up on that explosion. The next incident was all arranged. And it would happen soon.

I hadn't expected that. Logic dictated that Krüger would prefer to be firmly on U.S. soil *before* the next bomb detonated. He'd be better able to distance himself from the disaster, physically and politically. I'd assumed his only real goal was self-preservation. I'd been wrong. Protecting himself was essential to Krüger. But so was making me suffer.

A commercial airliner would blow up while my father was still his hostage. If I did nothing to prevent the explosion, I'd become an accomplice to the terror I'd spent my professional life fighting. Yet if I alerted anyone to the danger, Krüger would make sure my father died.

Now, he closed the stove door and came back to the table. "A simple choice."

The muscles tightened in my chest. I struggled for air, suffocated by my dawning realization that I had no way out of his trap. His scheme wasn't invulnerable—no intricate strategy was. But I wouldn't quickly spot the points of weakness. He'd guaranteed that with his fanatic attention to detail. And the predatory patience with which he'd stalked me, waiting for this moment. He could predict my every move.

He was watching me now, his face bland. He looked and

acted like a dispassionate technician who might design pollution-free processes for the paper industry. But I'd heard his deceptively courteous voice. I'd looked into his muddy eyes. I knew Reinhardt Krüger was more than an inventive draftsman. He was a brilliant engineer of death. And he'd turned his evil genius on me.

I felt it then, a rage so visceral I couldn't speak. This man might not brutalize me physically. But he would destroy everything I held dear. No matter which awful choice I made.

Then the rage faded, blotted out by anguish.

He'd beaten me. Utterly. Exactly as he'd planned to do.

I drew in a shuddering breath. "Give me something I can send to Washington," I said. "Something good."

19

I left Krüger's cabin at seven. The Sunday evening temperature had dropped, though the air remained moist. Mist glazed the frozen roads. I drove with my hands on the wheel at ten and two o'clock, as if my father were coaching from the seat beside me.

"Got a film of ice on the asphalt tonight," I said aloud in my imitation-airline-pilot voice. "We'll hold to a steady pace, keeping an eye out for cross traffic. We'll be looking to avoid your sudden moves on this trip." I added a crinkly-eyed chuckle. "So don't worry about a little turbulence up ahead. No danger we'll be spinning out of control." I imagined my father laughing, then tipping his hat brim down to cover his eyes, faking sleep. Only a too-firm grip on the right-hand armrest would give him away. I kept my bright chatter up for the next two hours, muscles tensed and mouth loose for periodic volleys at my nonexistent companion. It kept me from thinking about Stefan.

For more than a decade, he'd been the love of my life. Yet I hadn't known him at all. I'd deal later with that crippling truth. Now I had to stay strong to help my father. I couldn't—I *wouldn't*—think about Stefan.

On the south side of Berlin, I followed airport signs to the long-term lot at Schönefeld and parked the Ford with the keys under the seat, as Krüger had instructed me to do. I found a pay phone in the terminal and called an answering machine to leave the signal for Erika with a coded reference to my location. If I'd had any other way to communicate safely with Harry, I would have used it. I would never have contacted Erika again. But I was out of options. I had to go through her. I went outside to wait for her to retrieve my message and dispatch someone to pick me up.

I couldn't linger inside the terminal. My photo might be posted in the gallery of wanted women terrorists. For sure the FBI would have passed my description to all airport personnel. Outdoors, I huddled in a bus shelter, while around me foul-scented mist haloed the streetlights and dulled the sheen of passing cars. An interior fog seeped through me, dimming my vision, muffling sounds, coating my tongue with mud. It was as if Krüger's malevolence had corrupted everything in the world. Including me. I knew he was going to kill more people. Yet I would do nothing to stop him.

I shuddered, hugging the borrowed coat around me. The fur smelled rankly of moth crystals and the ancient pelts were too thin to keep out the damp chill. I stood there, growing colder and more exhausted each minute. When the Jetta eased up to the curb at nine-thirty, I collapsed into the passenger seat. Erika was behind the wheel. I kept my eyes straight ahead, my hands busy with my seat belt.

She cut smoothly back into traffic. After a minute, she said, "We underestimated Krüger, I admit that."

"You can hardly deny it," I said. "He knew Stefan wasn't dead. And he knew everything about me." My throat tightened, choking off my voice.

"Clearly, he's been interested in you since you became involved with Stefan."

"Interested? I guess he's been 'interested.' If I'd known sooner . . ." I ran a hand over my scalp. "It didn't occur to any of you that my father might need protection?"

"As soon as Stefan realized you were going to meet with Krüger, he demanded a guard for your father. But by the time our man in the States got into position, your father had disappeared."

"Why are you surprised?"

She glanced over at me. Awareness gleamed behind those cool eyes. "You can't believe Stefan—"

"They're brothers, aren't they? A fact Stefan failed to mention to me." My voice was shrill and I turned away from her gaze. We were traveling west from the airport on a broad city street. Christmas decorations still hung from the lampposts, the season of Brotherly Love in Europe extending into the first week of the New Year. Glass storefronts shone below a rush of neon, the colored lights dancing off the icy sidewalks in front. I forced myself to breathe calmly, regain control.

Erika got us northbound on the motorway. Then she said, "Did Krüger claim that Stefan was working with him?"

I replied with undisguised sarcasm. "He pretended that he fears Stefan so much, he has to use me for a shield."

She was silent for a moment. "I'm taking you to our operations center."

"Operations center?" The phrase jarred me.

"Nothing grand. A building that Stefan leased and stocked last month, before Global 500 exploded." She negotiated an exit near Steglitz. "You and I need to sit down, review everything that happened. Then we can decide how best to handle it."

"*We* can decide? There's no 'we' in this anymore. Krüger's seen to that. There's only him and me."

"You can't deal with Krüger on your own," she said.

"You can't help me."

"*You* called *me*." Erika turned off the main road into an industrial park. The entryway was slick under the jaundiced streetlights. "Tell me what you want."

I pulled a crumpled paper from my pocket and waved it at her. "Get this message to Harry Martin."

She parked in front of a squat structure at the end of a row of rectangular storage facilities. The building was separated from its nearest neighbor by a graveled field, half of it covered by pallets filled with ornamental cinder blocks. She unlocked the entry door and I followed her into a warehouse. The only light drifted down from the skylights above, the faint yellow of the outside security lights reflected from the clouds to cast a ghostly glow on the concrete floor below. Off to my left, I saw a pair of telephone poles lying like forgotten pick-up-sticks near a huge wooden spool empty of cable. The air smelled faintly of creosote.

I trailed Erika toward a cluster of objects at the rear, the staccato sound of our footsteps disappearing into the emptiness. She snapped a switch and a trio of fluorescent shop lights on the back wall sluggishly blinked up to full power, illuminating a rudimentary kitchen. The only furniture was the metal-legged rectangular table in front of us and a half-dozen folding chairs. Erika draped her jacket over one, then sat.

I sat, too, and slid my paper across the table to her.

Erika picked it up. "Krüger wants a U.S. military flight from Templehof?"

I nodded.

Her eyes went back to the paper.

Mine roved the shadows beyond our island of blue-white light. A pair of cubicles had been partitioned off in the back corner, leaving the rest of the enormous room virtually empty. Erika had referred to this place as their "operations center," but it contained none of the snaky electrical cords and high-tech communications equipment usually associated with that term. The absence underscored with bold, black marker the one fact about this mission I tended to treat too lightly. Holger Sorensen was behind it.

Holger's strength was people, not electronics. He traded for any data he needed from the big-time spy agencies. And he'd proved long ago that a single gem from a field agent could buy a roomful of satellite photos. This "center" typified the way he structured his operations—low on technology, high on human intelligence, comfort irrelevant.

Erika flattened the paper on the table and looked up at me. "In return for this information, they'll send the plane."

It wasn't a question. Krüger had named an Army intelligence analyst who'd spied for Department Nine while working in West Berlin from 1982 to 1984. He'd gone on to Fort Huachuca, where he copied classified Star Wars documents and passed them back to his HVA contact. Now he was happily retired, with a military pension and a secret stash from HVA. Just the type of guy the FBI loved to make miserable.

And Krüger promised he'd give up more traitor Americans when he was safe there, collecting the high price in future security he'd demanded.

I said, "If this is legitimate, Krüger can write his own ticket."

"Information like this will ultimately make him powerful," Erika agreed. "And dangerous to you. I fear that getting him to the U.S. won't end your problems."

"I can't sacrifice my father."

"Of course not." Erika kept her eyes on my face. "But you have reached one incorrect conclusion. Stefan did not betray you to his *half* brother." Her last sentence echoed off the walls, it was so heavily powered by conviction.

He'd made a fool of Erika, too. "Stefan's a great lay," I said, "but don't let the sex blind you to the facts."

Erika leaned closer, her voice low and compelling. "*Two* incorrect conclusions. Stefan Krajewski has never been my lover. Don't let that misconception blind you to the truth."

"The truth? If you weren't sleeping with him, what was going on in my hotel room the first time I met you?"

"When you showed up in Brussels, I resented the intrusion. I wanted you to feel excluded. I acted badly."

"Acted?" I repeated stupidly.

"I apologize for misleading you then." The bright light on her face washed the skin to pure white, without shadow. In that snowy expanse, her eyes glowed indigo, that bottomless shade of blue that the sky takes on at twilight.

I looked for the duplicity that had to be there. But I couldn't see it. Only her calm assessment of me.

I'd been so certain about Stefan and Erika. And if Stefan had broken faith with me in that way, I had to assume he'd deceived me in every way.

But if he and Erika hadn't . . .

I'd been holding my breath. I inhaled a huge draft of air through my mouth, my lungs expanding as if a weight had been lifted off me. She was telling the truth. I saw it in her eyes, knew it with my heart. Stefan hadn't betrayed me.

Erika made a sound, a delicate mutter of satisfaction. As if she'd seen something in my expression that pleased her. "Krüger was not pretending to fear Stefan," she said, her voice intense. "Their enmity is a fact—one that can be verified. Krüger's mother was a German Communist, forced by the Nazis to spend the war as slave labor in one of their Baltic factories. That's where she met Tadeusz Krajewski, sent there from Poland for similar reasons. They were both sixteen years old and they quickly became close. When the war ended, Gerda Krüger was pregnant with Krajewski's son, but she refused to go to Poland. She'd paid her dues and she saw a bright future for herself in the Communist GDR. Though Tadeusz Krajewski married someone else, he didn't break contact with Gerda's child. But no one who saw him with his two sons could doubt which one he loved more."

Lifelong hatred rooted in something so banal as a father's preference for a younger son. For Stefan. I said slowly, "And that rivalry worsened as they became adults."

"Aggravated by events. The father launched both boys on careers in sister foreign intelligence agencies. For many years their adult relationship was cool, but not hostile."

Erika kept her eyes on me as I worked out what had to have happened next. After martial law was instituted in Poland in 1981, both Stefan Krajewski and his father had become disenchanted with the Party. It was then that Stefan began working with Holger Sorensen to end what he considered the greatest evil forced upon Poland by its Soviet masters—cooperation with international terrorism.

"And then Stefan and Krüger became antagonists," I concluded.

"Yes," Erika said. "You were there when Stefan changed sides. You know he held nothing back when he fought that battle."

"Why didn't Stefan tell me about Krüger?"

"Ask him."

"But you could have told me they were brothers. Why didn't *you* tell me?"

"Stefan insisted."

"And you went along with that?"

"I objected. I was overruled."

"But keeping that information from me—"

"Unwise. I agree. But now you know." Erika leaned back and the metal chair complained. "It was in 1986, at about the same time that you met Stefan, that Reinhardt Krüger became embroiled in terrorist activities. Of course, Stefan didn't know that then."

"How do you know it now?" I asked.

"It's all in the Stasi files."

I made a sound of disbelief. "Krüger's too smart for that. He'd have cleaned out his files."

"True, he destroyed his personal files. But alert Germans preserved a two-hundred-kilometer shelf of Stasi records." She laughed. "Such pedants in the Ministry of State Security. They wrote everything down. From the secondary files and expense reimbursement records, we've pieced together a clear picture of Krüger's activities. His first terrorist action was the bombing of the LaBelle discotheque in Berlin. He was in on the planning from the beginning."

I spoke slowly. "What Stefan and I did in 1986 was instrumental in proving Qadhafi was behind the Berlin disco bombing."

"Yes," she said. "And some people were certain that Stefan had first learned of that connection from his half brother. When the U.S. attacked Libya in retaliation—"

I finished her sentence. "Krüger's career was jeopardized."

"Not only his career," Erika said. "His life. Libyan intelligence wanted a scapegoat."

"And they picked Krüger."

"Though in fact he wasn't guilty. He had never revealed that information to Stefan."

"But Krüger assumed Stefan had set him up to look guilty."

"Because that's what Krüger would have done." Erika's expression was grim. "He survived. He managed to implicate a young Libyan named Muhammed Asher. That one was assassinated in Berlin by Libyan intelligence—with obvious Stasi assistance. And Krüger became rabidly involved in terrorism."

"To prove his loyalty," I said, thinking out loud.

"Partly. And it's his natural inclination. He likes to attack planes." She held up three fingers of her left hand, then bent them, one by one, as she ran down the list. "The Pan Am hijacking at Karachi. The UTA flight from Brazzaville. Pan Am 103. And those are only the crimes we can prove conclusively."

"I don't understand." I rubbed my hand over my scalp again. "If there's proof, why don't the Germans arrest him?"

"Their prosecutors build cases only against the living. The German investigators disregarded references to Reinhardt Krüger, who by 1990 was conveniently dead. It is my friends"— Erika paused so that I'd understand she meant the Mossad— "who scrutinized all evidence of institutional support for terrorism. They indicted the Stasi itself, and in so doing, they collected the clues which so dramatically implicate Krüger."

I said, "Harry discounted the idea of a single evil fiend within the Stasi, masterminding terrorist plots."

"Harry hasn't met Reinhardt Krüger."

Erika reached across the table. Her fingertips were cool on the back of my hand. "We must get to him. Before he kills more people."

The same gesture, the same intimate tones that Krüger had used only hours before. The contrast between them was electrifying. Erika's fierce vitality made her touch galvanic, sending a hot rush to my brain. *Get him. Get Krüger. Stop that bomb from going off.*

And then the rush vanished. "My father . . ." My voice faded away. I shivered. The creosote-tinged air had grown colder. I clenched my teeth to stop them from chattering. Stefan was on my side, not Krüger's. But that was no help to me now. My situation was hopeless. I couldn't escape from Krüger's trap in time.

Erika tapped the paper against the tabletop. "You must send this message. Order the jet for Wednesday at Templehof. It is likely that Krüger will know you've done that. He has people in the States reporting back to him. For at least the next forty-eight hours he won't be worrying about you. We will have time to get your father out of there."

"We?"

"Yes. You and me and Hans and Bert. Also, Danièle and Hilly-Anne. They are on their way to join us."

"The six of us? We can't go against Krüger."

"You give Krüger too much credit. Don't ignore our successes. We've unmasked him. Thwarted all his attempts to kill Stefan. Forced him to work through you to escape the Mossad." Erika's fingers curved around my palm. Her hand was warm in mine, the skin smooth, the fingers slender. I smelled her shampoo, lemon and sunshine. Her grip on my hand tightened. "We *can* rescue your father."

There was such power in her voice, such warmth in her touch. Hope thudded in me. The air in the room felt the way it does before a thunderstorm, protons and neutrons jittery with incipient chaos.

Something tapped lightly against the door. I jumped. Erika slid her chair back and hurried to the entry. She checked the peephole, then unbolted the door and drew it open.

Icy air sliced through the room. Bert stepped across the threshold, stomping his boots to dislodge grit. He crossed toward us. As he passed behind my chair, he brushed my shoulder with his fingers. "You're back" was all he said, but the relief in his voice gave his light touch the weight of an embrace. He pulled open the refrigerator door and began setting packages on the counter next to the hot plate.

Van Hoof followed him inside. When he reached me, he slapped a stack of papers on the table.

"Bert and Hans made a call on my friends," Erika said, taking the chair beside mine. She raised an eyebrow at van Hoof. "They were helpful?"

Bert answered. "Went like you said it would." He waved a dark brown loaf of bread at her. "Assholes didn't want to talk to us. Especially not about Casey's dad." He thumped the loaf onto the breadboard, then tore the butcher's wrapping from a dozen dappled bratwurst. "The major, though, he's good at that. Getting people to talk to him."

Chair legs grated against the concrete as van Hoof seated himself across from me. "These fellows, they're young, eager.

They forget that we old soldiers know a thing or two. I gave them a short lesson in respect." He shook his head. "They knew your father was in Berlin. Had it in their records."

I fanned through the papers on the table. No red-stamped CONFIDENTIAL marked them. But they were intelligence files. Surveillance reports. Photocopies of records kept by border officials. Smeared carbons of hotel registrations showing which guests had foreign passports. The written record of the Mossad's efforts to track movement in and out of Berlin.

Behind me, Bert was busily putting together a late supper, like a mother who delays feeding the family until all the children are safely home. The lights were at the level of his torso, brightly illuminating his dirt-specked sweater, casting a glow upward onto the spiky stubble of his beard. He spoke over the sputter of bratwurst heating in a skillet. "Little prick made a lot of pissy remarks about amateurs. I told him it was real amateurish, letting Casey give 'em the slip that way."

Erika frowned at me. "How *did* you evade the team Bert sent after you?"

I explained how I'd ditched the pair in the alley. "Brunhild should never have gotten out from behind the wheel."

"Brunhild?" Erika asked.

"She looked like a Brunhild—so tall, with all that braided hair coiled on top of her head."

Erika's expression grew more intent. "The man with her— was he short and heavy?"

"He didn't get out of the car. But he was short," I said, recalling what I'd seen in the rearview mirror. "His chin was hidden by the dash."

"Assassins." Erika's word hung in the air like a curse. "They sent their best hit team in with you."

Van Hoof said, "Interrogating Krüger was never their goal." The glaring light sharpened the contrast between his bronzed skin and black hair, so that the anger in his face had a brutal edge to it. "They had the evidence they needed to convict him. All that remained was the execution."

"You didn't know they were using me to get to Krüger?" I asked Erika.

"No," she said. "I wanted to stop him from blowing up any more planes. Capture him, then interrogate him. But obviously, at least some of the Israelis think terminating him is the wiser course."

I said, "Krüger's got the next bombing all planned. It's not likely that killing him will stop it."

"You know that?" van Hoof asked.

"That's my analysis of the situation. Based on the Lockerbie Two incident and what I've learned about Krüger." The vocabulary of my job sounded strange here. The words didn't convey the daunting nature of the intelligence I'd acquired. My hopefulness vanished, replaced by icy despair. I struggled to keep my voice level. "I can't prove it. The Mossad reached a different conclusion. Either their analysts doubt another incident is planned or they're confident they can find the device before it explodes. They see no risk in executing Krüger."

"We underestimated him," Erika said. "The Mossad has made the same mistake."

For a moment, the only sound in the room was the popping of fat in the skillet. Then Bert said to Erika, "That little prick claimed he didn't realize Victor Collins had any connection to Kathryn Collins. Like you said he would." He laughed. "Won't pull that crap again, not on us."

Van Hoof bent toward me, his hand on the papers. "They didn't bother to inform us. Your father arrived in Berlin on Friday. January first." He pointed to a registration slip from a new luxury hotel a few blocks from Alexanderplatz.

Krüger had housed my father like a well-heeled tourist. "That fits with the ploy Krüger used to get him to Germany."

"Then your dad's probably still there," Bert said. "Along with that pair we saw with him in Potsdam." Deftly, he plunged a stainless-steel knife into the bread. I smelled the heavy sourness of sliced pumpernickel. "We've got him, then," he said to van Hoof.

"The girls are coming from Antwerp?" van Hoof asked Erika.

"They'll arrive tomorrow," she said.

"Ideal chambermaids," van Hoof said, and his sharp-edged grin was wolfish, a predator who'd stumbled on a poorly protected flock of sheep.

"Good thinking," Bert told Erika, and appreciation flavored his tone. "Sending us to shake up your *ex*-friends. Sending for those girls." He lifted a white dinner plate from the china stack and forked bratwurst onto it.

Erika stood and took the plate from him. "You and Hans also did well, bringing all this data back to us." She added a slice of bread to the plate and passed it to me.

Van Hoof handed me a knife and fork. "I have some excellent ideas how we can extract your father from there."

I opened my mouth to protest. He shared Erika's fantasy, that we could defeat Krüger. Our ragtag bunch against Lucifer? I shut my mouth without speaking. My father was Krüger's prisoner. Soon I would be, too. Why bother to argue with van Hoof?

He took a filled plate from Erika and bent over it. If defeat showed on my face, van Hoof didn't see it.

Erika and Bert joined us at the table. I looked down at my meal. The sausage was marked by stripes of dark brown, dotted with drops of fat. It smelled of garlic and thyme, the scent so rich it made me light-headed. The other three ate European-style, using their knives to pile meat and bread onto their forks, efficiently clearing their plates.

I shivered. Chilly air currents flowed from the dim corners of the room, slid beneath the table, wrapped themselves around my legs. My lower body was going numb. My brain felt numb, too, anesthetized against the horror of what I had to do. I picked up my fork and made a weak stab at the sausage. It slid to the other side of my plate, leaving a shiny trail across the porcelain. I laid the fork down. Eating was too difficult.

Bert saw my untouched meal. He reached behind him and snagged a glass jar off the counter. "Needs mustard." He unscrewed the lid, jammed a spoon into the jar and slid it to me. "My own recipe."

Unable to refuse, I spooned mustard onto my plate.

"Try it." Bert beamed at me, waiting.

Reluctantly, I cut a sliver off the sausage and dipped it in the puddle of yellow brown, then raised the meat to my mouth. I smelled mustard, then felt the miniature seeds roll over my tongue. I tasted vinegar made from exotic fruit and a fiery spice that glowed, emberlike, in my mouth. The heat swelled, cascaded down my throat, spread out across my midsection. Sweat beaded around my eyes. I felt the noonday sun on my face, the air as hot and moist as it is at sea level in the tropics.

"What is it?" I asked Bert.

"*Pili-pili* is the secret ingredient," he said. "I call this mustard 'jungle love.' " He leered at me. "You find yourself feeling romantic later, remember, I'm available."

I choked on my sausage, started to cough.

Bert peered at me. Had I once thought those eyes were ice-blue? Nothing icy in them now when he looked at me. He winked. "Made you smile," he said. "That's a start."

I wiped my eyes and said, "Great stuff."

Erika made a sound too dainty to be called a grunt, yet the satisfaction in it was animal. She reached for the jar. "Let's see if this *pili-pili* has an equally good effect on me."

Good effect? But she was right. As if I'd come back from the dead.

Suddenly, I was ravenous. All that warmth inside me. And around me. I'd been cold, paralyzed with cold. As if Krüger's icy heart had frozen my own. Spiritless, I'd undervalued the forces at work on my behalf. Krüger's victory wasn't certain.

The struggle with him wasn't over, not yet. I wasn't alone.

I cleared my throat again. "You think we can rescue my father?"

They all heard it.

Van Hoof grinned. " 'We'?"

Bert said, "Piece of cake. Getting your dad out of a hotel, be like a kid's game for me and the major."

Erika leaned toward me. "We will require some support from the Mossad. But now we know they have a different agenda. We are prepared. Rescuing your father is *our* priority. You can be sure of that." Her fingers touched mine again.

Again, that shock.

This time it felt like renewal.

"Okay," I said. "Then let's get things rolling. Let's send that message to Harry."

"Eat first," Bert said sternly.

So I did.

But as soon as I finished, I rechecked my request for the Wednesday jet, and Erika summoned a courier to take it away for transmission. Then she and Bert and van Hoof and I went to work.

We confirmed that my father was still registered at the same hotel and we roughed out a plan to get to him. Nothing fancy, the six of us entering the hotel in various guises, then converging on my father's room when the hallways were crowded with staff and other guests. The combination of surprise and a ready audience would work to our advantage.

While van Hoof double-checked the hotel's layout and schedules against reports from someone who'd been inside, Bert pulled together the clothing and weapons we'd need. Erika went to the Mossad safe house to collect the latest intelligence and make sure my message had gone to Harry.

I had only one task to perform in the operation. When we got inside my father's room, I had to instantly convince him to come with me. Simple, but critical.

I found my down jacket and winter boots stacked with my few personal items on a cot in one of the partitioned-off rooms. I carried my toothbrush with me to the cramped lavatory, fantasizing about a steaming shower, foaming body wash and fresh underwear still warm from the clothes dryer. None of that was available this night. As soon as my father was safe, I'd figure out how to get clean again. Then I'd figure out how to get to Stefan. I wanted to ask him why he'd kept Krüger a secret from me. I hoped—I prayed—he would have a good answer.

I returned to the cot and tried to sleep. I needed to be ready to do my part. Our plan wasn't foolproof, but with careful attention to detail and a little luck, we'd have my father safely under our care by noon.

But at ten o'clock that morning, the whole thing fell apart.

21

I woke up to a lousy taste in my mouth and the news that my father was on the move. The Mossad's watcher at the hotel had reported that Victor Collins had boarded the airport limousine bound for Schönefeld. Luckily, Erika was at Mossad headquarters when the message came in. She realized instantly what my father's unexpected travel meant. Krüger had given up his hostage—and his shield—and abandoned any plan to seek safe haven in the U.S. She grabbed the phone and called van Hoof. He roused me and, ten minutes later, we were racing toward Schönefeld.

We had to assume that Krüger would carry out his threat. We had to stop my father from boarding an American carrier. We had to keep him off a doomed flight.

Bert drove the Mercedes taxi. Van Hoof and I were his passengers, dressed once again in our blue coveralls and yellow hard hats. We got to the airport ahead of the limo from downtown. Bert waited outside the terminal for Erika. They'd spot my father when the limo arrived. Bert would follow him in; Erika would have the car ready when I brought him out.

Van Hoof and I strolled inside and placed ourselves in the coffee shop, trying to look like members of the remodeling crew taking a break. By the time we'd been there ten minutes, my knuckles were red against the dull silver of the coffee spoon, my body rigid with the effort to appear relaxed.

"Lufthansa to Frankfurt. First call for boarding." The woman's voice was musical, but her Teutonic enunciation of the English turned the mundane announcement into a command. "Passengers will proceed directly to Gate Thirty-two."

I bowed my head over the cup, resisting the urge to study the faces of everyone who passed.

Van Hoof made a casual eye-sweep of the area in front of us. "If he wants to make that flight, he'll have to go straight to the gate. You know what to do."

I repeated the words he'd drilled into me. "I intercept him before he reaches the metal detector. You take care of his watchers. I get him outside to Erika."

I stirred the coffee, concentrating on not slopping any from the cup. I couldn't drink it, pour caffeine on top of the adrenaline overloading my system.

"Get him out as quickly as you can," van Hoof said. "And remember: Krüger may have people outside."

"And Interpol may have shown my picture to everyone inside. Enough. I know the odds."

Van Hoof's chair legs scraped against the tiles. "Here he comes."

I stood. The electrician's belt shifted on my hips, and the wire cutters clicked against the ball peen hammer. I let my gaze wander across the concourse. I sucked in air. *There.*

A hundred feet to my right, my father shambled toward the short line in front of the security checkpoint. He was bareheaded, his hair like a drift of white feathers across his pink scalp. His gray raincoat was the same style he'd always worn, two-inch buttons holding it closed across his chest. He was canted to the left, weighed down on that side by a white plastic bag, the largest size from some duty-free shop, blazing a three-color ad for Prince cigarettes. His right hand clutched a ticket folder.

My heart felt buoyant, lifting inside my chest. My subconscious, yearning for that simpler world I'd lived in as a child. *Dad's here. It's all right now.*

Not this time.

Fewer than ten paces behind my father were the two beefy thugs who'd been with him at Potsdam. They formed a triangle with my father as the apex, moving in stately formation. The goon farthest from me was chewing gum steadily, in rhythm with the slow pace. Twenty steps behind him was Bert, hobbling along as though he needed the cane tapping the floor in front of him. The thug nearest to us had a port wine stain discoloring his lower jaw and neck. It darkened further as he registered van Hoof's sudden approach. He missed Bert, moving up swiftly on his right. Before Port-Wine could react, he was pinned between the two Belgians, his limbs paralyzed by the stun charge from Bert's walking stick.

Chewing-Gum threw himself against Bert, slamming him down. Bert's special-purpose cane rattled against the floor, rolled out of reach. A heavy boot smashed into Bert's shoulder. He screamed.

The guard at the security checkpoint turned to look.

Van Hoof tossed Port-Wine aside and caught Chewing-Gum under the chin with a two-handed uppercut. He fell across Port-Wine, but van Hoof hadn't knocked the second goon unconscious. Chewing-Gum's right hand slid under his jacket and his lips moved, but whatever he said was lost in van Hoof's shout. "A gun! This man has a gun!"

The security guard drew his weapon. He started toward them. My father was blocking his way. Without a sideways glance, he straight-armed my father and shouted something in German at the four men in front of him.

My father stumbled.

I grabbed for him, taking his weight to keep him from falling. "Dad—"

"Casey," he said, and his face eased into a grin. "Casey,

girl." Then his forehead creased. "Give me a hand with the bag?"

We both looked down. The contents must have weighed at least five pounds, pulling the cutout handles of the plastic bag so tightly against my father's hand they looked like a single white strip. Through the taut openings I saw silver-foil paper covering a rectangular box bedecked with a paper flower made from the same gift-wrap. Not likely anyone in Berlin had taken my father shopping. Krüger had given him this present, I was sure of it. I reached for the package. "Give it to me," I said.

"Can manage now," he said, his tone a mixture of affront and slyness. "I got it." But his fingers uncurled. The white strip slid down from his palm to the first joint of his fingers. It rested there. The bottom of the bag was a foot above the floor.

I reached for the bag.

My father stepped back. "I got it."

I watched the white line slide toward the next joint. Five pounds falling from a height of one foot. Enough impact to set off certain detonators.

The plastic slipped again, the strip now grazing his fingertips.

I lunged forward. Jammed my hand into the opening. The bag was an inch from the floor when I felt the full weight on my palm. I exhaled. Tightened my fingers into a fist, the strips of white plastic locked inside my grip. The bag swayed gently against my thigh. I extended my arm, held it carefully away from my body. Breathed again.

My father rocked back on his heels so that he could see my face without having to tip his head back. "Said you weren't coming," he said, slurring the initial *S* so that the word sounded more like "Shaid."

"He lied." I put my left hand on his arm. "Come with me." I wanted to run with him to Erika, waiting outside in the Jetta. But the arm I gripped felt withered, as though the muscles had atrophied. Sweat shone on my father's forehead as he strained to put one foot in front of the other. We inched forward.

I looked back. The security guard knelt beside Bert. The two thugs huddled to one side, kept from bolting by an equally stocky airport policeman, tapping a nightstick against his palm. He was listening to van Hoof, whose mouth was moving fast. Then van Hoof turned toward Port-Wine as though he'd been interrupted. I saw van Hoof's arm move. He slapped Port-Wine in the face. Nightstick shoved between them and jerked Port-Wine's hand up the center of his back.

My father and I were now fewer than fifty feet from the exit doors. Airport noises swirled up under the high ceilings, bounced off the expanses of glass and combined the way that colors do, so that the spectrum disappears into a single new color. I felt as though we were crossing an immense Arctic plain, buffeted by roaring whiteness.

"Can't breathe," my father wheezed. "Got to rest." His skin was ashy beneath the film of sweat.

The heavy bag dragged my arm down. My shoulder ached with the effort to hold the package steady. Other travelers surged around us. An information kiosk was centered in the area off to my right. A navy-suited man leaned across the counter. He waved and mouthed something at me, as though trying to get my attention. Maybe he wanted to offer the kindhearted airport maintenance worker the use of a wheelchair for the elderly tourist. Maybe he wanted to get a better view of my face, see if I matched the Wanted poster under the counter.

I nudged my father. Beyond the glass entry doors I saw the Jetta idling in the passenger-discharge lane, its exhaust like a white plume. I put more pressure on my father's arm. "We've got to keep moving."

He gasped. I thought I'd hurt him. Then I saw her. Short and compact, with straggly hair tinted the henna shade favored by women who learned their beauty secrets in the former East Bloc. In an instant she was beside me, the muzzle of her pistol a hard circle pressed into my back. She said something in German, a command that had to mean "Come with me."

I dropped my father's arm and half turned toward her. The circle became a sharp line running along my kidneys. I hugged the bag with both arms against my stomach. "You won't shoot me," I said. "I've got enough Semtex to take us all to kingdom come."

She hesitated. Then the pressure on my back eased. As the muzzle moved toward my father, I chopped down on her wrist with my left hand. A twenty-five-caliber Glock hit the floor, the clatter of plastic against concrete lost in the white noise. My face was separated from hers by fewer than six inches.

Her eyes shifted toward the floor, searching for the gun. But before she could go for it, my ball peen hammer caught her on the bridge of her nose, perfectly centered between those eyes. She dropped to the floor like a marionette whose strings had been cut. The Glock was under her sprawling body. Nearby, a woman squealed. The clerk in the information booth shouted, but I couldn't understand the words. I shoved the hammer back into my belt. Someone screamed as if terrified.

Time to run. But running was impossible. My father stood there as though he were the one who'd been coldcocked. I gently bumped him forward. "Come on, Dad. My car's outside." He seemed to register the Jetta then. Slid one foot in that direction. Then the other. Step by slow step, we made it through the door, over to the curb.

I yanked open the door and helped my father lower himself into the rear of Erika's car. I slammed the door. Ran behind the car, jumped in the other side. The Jetta slid smoothly away from the curb.

I balanced the bag firmly on my lap as I unbuckled the

electrician's belt. I couldn't get enough air. "I've got a bomb," I said to Erika.

"Hans is skillful with explosives," she said, carefully steering us toward the street. "He'll disarm it."

"Sure," I said. *If he catches up with us before it explodes.*

22

I reached over and fastened the seat belt across my father's lap. He sat as if in a stupor, his chin forward on his chest, his eyes closed. His breathing was labored and the air whistling out smelled of acetone, like the breath of a feverish child.

Erika was watching us in the mirror. "Is he okay?" she asked.

"No." My fingers touched the back of his hand. "Dad?"

He didn't react. Maybe he was hurting from all the sudden movements, but that didn't explain why he seemed so out of touch. I had to get help for him.

But first we had to deal with his carry-on luggage. The plastic bag was slick beneath my fingers, the weight ominously heavy on my lap. I yearned to pull up beside the next Dumpster and heave it away. But that would endanger anyone nearby when it exploded. We had to dispose of this present ourselves.

Unless it disposed of us first. "Want to guess when this will go off?" I asked Erika.

Her eyes met mine in the edge of the mirror. "Most likely Krüger set the timer to explode over the Atlantic."

"On the Global flight from Frankfurt."

"What?"

I held up the ticket I'd been studying. "My father was using his return ticket. The one he bought on December thirtieth. He was trying to catch the Lufthansa flight to Frankfurt. He'd have taken Global from there to Kennedy."

My face was warm, my whole body overheated by dread. Sweat soaked my T-shirt under both arms, dampened my bra between my breasts, made a wet circle on my back. I smelled the rancid odor of my fear.

Above us the sky was cloudless, a piercing blue that intensified the winter sunshine, the harsh beams bouncing off the concrete and assaulting my eyes. My father and I sat like two hunchbacks, he bent by his pain, me unthinkingly curved around my parcel as though I could contain it. I repeated Erika's calming words. The bomb was probably set to explode four to five hours from now, when my father would've been over the Atlantic. But maybe Krüger thought it would be more fun to have it explode on the ground. Tracking my father to the airport had been too easy. Was I now sitting at ground zero, right where Krüger wanted me?

My heartbeats magnified. They exploded inside my head, the giant ticks of a clock counting down to our doom. I heard them, each and every one, at least a thousand total in the ten additional minutes it took for Erika to get us back to the industrial park.

We left my father's package in the car while Erika and I brought him indoors. Then she went back outside and moved the Jetta to the far side of the lot, beyond the rows of concrete block. I heard every rumble of the engine, every grating of rubber against gravel. My wet T-shirt turned icy against my skin and my sour scent filled my nostrils.

I tried to get my father to talk with me, tell me where he'd gone and what he'd done for the past few days. He was as cranky as a child, cheated of his sleep. Kept insisting it was time for "a little lie-down." I helped him into the cubicle where I'd rested the night before. He curled up on the cot at once, pulling the bedroll up to his chin and squeezing his eyes shut as though that would make me leave him alone.

I'd never heard of a drug that worked like this one, but his strange behavior had to be chemically induced. I reached out to touch my father's shoulder, then drew back my hand. Let him rest. Let it wear off, whatever it was.

Erika was still outside. My movements were jerky with tension. I went back into the main room and forced myself to do something, anything, besides listen for the sound of Erika being blown to bits. I ran rusty water from the spigot until it turned clear, the thin stream tinny against the steel-bottomed sink. I filled a teakettle and set it on the hot plate. As the coils reddened, the spatters burned off, filling the room with the scent of scorched fat. On the shelf above the hot plate I found a jar of instant coffee and a battered container of Earl Grey. I set both on the table, along with mugs and spoons.

The kettle shrieked. Erika came inside. My shoulders dropped. She was okay. She made a phone call, then said, "A doctor will come to check your father."

Outside, gravel again scattered beneath a set of tires. Erika hurried to the door and opened it. "Hans," she said over her shoulder to me. She spoke to him, then came back in. "Bert may have some broken bones. The police took him away for X rays."

"The cops didn't figure out Bert's connection to van Hoof?"

"No," she said. "And they won't learn anything from Bert."

A car door slammed.

I started.

"Calm down," Erika said. "He's good at this."

I spooned instant coffee into a cup, poured hot water over it. The crystals foamed up. I didn't want coffee, but I had to do something. Had to stop listening for explosions. Had to stop thinking about my father. Had to concentrate on Krüger. He'd abandoned his plan to come to the States with me. I wondered why. But the more critical question was, what would he do instead?

Erika sat down and clinked a spoon against the edge of her

cup. I poured more hot water in. She kept stirring with the spoon, swirling whitish scum in circles.

I sat down. "At least we can defuse this one."

Her eyes were on my face. "You think there is another? That your father's flight was not the one Krüger's been planning to blow up all along?"

I shook my head. "Giving that bomb to my father was not part of Krüger's original plan. No, Krüger's been working up to a major incident since long before I became involved." I ran my gaze around the room, automatically searching for a calendar. I didn't need to check. "Wednesday. Everything he said points to Wednesday as the day. A farewell blast timed to occur after he leaves Germany for a safe haven."

"He must have picked Global 500 as his initial target *before* he decided to seek safety in the U.S.," Erika said. "It defies common sense, killing so many Americans, then going straight to their homeland."

I picked up my coffee cup, then set it back down. I'd given this point a lot of thought, puzzling out why Krüger had seemed so arrogantly confident that he'd retain his power over me when we reached the U.S. I said, "Remember, he's using Lockerbie as a model. He concealed his role in that one. He'll do it again. Both the Global 500 bombing and the next one will be clearly identified as the work of terrorist groups."

"But how could he be sure no one would discover he was the one who planned the bombings?"

"He'd definitely have covered his tracks well. And, given the valuable information he was bringing with him, nobody in the U.S. would have looked hard for a link either. Just like Harry—they'd have wanted to go on believing he was clean enough to do business with. All the people involved with him would have had a strong interest in *not* connecting him to international terrorism."

Erika frowned. "What you're saying is reasonable, but I think he started this with a different safe haven in mind."

"Of course he did. Libya is the obvious choice. But there are hazards in being the guest of Qadhafi. When I came on the scene, he saw a way to arrange a more attractive future in the States."

Erika clicked her teeth together, her forehead still creased. "Going to America was an inviting option. But after he met you, he realized that plan contained too many variables beyond his control."

"Maybe." I didn't think Krüger had gotten cold feet. I'd detected no doubt in his cavalier assumption that I'd do as he wished. And so long as he held my father hostage, he was right. "He wanted me to know he was going to blow up another plane."

"To guess what he planned, but to tell no one."

"And to save my father, I had to share his guilt." I remembered Krüger's cool assertion that without his help I'd have no way to solve *my* problems. "He was letting me know that he could make my situation worse whenever he chose."

"Perhaps not going to America achieves that in some way I can't yet see," Erika said slowly.

I couldn't see it either. "We need to figure out what he'll do next."

"He can't remain in Europe," said Erika. "I'm certain the Israelis intend to kill him."

"He'll go to Libya," I predicted.

"Qadhafi will know that he orchestrated the next terrorist action. Krüger will be a hero in Tripoli."

"He wants his arrival there to coincide with whatever he's planned for Wednesday." I saw the problem clearly now. To stop the next bombing, we had to catch up with Krüger before he reached safety in Libya. We had to extract all the details of his plan from him. If the Mossad killed Krüger before we got that information, our only hope of preventing the incident would die with him.

The door flew open. In van Hoof's hands were the two

halves of a boom-box case. He slammed the door shut and then crossed the room to drop the plastic on the table between us. *Toshiba.*

"They'd have stopped your father as soon as he put this on the security belt," van Hoof told me. "It was a setup." He slapped a piece of gift-wrap on the table. "Krüger wanted him caught with this."

I drew the wrinkled paper toward me. The tag was glued to the silver gift-wrap. It read, "To Dad from Casey with love."

"And inside the player?" Erika asked.

"Semtex all over the printed circuit board." Van Hoof tapped the casing. "Identical to the one used to blow up Pan Am 103. Everyone knows this piece of equipment."

"But my father would've told them . . ." I let my voice trail off. I couldn't guess what my father truly believed about my involvement with Krüger. I said, "That's why Krüger let my father travel to the airport so openly. It didn't matter how I reacted."

Van Hoof said, "Given the tight time frame, odds were you'd botch any attempted interception. Be caught by airport security with the bomb."

Erika said, "And if they stopped only your father—"

"They'd have tied the bomb directly back to you," van Hoof finished.

Erika's eyes seemed to turn a darker blue. "That's why Krüger made your father use the same ticket," she said.

"He was making his return trip precisely two weeks after the Global 500 bombing," I said slowly.

"The investigators would conclude that you had been involved in the preparations for both disasters," van Hoof added.

"Causing me trouble won't count for much in Tripoli." I frowned, trying to make sense of it. "Why is Krüger wasting his time?"

"Stefan loves you." Erika's fingers were cool on the back of my hand. "And Reinhardt Krüger hates his brother. He knows that harming you will harm Stefan."

Stefan. I felt a sudden surge of panic. "Where is Stefan?"

"We have a bungalow in Limburg, in eastern Belgium, situated on a ridge above the Maas valley," Erika replied, her voice soothing. "A safe location. Danièle and Hilly-Anne took him there."

Stefan hiding out from his brother. Unless I could defeat Krüger, I'd have to do the same.

My stomach clenched, a gut-twisting bitterness unrelated to all my motives for capturing Krüger alive. He'd tried to kill two people I loved. Savaged my career. Wrecked my life.

I wanted him to suffer. Suffer hideously. Then die a horrible death. Van Hoof's eyes were on me, and suddenly I knew—*I knew*—what drove him.

That desire for vengeance blazed up. Just as quickly, dread snuffed it out. Bloodlust left an aftertaste like ashes in my mouth. And fear knotted my stomach. "I think we need to take a hard look at what Krüger's after—" I began.

Erika held up a hand, her head tilted toward the door.

I heard something disturb the gravel outside. Van Hoof moved to the right of the entry. He hand-cocked his Browning with a sharp click. I was on my feet, too. I moved into position on the left of the door, behind Erika. I felt the handle of the hammer in my fist. I didn't remember grabbing it from the counter.

23

Erika said, "Danièle and Hilly-Anne are here."

Van Hoof said, "If you're going to run this place like a convention center, I better set up a guard post."

"My friends will make excellent sentries," she said, opening the door.

The Vespa idled ten feet from the entry. The two women were both in motorcycle leathers now, their heads and most of their faces covered by glistening blue-black helmets with smoky plastic shades over the eyes. But their mouths were visible, their teeth gleaming. Erika stepped outside to talk to them.

I shut the door and dropped the hammer back on the counter. I pointed at van Hoof's weapon. "Got one of those for me?"

"Certainly," he said, moving to a padlocked storage locker. When he opened it, I smelled gun oil. Inside were at least a dozen Browning pistols and four times that many boxes of nine-millimeter parabellum cartridges.

How many Browning weapons had I seen in the past week? "Is this the only gun available around here?" I asked van Hoof.

"The finest firearm in the world," he said.

I hefted one in my hand. "Designed by a Mormon from Utah."

"And crafted by artists in Belgium." He handed me a box of cartridges.

I fed the bullets into the magazine. The gun was manufactured by the Fabrique Nationale d'Armes de Guerre of Liège, a town whose armorers had been supplying weapons to all sides since the Middle Ages. A Modèle 1900 had been used to kill Archduke Ferdinand during his Sarajevo visit. FN's guns had gotten even more accurate in the eighty-odd years since then.

Van Hoof handed me a leather belt with a small-of-the-back holster. I buckled it on and stuck the pistol into place. The belt fit perfectly, the gun solid at my back.

I watched van Hoof catalog the weapons store, stroking each piece as he checked it. Erika had told me that Stefan had stocked this warehouse a month ago. But then Stefan had been trying to buy information from Krüger's business associate. He wouldn't have needed a dozen well-polished pistols. I bent down beside van Hoof. "This your private cache?"

He grunted. "Sometime back, I saw a way I could cause a problem for Krüger. I was setting things up when Erika and Stefan contacted me." He gave a sour chuckle. "They preferred a more subtle approach."

But their strategy had failed. I asked, "What were *you* planning to do?"

He carefully shut the locker. "I discovered Krüger had an unusual interest in a tight little group working in Berlin. Supposed to be running an information service for Third World translators. But I saw that only Libyans were going into that office. Seemed more likely it existed just to coordinate their terrorist activities."

"So you wanted to attack them."

"I have some expertise in urban assaults. Seemed a pity not to use it. We would reduce the number of Libyans in the world. Demonstrate the unwisdom of associating with Krüger." He shrugged. "I was overruled. The others thought the plan too dangerous."

Cool words. But when van Hoof's eyes met mine, I saw heat there. He'd given in to superior logic. He'd shelved his battle plan. But the passion behind it remained. He wanted revenge. He wanted blood.

I was the one who looked away first.

I went back to the table and began clearing the coffee cups. Sunlight cascaded down from the rooftop windows, dust motes made into Christmas glitter by the beam, the particles dispersing randomly, as if driven by individual motors.

As different as those particles, van Hoof, Erika and I had been brought here by different motives. But ultimately by one person: Holger Sorensen. A man who'd skillfully welded our separate agendas into a single mission. A man who'd been my ally for more than a decade. A man who'd awed me with his incisive understanding of the issues involved in international terrorism.

Yet this paragon had withheld vital information from me. He'd encouraged me to believe that Stefan had died in Scotland. If he'd told me about Reinhardt Krüger then, I'd have handled Mike Buchanan differently, perhaps never been forced to flee in Lura's jet.

I set the coffee cups in the metal sink, the thick china resonant against the stainless steel. I hadn't seen Holger again until he brought Harry to me. No time then to confront him. We'd been too busy maneuvering Harry into the role we'd picked for him. Or so I thought. But Holger had made a conscious choice to continue keeping his secrets. Not telling me that my father had disappeared. Not disclosing that Stefan and Krüger were half brothers. As though he didn't trust me to handle all the facts, all at once. Need-to-know is the oldest rule of the game, but Holger had made poor choices when it came to deciding what it was that *I* needed to know.

What was it Harry had said? *That bunch of Viking vigilantes will burn you all over again.* Time to start paying better attention to Harry's advice.

The entry door swung open. Then slammed shut. I turned to see Erika ushering in a man. He was as short as she, not more than five feet five, and half that wide. Shoulder-length blond hair, three gold rings in his right ear, Hard Rock Cafe T-shirt, stained white carpenter's pants, carrying a black medical bag so new he had to be still a student. As I got closer to him, I smelled that hospital blend of rubbing alcohol and burned toast.

After Erika introduced him as the doctor, I described my father's disorientation and physical feebleness.

"And this is a change from when you last saw him?" the doctor asked in the unaccented English spoken by well-educated Europeans.

"Yes," I said firmly. I'd spent the four-day Thanksgiving holiday in Oregon with my father. He'd seemed normal for a man of seventy-five. Slower, more forgetful than when he was younger, but not so weak and confused as he'd been earlier today. "Check for a drug reaction. Either he's not been taking his medication, or he's been given something that's dulled his reactions. He functions better than this."

"Let me see him," the doctor said.

I led him into the cubicle. My father lay curled on the cot, the wispy hair now thickened by sweat, the damp locks striping his pale scalp. He drew in a rattling breath.

"Dad," I said, gently moving his shoulder.

His eyelids opened. I looked into vacant gray-green eyes. Awareness slowly came into them and he asked, "Time for the news?"

"The news?" I repeated.

"News," he said. "That German fellow lets me watch it every day." His brow furrowed. "Need to keep track of how much trouble you're in."

"I'm not in trouble," I said.

He sniffed. "Not what I hear." Then his expression grew ingratiating. "Turn on the TV for me, okay?"

"Sorry," I said. "We don't have a television."

"No TV?" He looked desperately around the cubicle and his eyes landed on the doctor. "Young fellow, can you get me a TV?"

"Dad," I said, "he's a doctor, come to give you a checkup."

"Don't need a checkup. I need the news. Go talk to that German fellow. He understands. He'll explain." His voice took on a wheedling tone. "Be a good girl, now, Casey. Go find your old dad a television."

I ran my hand across my scalp. Damp as usual and I was wet under my arms, too. What was going on? After everything that had happened, all my father wanted to know from me was where his next news fix was coming from? Something tightened in my chest, seemed about to explode inside my head.

I felt him touch my arm.

I looked down, saw his hand, clawlike, plucking at my arm. Saw my own hand clenched into a fist. I was suddenly so angry, all I could imagine was knocking him back down on the bed.

Wrong reaction. And I knew it. Recognized that rush of fury for the defense mechanism it was. As an adolescent, that was how I'd distanced myself from my mother. Compassion would have kept me at home by her side forever. Angry resistance set me free. Now I was reacting the same way to my father. I forced my fingers to unclench and said, "Talk to the doctor for a minute, Dad. I'll go try to find a *Time* magazine for you."

His expression was doubtful, but he let me step aside. The doctor took my place beside the bed. He moved my father's arms and legs the way you would with a child unable to understand what was being asked of him.

I went back into the main room and rummaged around until I found a month-old edition of the *International Herald Tribune*. I opened it to the crossword puzzle. When I returned and held it out to my father, he seized it. "I need a pencil."

"I'll get it," I said, following the doctor back to the main room.

He said, "He's dehydrated, but otherwise in fair condition, given his age." He tugged at the ringed ear. "He suffers from arthritis?"

"A variant of arthritis." I pulled the name from memory. "Ankylosing spondylitis."

"Yes," said the doctor. "Affecting the backbone, forcing the poker-spine posture."

"He's had it since his late twenties," I said. "It's gotten worse over the years. But that doesn't explain why he's acting so mentally out of it." I leaned closer. "Is it drug-induced psychosis?"

"Unlikely," the doctor said. "If he had been given drugs, their effects would have become less marked now, not more so. No, his behavior suggests an organic problem. Something age-related. There are several ailments with similar manifestations."

"Such as?"

"A B-12 deficiency, severe atherosclerosis, cerebral vasculitis. And, of course, early-stage Alzheimer's." He gave me an inquiring look. "Does his family have a history of any of those?"

I looked at my feet. Beneath the laces, the tongue of my boot had slipped off-center. I bent down to readjust it, spoke without looking up. My voice was muffled. "His mother."

"Had what?"

I straightened up and faced the doctor. "They didn't make the diagnosis so easily then. But it was Alzheimer's."

"Then this is no surprise to you."

"But he was fine last November."

His expression grew skeptical.

My father had been almost fine. I'd seen the weekly magazines piled on the coffee table, more material than even a bored retiree could read in a week. He'd shown me the digital watch that came with one free trial subscription. It displayed the wrong time. Not so strange that a senior citizen couldn't depress the minuscule buttons in the correct sequence. But every time I set it correctly, he fiddled with it until it was wrong again. Irritating, I thought. But older people can be stubborn.

His ten-year-old Ford was marked by recent scratches, dents and dings. Parking lot stuff, he told me. He was a careful driver. And I agreed that the lots were more crowded, the spaces narrower, other drivers more impatient.

He didn't behave oddly enough to alarm me. But he was in his home, in the place where he'd lived for fifty years. Much easier for him to conceal his diminishing capacities there. The mental and physical erosion that now, in this strange environment, had become undeniable.

My growing awareness must have shown on my face. The doctor shrugged. "Perhaps it was not so sudden, yes?"

"Isn't there something you can give him to help him get around better?"

The doctor shook his head. "If it is Alzheimer's, we can only slow the decline. We cannot repair or even halt the deterioration of physical and mental function, impairment of judgment, loss of communication skills."

"A lot of sudden changes, stress, violence—all that would hasten the process, wouldn't it?"

"Very likely. It can only be harmful, exposing him to a hostile environment." He made a noise that he must have thought was sympathetic. Then he headed for the door. Erika hovered beside it, waiting to usher him out.

I turned back toward the room that held my father. He'd never be okay again. He'd keep on shriveling up inside. And then, when his shell was completely empty, he'd die. And there wasn't a damn thing I could do about it.

My father was watching me from the doorway. "What about that television?" he asked, his voice querulous. "You doing anything to get me some news?"

I settled him back on the cot with the newspaper and the

crossword and a renewed promise of *Time*. I hoped he'd forget about the magazine. But I wasn't betting on it. The memory failures were never helpful. Only hurtful, in a slow, cumulative, dreadful way.

I'd been only eight when my grandmother's failing powers became too obvious to ignore. By the time I was ten, she was unable to leave the nursing home to join us for Christmas dinner. A relief, really. So unpleasant was she, no one wanted to be around her.

I'd been so preoccupied with my father, it hadn't registered with me that Bert was back. I found him sitting at the table, his arm in a sling. Van Hoof stood by the counter, a dish towel draped over his front, a chef's knife in his right hand, an oven mitt covering his left. The smell of grilling onions came from a cast-iron Dutch oven, jammed onto the hot plate beside him.

Bert said to van Hoof, "The chicken goes in next." He grinned at me. "Got the major doing the work for a change."

"You sure you should be out of bed?" I asked.

"Three cracked ribs. Broken clavicle. Bruises, contusions. The usual. No need to coddle myself."

Erika joined Bert at the table.

Behind them, van Hoof removed a platter from the refrigerator and held it above the Dutch oven. Resinous vapor floated from the heating pot, another more exotic odor mingling with that of the onions. Van Hoof prodded the contents of the platter with the tip of his knife and oily chicken parts cascaded into the mixture, setting off percussive explosions. I peered into the pot. The steam left an oily film on my face and I smelled a piquant spice I didn't recognize. My lips burned as if I'd rubbed them with a slice of chili pepper.

"Palmnut sauce with *pili-pili* and onions," said Bert. "*Moambe*'s the name of the dish. Congolese fare. Put you in fighting form."

"Fight's over," I said flatly. "Krüger has us beaten."

Erika said, "We can't give up."

I disagreed. "We have no choice. Bert's out of the action now. We can't count on support from the Mossad. There's no way we can capture Krüger and make him talk."

"We rescued your father." Van Hoof's face was grim. "Now we must stop Krüger. You said as much yourself."

"I said it. But I can't do it. Not now."

Erika kept her eyes on my face. "The doctor says your father's mental function is not good?"

"He wouldn't be in such bad shape if it weren't for Krüger." A pain like heartburn flared in the center of my chest, made my voice harsh. "He's like this because he tried to help me. I've got to take care of him now."

Van Hoof slammed the knife onto the cutting board, left it upright, quivering. Vapor from the pot clouded the air around his face, so that it looked as if his anger were boiling out of him. He yanked off the oven mitt and said, "You will have no life, Casey Collins, so long as Krüger goes free."

Hot words. Cold truth. Krüger wanted to destroy me, would destroy me, perhaps had done so. I wasn't brave enough to face him again. Despair rose from my guts like a wave of nausea as I saw my future. Me, alone and scared, stumbling through a desolate wasteland of a life. Trying to drag my bewildered, complaining father along with me as I fled from a hundred enemies. A future I could not bear.

24

The pot bubbled noisily behind me. I braced myself against the counter, waiting.

Van Hoof stared at me silently for fifteen seconds. Then he pulled off the dish cloth and tossed it down next to the knife. He dropped into the chair beside Erika and said to her, "She's right about the Israelis. We can have no further contact with them."

"Agreed," she said.

"You?" I asked Erika. "You'll keep on with van Hoof?"

Erika moved in her chair.

"You will," I said flatly. "The two of you, on your own, without the Mossad to back you up. Impossible. How can you find out where Krüger is?"

"Holger Sorensen is on his way," she replied.

"The Father-Major's no match for Reinhardt Krüger. You don't need a desk jockey getting in the way. You need a larger force and more resources."

"That's why Holger's coming to Berlin," Erika said. "To provide us with immediate access to his source here."

"Gorm," I said, recalling the code name. He was the former Stasi file clerk who had continued working for Holger after German unification. "Better intelligence isn't enough."

Van Hoof's face contorted with fury, his mouth open to speak.

Bert interrupted in Flemish, his tone reasonable, as if he were asking van Hoof to do something.

The foreign words startled me. Until this moment, everyone had spoken a language I understood, too.

Off-balance, van Hoof barked out a single word. If he'd been speaking English, I'd have thought he said, "What?"

Bert repeated his request, the pace more urgent this time.

Van Hoof gave him a disgusted look. Then he glanced at me. Then back to Bert. "I'm going outside," he said.

English again. For my benefit?

The legs of his chair screeched angrily on the cement. "You coming?" he asked Erika.

She stood without answering. I watched their backs as they went out the door.

Bert said, "Simmer down, I told him."

When I didn't react, he spoke impatiently. "The broth has to simmer now." He waved a hand toward the hot plate. "Lower the heat under the pot, will you?"

I reached over, turned the dial on the hot plate counterclockwise. Color ebbed out of the coils beneath the pot. The boiling grew less rowdy. "It's simmering," I told Bert.

"And so's the major." He winked at me, his grin sly. "Sit down a minute."

"You going to start in on me now, too?" I asked, taking the seat beside him.

He rubbed his jaw, his fingers grating against the half-inch stubble. The skin beneath the beard was mottled by a purple bruise. "This thing Krüger did with your dad, it was pure evil. You can bet the bastard's got more tricks. I don't blame you if you don't want to give him a chance to play them."

Air came out of me in a gusty sigh. "You see how he's come after me—me, personally?"

"I see." He softened his voice. "Of course you're afraid of him."

Afraid. Yes. "You. My father. If anyone tries to help me, he hurts them. You better believe he scares the hell out of me."

"Sure he does. Man's got a thing about his brother. All that hate's spilled over onto you. There's no guessing what a fellow like that will do." His body twitched, an involuntary shudder that jerked his shoulder, made him wince.

I realized he was talking about himself as much as about me. "You've been through it, too?"

"Long time ago. And the major didn't cut *me* any slack either." For a second, a shadow darkened the crystalline blue of his eyes. "The best thing for you to do is get your dad away. You got to look after your own."

Curious, I asked, "Did you?"

"Look after my own?" He laughed. "It wasn't the same thing. I'm a soldier. Looking after the major, that's my job."

"You can't do that now, beat up like you are."

He tried to shrug, winced again. "And the Dane's on his way. That Father-Major fellow." He snorted. "Two majors. Quite a treat for a crippled old sergeant."

"A treat for us all," I said.

Whatever Erika and van Hoof were cooking up outside, I wanted no part of it.

Especially if Holger Sorensen was stirring the pot.

Five minutes later, he arrived. Erika and van Hoof followed him, three sets of boot heels slapping decisively across the concrete floor. Holger took the chair facing Bert and me. Erika and van Hoof sat on either side of him. My muscles tensed, the arrangement into opposing camps too obvious. Holger shook hands with Bert. To me, he said, *"Hellig tre Konger."*

Three Holy Kings. I heard the mournful minor notes of the English carol: "We three kings of Orient are . . ." The three Wise Men paying homage to the infant Christ. *The Epiphany.* Krüger had used the word. Oddly out of place, but I hadn't paid attention then, I'd been so focused on other problems. But now, as part of the religious calendar, I got the connection. I said, "January sixth. Wednesday is January sixth. Wednesday is Krüger's epiphany."

Holger said, "Epiphany, yes. Gorm made the association. Something terrible will happen on Wednesday."

"Casey reached the same conclusion," Erika said. "Most likely another airplane bombing."

"Gorm suspects it will be a much bigger disaster," Holger said.

"He's upped the ante," I said slowly.

Holger said, "He is holding the information closely. Gorm cannot extract more without risking exposure. We must get the details from Krüger."

"You know where he's hiding?" Bert asked.

"Not precisely," Holger said. "We will have to draw him out." He stopped there, his gaze resting on me.

"And you want to use me as the lure." I shoved myself to my feet. "I proposed the best deal I could put together. Krüger rejected it. What else could I possibly offer him?"

Holger leaned back in his chair so he could see my face. "This time, Krüger claims he has something to offer you."

"Something for me? What are you talking about?"

Erika drew in her breath, a gasp of sudden understanding.

And then I got it, too. "Stefan," I said to Erika. "He's not in Limburg, is he?"

"No," she said. "Danièle and Hilly-Anne took him there Friday. He was alone in the safe house when they left Saturday morning. Sunday, yesterday, they stopped by on their way here. He was gone."

"Do you think Krüger's people—?" I couldn't finish the sentence.

"No sign of violence," she said. "It looked as though Stefan waited until the women departed on Saturday. Then he left the house."

I rubbed my forehead, let my hand slide down to cover my eyes. Stefan hadn't run away. He wasn't a man who ran *from* trouble. Of course Stefan had come to Germany. "Krüger has him."

"So he claims," Holger said.

"But how did Krüger find him so easily?" I asked.

"I think it more likely that Stefan found him," Holger replied. "That cabin where you met Krüger? Stefan once told me that he and his father made a secret visit to such a place years ago. A clandestine retreat for Krüger's mother. One that afforded maximum privacy. That cabin would be the first place Stefan would look for Krüger."

"You think Stefan was trying to get there before me?" I asked.

Holger said, "We all know he did not want you to come into contact with his brother."

"But how could he prevent that? At best, he'd have arrived only hours before me. To stop us from meeting, he'd have had to kill Krüger. And he couldn't do that—"

"Or Krüger's associates would have eliminated your father." Holger shook his head. "For that reason, I'm certain Stefan didn't intend to execute Krüger. I think he hoped to negotiate."

"Offer himself in place of my father." I had difficulty saying the words.

"He knew Krüger would give anything—even his American future—to capture him," Erika said. "And if Krüger brings Stefan along, Tripoli becomes a more dependable refuge. When he turns his half brother over to Libyan intelligence, he'll prove where his loyalty lies."

"Exactly," van Hoof agreed. "He's got Stefan and he's taking him to the Libyans."

"That's insane," I said. "He shouldn't have done it."

Erika covered my hand with hers and tilted her head to look up at me. Compassion darkened her indigo eyes. "Stefan made the best move he could to force a change of plans."

"Krüger abandoned his scheme to go to the U.S.," van Hoof said. "And he released your father. That created a new opportunity for us."

"But we can't allow Krüger to give Stefan to the Libyans." And then I realized what my words implied. I glared at Holger. "That's what you want, isn't it? That's what your famous loyalty to your agents comes down to. To save Stefan, you'll let Krüger have me."

"No . . ." Erika's shocked tones were drowned out by Bert. "That son-of-a-whore," he said. "What he'd do to her—"

Holger interrupted. "An exchange of Kathryn for Stefan is not something I would consider." His eyes held mine. "You know that."

No, he wouldn't trade me away. But Krüger was the one forcing this meeting. He'd asked for me—no one else. My fate was sure to be at the top of his agenda. I had to make them understand that.

But van Hoof spoke before I could. "We won't allow the man to touch you." He unfolded a map and smoothed it flat on the tabletop. "You were at Potsdam," he said to me. "Where did you actually meet Krüger?"

I traced my route to Krüger's cabin on the Spree.

"I know this area northeast of Dresden well," van Hoof said, his finger replacing mine on the map. He spoke to Holger. "If you can persuade Krüger to meet her down here"—his finger slid toward Dresden—"we can snatch the bastard before he does her any harm."

I put my palms on the table and leaned toward Holger. "Here we are," I said. "Right where you wanted us."

I moved my gaze to van Hoof, then to Erika, before I turned to take in Bert. "*He's* got an undercover man who travels in the same circles as Krüger. Gorm could try harder to find out what plane Krüger's going to blow up next. But *he* won't risk blowing

Gorm's cover. Please, Holger, explain: Why is it you prefer to risk all of us?"

"I have to trust my agent's judgment," Holger said. "Gorm insists he cannot learn more about the bomb. He says that Krüger holds that information too closely. Therefore, a second attempt to entrap him is the only workable option. We have fewer than forty-eight hours left. Krüger's willing to expose himself in order to meet with you. We must exploit that opportunity."

The situation was eerily familiar. Four days ago in an Antwerp cathedral, Stefan had tried to stop me from meeting with Krüger. I'd pushed his objections aside. I'd been ignorant then of Krüger's hatred of his half brother. Unaware that he'd probed my life for any point of weakness he could exploit. Four days ago, I hadn't known my enemy. "We have to rescue Stefan first," I said. "Where is Krüger holding him?"

"Gorm has identified three probable locations," Holger said. "I've got people working on it, but we will not pinpoint the exact spot in time."

"But I'm vulnerable while he's got Stefan," I said. "If he were to bring him to the meet—"

"We can rule out that contingency," Holger cut in. "Krüger will expect you to have backup. He won't take a chance on losing his only bargaining chip. He's got Stefan safely stowed away and he'll leave him there until the deal is arranged."

"Stefan first," I said again, the two words crushed into one by my urgent need to make Holger understand.

"Not enough time to locate the prisoner, let alone set up the operation." Bert shook his head, his voice thick with regret. "Can't rescue somebody, you don't know where he is."

I said to Holger, "You can access satellite photos of those locations. With intensive analysis, we can find him—"

"Can you not recognize the flaw in your logic?" Holger's voice was pitched low and it rolled across my passion with the force of an icy wave from the Baltic Sea. "If we could rescue

Stefan, what would be the point? There would no longer be a basis for credible negotiations. Krüger would not show up at the meet. At this juncture we cannot help Stefan. Later, yes. But now we must focus on capturing Krüger."

A scream was in me, trying to get out. Krüger had used my father against me. Now he was holding Stefan's life in his hands. I was helpless in the face of that threat. Yet Holger wanted to send me to him again. I managed to say, "No. Not Krüger. Stefan is—"

"*I* have suffered." Van Hoof's voice slashed through mine, brutal as a bullwhip. "In this struggle, I have lost a child. A wife. I don't want to lose yet another comrade. But we have no time to waste flailing against reality. Accept that discipline, as I have."

My face was hot and I knew I had to choose my words carefully. Yes, he'd suffered. Erika, too. But their loved ones had been killed by faceless terrorists blasting into anonymous crowds. Stefan had been singled out by one man who wanted to hurt him badly. Krüger had spent months—perhaps years—figuring out how to inflict the most damage on Stefan—and on me. Finally, I said, "Sending me to that meeting is the same as giving me to Krüger."

"Enough!" van Hoof said. "If Holger tells us he has no better way to get the information, we must accept that. He's not 'giving you' to Krüger. Your role is to draw the man out of hiding. If you do your part, we have some hope of preventing a great loss of life. Are you so frightened you can't do that much? So selfish you care only about your own safety?"

"I care about the safety of everyone." I spoke with difficulty through the rage tightening my throat. "If you've miscalculated, this operation won't save people. And Krüger will have me. I can't risk that. My father needs me too much."

"And all the other fathers who will be on those planes?" Van Hoof's tone was murderous. "They don't matter to their daughters?"

The cruelty of his words robbed me of any response.

Metal shrieked as Bert shifted in his seat. His back to me, he turned off the hot plate. When he settled down again, he'd moved his chair an inch closer to van Hoof. Of course. He was looking after his own. I'd lost Bert.

Didn't anyone realize what this so-called negotiation came down to? Krüger was offering me Stefan—but what did he want in return? "Erika . . ." I began.

When she raised her chin and looked at me full on with those bottomless eyes, I saw only pity there. She said, "We must follow Holger's lead in this. Only he has a complete picture of what is going on."

"Don't you see what you're asking me to do?"

"Try to look at the situation objectively," Holger said. "We know Stefan's value to Krüger. He would exchange Stefan only for something of greater long-term use to him in his relationship with Qadhafi."

"Me," I said.

"You, yes," Holger agreed quickly, "but not as a prisoner. Stefan is a far better choice for show trial and execution. No, you are more valuable to Krüger as a pawn."

"What do you mean?" I asked.

He waved his hand impatiently. "I could list a half-dozen problems you could solve for Qadhafi if Krüger could convince you to exploit your knowledge and connections on behalf of Libya."

"Convince her?" Erika echoed. "But after he released Stefan, how could he maintain a hold over Casey?"

Holger said, "I'm sure Krüger does not view that as a problem."

His voice was cold, the sound so chilling that I felt a lump like ice forming in my midsection. Holger was right. I had no doubt that Krüger saw a way to control me for the rest of my life. "That's what I'm trying to get you guys to see—"

Holger cut me off. "You fear him, we all understand that.

But we have no more time for debate. We must proceed with the plan to draw Krüger toward Dresden. You may participate or not, as you choose. But for the rest of us, there is no choice." He turned to van Hoof. "Agreed?"

"Absolutely," said van Hoof.

Erika didn't look at me when she nodded.

My chair was noiseless as I moved it back into place at the table. I centered it carefully between the table legs. I kept my body rigid, my footsteps silent, as I stepped toward the doorway to my father's cubicle. If I expressed a fraction of my anger, I'd explode. They weren't listening to me. They didn't grasp how monstrous Krüger was.

They were going to go ahead.

But without me.

I stopped before I reached the doorway. I couldn't maintain my pretense of calm in there. Not if my father asked me again for that unattainable *Time* magazine. I tried to look casual as I turned back toward the table. Van Hoof and Holger were debating how to deal with Krüger.

I stepped behind van Hoof's chair to reach the counter where the pot sat on the hot plate. The main room was so chilly that fat had congealed on top of the liquid. I picked up a spoon, while at the same time I extended my other hand to turn on the burner.

"Leave it alone," van Hoof said without looking at me. "*Moambe* must cool undisturbed." He resumed his conversation with Holger. "Krüger won't know Casey isn't with us. I'll have him in custody before he reaches the meeting point."

Holger said, "We must be ready if you don't succeed in your first attempt."

"We can make it difficult for him to recognize that I'm posing as Casey," Erika said. "Get him to come out in the open while I'm still some distance from him."

"You have to be close enough to cover the major," Bert said.

I stared at the *moambe*. The grease layer was thicker now,

the smell of chicken fat blocking the mingled odors of the spices. I still had the long-handled spoon in my hand. Carefully, I laid it on the counter.

"It will work," van Hoof said to Holger.

It wouldn't. Van Hoof and Erika against Krüger? An imbalance. One that only I could redress. I was the key to this. I wanted Stefan out first. But it wasn't going to happen. There was no way I could rescue him on my own. No way I could get myself and my father back home again without their help. I couldn't back out—I had nothing to back into.

I picked up the spoon. When I pierced the greasy layer of palmnut sauce, the steam that rose through the gap made the skin on my fingers tingle.

"No," Bert whimpered as though I'd hurt him.

I pointed the spoon at Holger like a sword. "All right," I said. "I'll do my part."

"Good," Holger replied. "With Kathryn the plan *will* work. We have the advantage now. We've forced Krüger into hiding. Eliminated the henchmen he used as guards. Cut him off from his terrorist connections. He's operating alone, in terrain that van Hoof knows as well as he does. He asked for this meeting, not us. This time, we are the stronger ones."

Holger stood, and for a half second I thought he was going to lift his arms in the same batwing gesture he used to end the Lutheran worship service, as if to invoke a divine blessing on our mission.

But he looked at me.

And his arms remained at his sides.

25

The Elbe moved swiftly between weedy banks, the swollen waters the same shade as the low-hanging overcast. Erika and I stood ten feet from the river, our bicycles leaning against a waist-high concrete wall. Buttoned into a padded blue cotton coat, her hair covered by a matching blue kerchief, Erika sucked hungrily on a cigarette. The smoke wreathed her head, another dulled-out shade of gray on this dour day. I glanced around, checking all directions for any sign that we'd been followed as we biked our way to this vacant lot near the river. I saw nothing alarming. On the hill above us, the spires of Albrechtsburg Castle stabbed upward, a brooding reminder of Meissen's golden age in the thirteenth century.

It was fifteen minutes past noon on Tuesday. My meeting with Krüger was scheduled to take place at twelve-thirty in Meissen's only tourist attraction, the museum attached to the chinaware factory. Since the early 1700s, this village had manufactured so-called Dresden china, each hand-painted piece identified on its back by the hallmark crossed blue swords.

Crossed. And double-crossed. As I'd feared, Holger had ended up orchestrating every detail of the mission. For safety, he and van Hoof had gone elsewhere to communicate with Krüger, physically distancing themselves from the rest of us in the warehouse. I couldn't fault the technique. But the secrecy made me ache all over, my muscles wired tight by edgy uneasiness.

Shut out of the planning, I'd found a deck of cards and inveigled my father into an endless game of solitaire. Then I'd focused on Stefan. After we captured Krüger, we had to move immediately to free Stefan. Bert and I reviewed the detail maps, checking out the three places in Germany where Gorm suspected that Stefan might be confined. We found them scattered along a north-south line running through Berlin.

Northwest of us, in Rostock, somewhere on the grounds of the former IMES armament factory.

Far to the south, a villa on the shore of Tegern See.

Outside Berlin, in a fenced-off section of the old Soviet garrison at Reisa. I was tempted to focus on that one, closest to Krüger's cabin. But it was also the most likely red herring.

Bert and I roughed out plans for a swift assault at each location. We rehearsed the best-case scenario, everything going right, Krüger ending up in custody, telling us where to find Stefan. And then Bert and I went through it again the other way, everything going wrong.

Unnecessary, perhaps, with business moving smoothly ahead on schedule. By midnight on Monday, Holger and van Hoof had agreed with Krüger on a supposedly neutral site for the meeting. Years ago, during my stay in Denmark, Holger had described to me how this game was played, the tedious bluff and counterbluff required. Step by careful step, he worked toward that point where it was his adversary who proposed the outcome Holger favored.

According to van Hoof, Holger's moves against Krüger had been "brilliant." The result was that Erika and I were in Meissen, a location that van Hoof deemed "ideal."

Nothing about it felt right to me. I scanned the riverbank in both directions. "I don't like this," I said.

Erika inhaled the last bit of smoke and dropped the butt to the ground. "You may not have to see Krüger. Hans could take him prisoner before he gets inside the museum."

"That would require a lot of luck."

"Not likely, I agree." She tugged her kerchief forward to the edge of her hairline. Then she reached over and adjusted mine to match. She and I were dressed alike in the pre-unification garb still doing service among thrifty women in the former GDR. We were two sturdy *fräuleins* in thick wool stockings and heavy shoes cycling through the cultural sites of Saxony—unfashionable and uninteresting. "But surely you can't be too concerned about this meeting. It's all preliminaries, working out details and safeguards for Stefan's release—the where-when-how. When I give the signal, Hans will move in on Krüger and we'll be finished."

I leaned out over the wall to look upriver. Nothing unusual in that direction. I turned back to Erika. "The whole thing assumes Krüger will act rationally. That's not a safe assumption."

"Let's take it one step at a time," she advised.

"Right." Foreboding flavored my tone.

"Apparently you have an unhappy outcome in mind."

"You bet," I said. "Van Hoof fails to capture Krüger. Instead, Krüger takes me in exchange for Stefan. He drags me along with him to Tripoli."

Her expression grew harder to read, as though she were evaluating me. "As long as you keep your distance from Krüger, he won't have an opportunity to force you to do anything. Make sure you can reach your weapon."

My hand went to the small of my back, where the Browning was concealed beneath the knee-length coat. I brought my hand in front again and fingered the buttons. I'd wait until I was about to go indoors, then open up the coat. I didn't want to expose my gun while bicycling through Meissen. I said to Erika, "Fine and good, so long as Krüger's alone. Can we be sure he will be?"

"He'll be alone," she said briskly. "He has too many enemies. He can't reveal his plot to anyone new at this late date."

"That's Holger's logic, but do you—"

She cut me off. "We can rely on Holger."

Holger's reliability wasn't my problem. Something else was bothering me, something I hadn't worked out.

Before I could explain, Erika said, "You trust me now, I think. Yet along the way you lost all faith in Stefan—a faith you now appear to have regained. But only at the expense of Holger Sorensen. Now your certainty of betrayal is focused on him."

Not betrayal. Something else. I said, "If you take a look at everything that's gone wrong—"

"Not relevant. Holger would not turn you over to Krüger." She paused. "You know Goethe?"

"You mean *Faust*?"

"Not Goethe's drama. His poetry." She spoke slowly, reciting. " 'Until one is committed, there is hesitancy, the chance to draw back, always ineffectiveness, concerning all acts of initiative and creation.' " Her voice went back to normal. "We start out fighting these terrorists because of love. Love of country; love of mankind; as with Hans, love of a child—. But the struggle changes us, changes our motive. And unless we guard against it, we become like them, motivated only by hate."

"You're saying that's what's happened to Holger—"

"No." Her fingers wrapped around my upper arms. "I'm saying that's what's happened to you."

"What are you talking about?"

"Hatred calculates acceptable losses. Hatred looks always for others who hate, who betray, who deceive. We cannot allow that distrust. We must keep faith with one another." Her hands were still on my arms, not moving.

I felt as if she'd shaken me, rattled something loose inside. Something close to truth. I'd begun this thing in December, driven by my love for Stefan. But that love was buried under the other emotions I'd heaped on top of it. Envy at first. Distrust, yes. And a feverish desire to punish Krüger. But this wasn't the moment to get into motives. "Dammit, Erika, I need to know how I'm going to protect myself in there—"

"Stop! Stop calculating odds." She pulled me closer. Our faces were inches apart and I saw the perspiration glistening on her upper lip, the perfect teeth in her mouth. "You must focus only on this task. Otherwise, at the instant when you most need to act, you will hesitate. And that hesitation will cost us everything."

"You'll try to protect me. But Krüger—"

"Runs on hate." My cheek felt Erika's lips, warm and pliant. She moved her head, and her breath was in my ear, a soft puff of warmth. "Love will win," she whispered.

We stood there, frozen, for at least fifteen seconds. Inside my chest I felt a soul-wrenching heart-soreness that left my eyes wet, my voice silent. I was overcome by a shapeless desire to cherish this moment. The top of Erika's head grazed my jawline. When my mother put her arms around me after I was fully grown, her hair always brushed me in that same way. My body remembered that physical sensation, the loving embrace of someone smaller than I was. I had an aching sense that a precious gift had been bestowed on me.

"Boldness," Erika said slowly, quoting a piece of the poem I'd heard before. " 'Boldness has genius, power and magic in it.' " She released my arms and turned her back, reaching for her bike. "It's time," she said, her voice matter-of-fact.

I was behind her as we pedaled away from the riverbank toward the porcelain factory. She stopped once, so suddenly that I bumped her rear tire. She waited for a rattling old-style Fiat to pass us in the other direction, making adjustments to her right pedal while she studied the driver. Satisfied that he was no threat, she got back on and continued. Even in the bulky clothes, she was graceful. After a minute, I found myself struggling to keep up with her. Or maybe I wasn't as eager to get to our destination. Once I was out of Erika's grip, away from her gaze, all my fears came back.

My front wheel skittered across a pothole and I had to catch myself with my right foot to keep from tipping over. I got the bike moving again, pedaling harder to catch up. The air was thick with river mist, the droplets wetting my cheeks.

I'd wanted to alert Erika to the pattern I'd seen, the misdirection that flowed from Holger Sorensen. She'd missed the point, thought I was accusing Holger of betrayal. And then she'd put herself in my corner in the most personal way.

Or was she only doing the trainer's job, saying whatever worked best to get the nervous fighter ready to face a stronger opponent?

The street cut between two halves of the factory, the walls rising from the curb on each side of us to create an ocher canyon, banded far above eye level by rows of windows. Their many panes were glazed with a winter's worth of grit. We parked our bikes in a rack where state-of-the-art Italian racing bikes mingled with balloon-tire two-wheelers that looked like they'd first seen use during World War II. I smelled clay dust and the chemical scent of paint. The place was recognizably industrial and I found myself listening for machinery, hydraulics— some factory noise. But I didn't hear even the whir of a distant forklift. Only the slap of Erika's leather soles on the damp cobblestones as she continued another fifty paces to the museum entrance. As we'd agreed, I stayed out of sight of the entry while she paid our admission.

The silence made me nervous. Holger preferred to set clandestine meetings in public places where the participants could come and go unnoticed. I'd hoped to find at least one tour bus parked outside and a score of earnest porcelain lovers in the museum. I didn't want another private chat with Krüger. But the street was deserted and even the factory workers seemed to be out to lunch.

The holster lay snugly against my back. I touched my coat button. No, it was too soon to open up. I couldn't see Erika. I ran a finger under the kerchief knot at the back of my neck. It was damp with nervous sweat. Why was it taking her so long? Was the vendor unwilling to sell her a pair of tickets? I listened, trying to hear her voice.

Wrong focus. It cost me critical seconds. Behind me, an iron door scraped across the curbstones. At the instant that I identified the noise, a hand was over my mouth, a strong arm around my torso, and I was moving backward into a loading entrance—all before I could make a sound.

The back of my head was jammed against the jaw of my captor. I smelled again his heavy aftershave. Overlaid now with the unwashed odor of a man who hours before had done sweaty labor and gotten a sexual thrill from it. I struggled, but the right arm banding my body only tightened. The gloved left hand over my mouth had the rough texture of cowhide. I bit down hard, but my teeth couldn't cut through the leather. I tasted something vile, like spoiled meat.

Inside, my captor spun us around so that he was between me and the doorway. He shoved me away from him, my face forward. My cheekbone crashed against the top riser of a set of gritty stairs. The metal door scraped shut again behind me, throwing the hallway into darkness. Splinters stabbed my fingers as I scrabbled, trying to pull myself up the stairs. I got my feet under me, but my leather soles were slick from the dampness outside. My right shoe slipped off the edge of the stair. I went with the momentum, swinging my leg back, trying to strike the man's groin.

He grabbed my shoe and jerked.

My forehead banged against the top two stairs. My knees thudded against the bottom tread. Kneeling, I fumbled at my coat buttons, trying to get to my gun.

"Hands above your head." Reinhardt Krüger's voice sounded bored. I felt pressure between my shoulder blades. Big and heavy. Something large-caliber.

"Where have you concealed your weapon?" he asked.

I twisted my neck to look at him, but I saw only a silhouette against the strip of light outlining the exit door. "I don't—"

"I will search you." He must have flexed his left hand. I heard a sound like pumice on skin, the gloved fingers sliding against one another.

The taste of the glove burned in my mouth. I thought of it touching my body and shuddered. "Holstered at the back," I said.

He motioned me to stand. "Unbuckle the belt."

If I could get my body between him and the gun, I might be able to find a way to take a shot at him. My hands went to my coat buttons as I moved to face him.

"Don't turn. And don't open your coat. Lift it so that I can see the gun. And then unbuckle the belt."

I did as he said. Before the holster touched the floor, he caught it with his left hand. He pulled the Browning free and shoved it into his waistband. "Go up the steps," he said. "I have something to show you."

At the top of the stairs was a door-lined hallway. He shoved me through the first opening on my right. I was in a rectangular room. The only light came from the multipaned windows. I looked out on the street where I'd been standing moments before. From here, Krüger had watched me and Erika, waiting for that moment when he could take me by surprise.

Centered in front of the windows was a worktable holding a potter's wheel powdered with white clay dust. Empty now, but it was clearly set up for demonstration purposes rather than for production. The space in front of the worktable was filled by a set of risers like those used by choral groups. At the far end was another door. The Meissen people probably used this room and others along the hallway for visiting tour groups. They could show, step by step, how they created highly polished porcelain. Very low-tech, very efficient, very East German.

I heard the tick-tick-tick of metal on metal, a key in a padlock. Metal chain links jingled together. I turned toward the sound.

The heavy glove now clutched a large steel ring attached to a length of chain. Krüger yanked on it, pulling upright a figure who'd been locked into a crouching position in the shadowy corner past the door. Krüger jerked to bring the figure closer.

"So," he said, "what is my little brother's life worth to you?"

26

$\int$tefan!

Not possible. Removing Stefan from confinement before we'd arranged the exchange was far too risky for Krüger. Or so Holger had argued. Wrong again.

Stefan beside me, close enough to touch. Krüger had made the one move for which I had no countermove.

My eyes jittered around the room. Suddenly, it was impossible to make myself look at Stefan. To see how much damage Krüger had done to him.

But I had to know how bad it was.

I managed to focus on the feet. Shackled at the ankles. The cross chain linked by a yard of vertical chain to another piece binding the wrists. The shortness of the vertical chain forced him to hunch his back and the ankle shackles shortened his gait, making Stefan stand like my arthritic father.

My eyes moved upward, to his hands. The tapering fingers were flaccid, powerless, the nail missing from the right thumb. Skin on the wrists on each side of the cuffs was raw. Shirtsleeve stained, torn half off at the shoulder seam. The skin on his jaw was swollen, reddish purple. His cheekbones disappeared into the puffy flesh. And his nose was bent crooked by a break. I cataloged each wound as if I were a scientist. No place now for feeling. Keep it away. Keep it distant. Get on with this.

I felt a puff of cold air against the back of my neck. A door to the outside had opened somewhere behind me. Erika? Van Hoof? If either of them was coming to help me, I couldn't let Krüger hear. Quickly, I said, "Stefan's almost dead. Not worth much to me in this condition."

"Disoriented, is all," Krüger replied. "Rather like your father." He shook his head. "Given your unfortunate genetic heritage, it was wise of you not to breed."

"Too bad your mother didn't make the same choice," I said.

He laughed, the sound hollow in the near-empty room. "I do look forward to the opportunity to enjoy more of your wit," he said. "I will leave my poor little brother for his friends to claim. And you will come with me."

"And if I won't?"

"We both know you're coming." His voice was thicker now, full of the pleasure of conquest, a word that has no meaning unless there is someone to be subjugated.

I said, "You roughed him up for my benefit, didn't you?"

Krüger laughed again. "I've studied you. I know how your mind works. Not by deduction, like your sanctimonious Danish friend thinks. But inductively, from the specific to the general. You can extrapolate from his current appearance how he will look after a sojourn among those who have vowed to punish him for his crimes."

Vowed? The unexpected word set off a ping somewhere in the back of my mind, like a phone jolted by electrical activity up the line. But the sound of it was pushed aside as I struggled not to imagine what would happen to Stefan if he ended up in Libya.

I couldn't take my eyes from the battered face. Each long eyelash lay as if etched atop the swollen flesh. My right hand went out and my index finger gently brushed the bruise along his cheekbone. In response, his eyelids slowly rose. My left hand formed a fist as I steeled myself, expecting to see in those eyes the same incomprehension I'd seen in my father's.

The awareness in his glance was so vivid, it seemed to light the room. His eyes bored into mine for a microsecond. Then his eyelids closed and reopened in a deliberate blink to show me again the clear hazel flecked with gold.

I sank down onto the lowest step. I bent over, my elbows on my knees, my head in my hands. "All right," I told Krüger, letting my voice crack. "I'll go with you."

"Of course you will," Krüger said, relaxing the tension on the chain.

Stefan sat beside me. I slid my arm behind his neck. "Let me say good-bye." I pressed my cheek against his and spoke loud enough for Krüger to hear. "*Moj skarbie.*" My treasure.

"*Sztuczka,*" Stefan breathed in reply. The harsh syllables sounded like nonsense. Possibly a slurred endearment. Not identifiable as communication unless you knew an obscure Polish word for "trick."

A chill filled the pit of my stomach. Krüger wasn't going to trade Stefan for me—the outcome I'd accused Holger of wanting. We'd both be going to Tripoli. This was a charade to pacify me long enough to get out of Meissen and headed south. I murmured, "*Rozumiem.*" The rumble of Polish that means "I understand."

"No conversation," Krüger ordered. He pointed the pistol at my sternum. "Move away from him."

"Please," I said in a pitiful voice. "A few more seconds." I maneuvered Stefan's head against my chest, pushed my face against his matted hair. I felt the warmth of his scalp and breathed in his scent. "*Tak,*" I whispered. Polish for "yes." Danish for "thank you." I used the word in bed, a coded signal my lover understood. It fit now, too. Swift, simultaneous, praise-the-Lord-type action was what we needed now.

Steel prodded my ear. "Out of the way," Krüger demanded.

I relaxed my embrace and let Stefan's head slump forward onto his knees. Krüger moved the pistol so that it no longer touched me. I stood and took a step to my left.

Krüger kept the gun in his right hand, pointed at me. The chain in his left hand was connected to the one binding Stefan's wrists. Krüger tugged on his end, trying to pull Stefan to his feet so he could drag him back into the corner, rechain him to the radiator.

But Stefan toppled forward instead, onto his knees. He screamed, a shriek without artifice, one forced out by real pain. I started toward him.

"Don't move." Krüger still had the gun pointed in my direction.

I stopped, but my nerve ends were tingling. I was on the balls of my feet, ready.

Krüger extended his left arm, as though to grab the handcuff chain, the better to drag Stefan's inert form the last few feet.

With a clatter of chain, Stefan exploded upward. His head slammed into Krüger's midsection. The German grunted as the air rushed from his lungs. He lunged backward into the worktable. The potter's wheel crashed to the floor, sending up a white whirlwind of dust and the schoolroom odor of modeling clay.

Krüger's pistol skittered across the floor toward me. I jumped forward and grabbed it.

But Krüger was quick. Standing again. Stefan in front of him, blocking my shot. Stefan's head tipped back, eyes shut, the length of chain a line of silver ovals across his Adam's apple. The ringed end was still in Krüger's gloved left hand. But now he held the other end with his right.

"Let him go," I said.

Krüger smiled. "Throw my pistol to me."

I held the pistol tightly in both hands and sighted down the barrel. One shot right between Krüger's eyes. That was what I needed to save us both.

The wire-rimmed glasses sat atop the bridge of Krüger's nose. Below was the smooth skin of Stefan's forehead. He gagged as the chain tightened across his windpipe. His skin was luminous in the shadowy room. Was he turning blue? Too dim to see. Too scant a margin of error to shoot.

I lowered the gun. "Let him breathe." I set the pistol on the floor. The metal rattled dully when I shoved it toward Krüger.

His right hand released the chain. Stefan fell forward onto his knees again. He gave a strangled moan and toppled sideways, his torso falling across the pistol. He didn't seem to notice, clutching at his throat with both hands, struggling for air.

Krüger's leg drew back as though he were going to kick Stefan off the gun.

Behind him, the window shattered, the clatter of breaking glass simultaneous with the report from Erika's Browning.

I threw myself down beside Stefan. His trouser leg was darkened around the knee and I smelled blood.

I shouted to Erika, "My gun—"

The crack of the pistol cut me off. Something bit into the soft flesh of my calf. I made a noise somewhere between a scream and a groan, then jammed my hand under Stefan's torso, my fingers trying to find the other weapon. His belly was warm and heavy against the back of my hand. I felt the weight of him ease as he tried to help.

I was on my stomach, my back to Krüger, my head toward the open doorway. Like an avenging angel, Erika slid into view. She stood, legs apart, the Browning in both hands.

Behind me, a click, Krüger hand-cocking the weapon he'd taken from me.

My fingers found the pistol grip beneath Stefan, closed around it. My leg throbbed, anticipating the hot tearing of my flesh.

"Kill him!" I screamed at Erika.

"We need him alive." Her voice was calm. "Drop the gun," she said to Krüger.

"All right," he said. And then he swung the barrel from me to her.

The force of the bullet drove Erika back into the hallway. Her weapon fired, too, the bullet smashing upward into the ceiling, knocking loose a rain of plaster.

I yanked Krüger's weapon from under Stefan. I rolled onto my back and fired toward where he'd been.

Krüger cradled his empty gun hand in the gloved one. He sprang across the room and vanished through the door. His boots thundered down the hallway. Like a thing apart, my conscious mind noted the noise. He hadn't gone out the door I'd come in. He was running the other way.

Stefan pushed himself to a sitting position. "You're hurt," he said, staring at my calf.

"Not as bad as you." There was a red streak across the back of my calf. If there was a bullet in me, I couldn't feel it. I stood, putting my weight on the leg. Not bad.

Gun in hand, I limped over to Erika. She was on her back, her limbs flung out to form an X, the thick blue coat as flat and lifeless as the cloth torso of a homemade doll. Her kerchief was gone, and with it, the top of her skull. I shut my eyes. I no longer could look at her.

I registered the sounds of a door opening and Krüger's footsteps growing fainter. And nothing else. Krüger must have bribed his way into these empty rooms, paid more to be sure we weren't disturbed. The blast of gunfire gave the workers another incentive to keep their distance from us.

My eyes were open again, but seeing nothing. My fingers worked at the knot holding the kerchief on my head. Chains dragged against the floor as Stefan crawled toward me. I ripped the square of blue cloth off me and dropped it. Covering Erika's face, I hoped. If I looked again at what Krüger had done to her, my heart would burst, my own head split apart.

"Someone will call the police," Stefan said. "We've got to get out of here—"

I didn't wait to hear the rest of it. Escape, yes, that was important. But stopping Krüger was more important. Before I reached the decision to go after him, I was running down the hallway. At the end was a carved wooden door. I flung it open.

A three-foot-tall porcelain nymph extended a graceful hand to me in welcome. Her skin was translucent, her white tunic was edged with gold and her cobalt-blue eyes were as hard as her kiln-dried heart.

The room before me was crowded with chinaware. The light glinting off the hand-painted colors pricked at my eyes. The designs were wild with ruffles and leaves and flounces, all edged in such sharp relief that they bristled like spines.

I was in the museum, the spot where I'd expected to have a sterile chat with Krüger. Where van Hoof was supposed to be in position. I moved carefully toward the rear, my eyes scanning for any sign of either man. Flush with the wall at the back was another metal door—another delivery entrance. A broken padlock lay on the floor in front of it, but the crossbar was still in its groove. If Krüger had gotten in here, he hadn't yet gotten out.

A dinner plate smashed into the wall beside me, fracturing into conchoidal pieces, like flakes of a broken seashell. I jumped aside and a bust of Homer whizzed by my ear, twenty pounds of unglazed bisque splintering against the floor. I ducked behind a display case, sweeping aside an ugly tureen shaped and colored like a tortoise. It fell soundlessly onto the carpet beside me, then disintegrated.

The barrage of china continued. Despite his wounded hand, Krüger fired steadily. Plates and cups flew by from a service for twelve.

I raised myself to bring my eyes level with the top of the display case.

The edge of a serving platter hit my temple a half inch above my left eye. The dish fragmented on the top of the case, a fountain of china shards forcing me to shut my eyes as I fired wildly toward Krüger.

Blood welled in the cut. When I did open my eyes, I could

see only out of the right one. I pressed on the wound with my left hand, pushed myself upward with the heel of my right, avoiding the now-jagged edge of the cabinet.

No missiles came toward me. Instead, I heard the sound of the crossbar sliding back. I couldn't get off a shot before Krüger was out that door. I wiped my bloody eye on my sleeve as I ran across the room, ignoring the pain pulsing upward from my calf. I jumped through the doorway onto a loading dock. A sleek black Saab was parked in front of it. Krüger was even with the driver's door, reaching for the handle. I dropped to one knee and aimed for his legs, sighting one-eyed; my first shot went wide. He yanked open the door and jumped inside. As the ignition fired, so did I. I got the left rear tire. But it didn't stop him. The Saab shot forward. I threw myself onto my stomach, braced my elbows. Blood oozed down my forehead as I aimed for the other tire. I pulled the trigger again. Nothing. Out of ammunition. And Krüger was out of sight.

Thick fingers tightened on my shoulder. "I saw," van Hoof said. "But I was too late."

"Set-up," I said, shoving myself to my feet, blotting again at the cut above my eye. "He was ready for us."

"And such a simple ruse to delay me," van Hoof said. "I saw through it at once, but alone, I had no way to speed things along. If I'd had Bert with me—"

"Save it," I said, leading him back inside. "We've got to hurry."

Stefan had dragged himself and Erika to the bottom of the steps beside the exit door. He looked up at us, the Browning cradled in his hands. "Saw you drive up," he said to van Hoof. He saw my face. "He got away?"

"Couldn't stop him."

Van Hoof was staring at Erika. Stefan had tied the blue cloth so that it covered her wound. He'd cleaned her face; her cheeks were no longer spattered by blood and brains.

Van Hoof touched Erika's cheek. Then his arms went beneath her neck and knees and he lifted her.

I opened the door. Stefan hauled himself upright, draped an arm across my shoulders. Stumbling and clanking like a chain gang of the living dead, we crossed that deserted street to the vehicle van Hoof had driven to Meissen. It had the shape of a VW minibus, a windowless once-white van typical of those used by repairmen laboring to preserve the crumbling Communist infrastructure. Van Hoof got behind the wheel. I lay between Stefan and Erika in the rear under a tarp.

The major quickly got us out of town and off the main roads. Once we were in less danger of discovery by the German police, I shoved back the tarp and found an iron file for Stefan. I used a rag and spit to clean some of the blood off my face and leg. While Stefan worked away with the file, he described his time as Krüger's prisoner, most of those forty hours spent heavily shackled and beaten to a near coma. "He wanted me immobilized, within sight every second."

"Within sight?" van Hoof repeated from the front seat.

"Chained to him most of the time. He loves me that much." His tone grew somber. "Casey, you should never have agreed to meet with him."

"She didn't want to," van Hoof said, his tone grudging. "But we had no better option, according to Holger."

"Holger." Stefan's voice was thick with something like anger, something like sadness. "His talent is analysis. Logical analysis. He says I become irrational when it comes to Reinhardt. But my brother isn't logical where I'm concerned. So many times, when we were boys . . ." His voice faded, as if he couldn't overcome his habit of hiding his brother from me.

"What, did you grow up with him?" I asked.

He shook his head. "He was ten years older, half grown when I was born. He came to us only for a month each summer. But that was enough."

"Enough?"

"The first visit I remember, he was already fifteen. I was only five. You can imagine the rest."

I could. "Didn't your father—"

"He punished Reinhardt, of course."

But fear of punishment hadn't stopped him from tormenting his little brother. "The police will be interested in Gunter Storch now," I said. "And his cover's gotten thin. They'll soon discover his true identity."

"My brother will have to flee Germany immediately."

"To Libya," I said, "in order to evade the Mossad."

"And to escape from us," van Hoof added.

Stefan said, "He has not shown much concern about you."

I was beginning to understand how Krüger had so easily outmaneuvered us all. I kept that thought to myself, though. "We're a sideshow he's running for his own amusement. The main event is the one he's planning for Wednesday."

"Yes," Stefan said. "He expects tomorrow's action to guarantee him a rosy future in Tripoli."

"Did you learn what he's planning?" I asked.

"Of course not. He's careful with me. But he let slip one odd thing." Stefan glanced at his leg. "He'd worked his way to my kneecap. Then he started talking as if he were an American gangster, the way he did after he saw the Godfather movie." He imitated Krüger's accented attempt at slang. " 'I shoulda fixed it so her old man got his plane ride. Give the suckers a real bargain. Two days early, but close enough. What the hell. Call it a baker's dozen.' " He winced, as if reliving the blow that must have followed those words. "I don't know that phrase, 'baker's dozen.' "

"One dozen plus one extra." Slowly, I worked it out aloud. "Krüger gave my dad a bomb to carry on board his flight yesterday. One extra, two days early." I paused. "*Hellig tre Konger*," I said.

"Right," Stefan said. "Tomorrow, January sixth, is Three Kings Day."

In English-speaking countries, Twelfth Night. Twelve planes on the twelfth day of Christmas. That was what Krüger planned. An epiphany for a madman.

27

"Could Krüger blow up a dozen planes in a single day?" I asked Stefan.

"The explosives would have to be virtually undetectable," Stefan replied slowly.

"That technology exists," van Hoof said. "The Global 500 bombing is proof."

Stefan added, "The men planting the bombs might have to change planes as often as four times to reach that many targets in twenty-four hours. It would require intricate synchronization. A plan of great complexity and technical brilliance."

"Krüger could formulate that plan." My voice was flat.

Stefan said, "Tactical precision has always been his special talent."

"And if the different terrorist groups supply the manpower—"

"With each bomb squad aware of only its own targets . . ." Stefan added.

"Then nobody can stop it from happening," I concluded.

Van Hoof cut in. "They could halt all air traffic to conduct a worldwide search, but it would be impossible to find all the explosives. And no authority would order so many planes grounded on the basis of an unsubstantiated threat."

"Krüger's people must be in position by now," I said. "And

he'll have made the plan fail-safe. They'll go ahead, all of them, without another word from him."

Van Hoof's palm slammed against the edge of the steering wheel. "We were so close. We could have captured him. We could have forced him to tell us which planes."

"He'll have made a list of them," Stefan said. "No one could safely rely on his memory for twelve flight numbers."

"You could," I said.

"Perhaps." He shrugged. "Reinhardt could not."

I remembered Krüger at our meeting in his cabin. Lips moving as he confirmed a date written on an index card. Perhaps he didn't trust his memory. But what did that matter now?

Van Hoof put my thoughts into words. "We don't even know where *he* is." He exhaled, a loud sigh of defeat.

Krüger had escaped. There was no way now to halt the murderous events he'd arranged for Wednesday. All we could do was return to Berlin and report our failure.

The route we took was safe but rough. Every pothole jarred us. Involuntary moans escaped from Stefan. I hurt, too—my head, my leg, my heart.

Erika's body pressed against my side. From time to time her leg would jounce against mine, then settle back. As though she were an exhaustion-drugged child restlessly napping beside an older sister, never waking, accustomed since birth to sleeping against me.

But the closeness I'd felt with Erika wasn't an old habit of sisterhood. That surge of affection between us was new, all-consuming in its newness, like the muscle-weakening rapture that sweeps through a new mother when she first touches her baby.

I'd wanted to stop time and marvel over that recent bond. Count its ten tiny fingers. Flex each of its perfect toes. Run my fingertips over its soft, pink skin. Inhale the heady, yeasty, brand-new smell. But Erika was dead before I'd begun.

The pain inside me felt as though bundles of muscles and

nerves were being peeled off my rib cage. I turned onto my side to look at Erika. Then pressed my face against her coat sleeve. I smelled smoke from her cigarettes and the residue left after she'd fired her weapon. The odor of ashes. A spasm shook my body, a convulsion that pushed me more tightly against her.

Stefan must have felt it. He moved, spooning his body around my back. I needed warmth. I let him stay close.

Van Hoof continued north. He followed dirt tracks across fallow fields, drove silently through a forest on a pine-needle carpet, idled slowly for a time behind a herd of reddish-colored milk cows on a muddy farm road. He didn't look at his map.

By the time we reached our warehouse headquarters, it was dark. Van Hoof swung the van to the far side of the stacked blocks, flashed the headlights twice, then turned off the ignition. He rolled down the driver's-side window and cold air surged into the van. After a half minute, Hilly-Anne's pale face was framed in the opening, her hand inside her jacket.

Van Hoof said something in Flemish. I heard Erika's name. Then, from the woman, an expletive powered as much by sorrow as by rage. Hurried footsteps on the gravel. A second face at the window, hair skinned back in a ducktail. Danièle. Van Hoof kept talking, giving instructions. He turned, asked Stefan a question.

Stefan slowly spelled out a long German surname.

Van Hoof turned back to the women.

"We must get out now," Stefan told me. "Hilly-Anne and Danièle will take the van."

I clutched Erika's shoulder. My voice came out too harsh. "Disposing of the body?"

"They'll bring her to a man who's helped us before," Stefan said. He put his hand on my wrist. "He'll take care of her and the paperwork."

I unclenched my fingers. But I didn't move my hand.

Stefan gently lifted it away. "Her parents. We'll send her home, to them."

Yes. They'd need that. I knew nothing of Jewish funerals. But I knew grief.

I sat up. When van Hoof opened the rear door, I climbed out to the ground. Together, we helped Stefan out. Then I slammed the door. Van Hoof supported Stefan as he limped toward the warehouse. I lingered for another minute, watching Hilly-Anne pull herself up behind the wheel. Her door thudded shut. Then, Danièle slammed the passenger door. They were both leaving. With Krüger on the run, we no longer needed sentries. The headlights cut a swath through the darkness. I smelled exhaust, felt the heat blow against my leg. Tires grumbled over the frozen stones. The van rolled slowly forward and out of the lot. I watched until the taillights disappeared.

I had to let her go. Erika, so newly my friend. She'd died protecting me. Oh! Standing there, alone now in that cold, lifeless place, it hurt me so to let her slip away.

I turned and walked toward the warehouse. I felt as if I were slogging through mud.

Inside, I went directly to the cubicle where I'd left my father. I found him playing against Bert in a game of cribbage. A space heater glowed in the corner and the air was thick with the smell of unwashed clothes. My father moved his peg along the board, counting under his breath. He looked up at me, annoyed, then resumed counting. He was winning. He hadn't beaten me at cribbage in the past couple of years. Why hadn't I noticed that? Why hadn't I let him win a game from time to time? Bert was better than I was at dealing with my father's illness.

"Bert," I began.

The seams in his face had deepened to grooves. "The major told me," he said in a worn voice. "You all right?"

"Alive." I took a deep breath, wanting to say more about Erika, not knowing how.

My father spoke first, his tone irritated. "Kathryn. You and the others have to leave us alone now. We're right in the middle of something." He gathered up the cards, formed them into a pile. "Come back later, there's a good girl." He shuffled noisily.

"I'll cut them, if you don't mind," Bert said to my father. He reached for the deck, waved me away without looking up. Maybe no better than I was at dealing with death.

I went back to the barren main room. The lighted kitchen area floated in the darkness, like a solitary vessel abandoned on a night sea. Holger sat in the center of the table's long side, empty chairs flung haphazardly around him. I'd never seen him smoke, but the ashtray in front of him was full of cigarette stubs. Smoky trails drifted in front of the shop lights and hazed his face so I couldn't read his expression. I started toward him.

Cold wind ruffled my hair. Van Hoof was holding the entry door open. The same German doctor came through it. Van Hoof waved a hand toward me, saying something about Stefan. The doctor nodded, then strode toward the table. Van Hoof holstered his pistol, shut and bolted the door and moved toward the second cubicle, a dim light marking Stefan's whereabouts.

By the time the doctor reached the table, I'd taken the chair closest to Holger and peeled the homemade bandage off my leg. The doctor prodded my wound and handed me a bottle of isopropyl alcohol and a packet of sterile pads. He glanced at the cut above my eye, gave a dismissive sniff. Van Hoof reappeared, asked a question in German. The doctor muttered a word I took to mean "superficial." He doled out rolls of gauze and adhesive tape, then hurried off to the room where Stefan waited.

Van Hoof rummaged on the counter, shoving the instant-coffee jar aside. Canned goods clattered onto the floor. His hand was around the long neck of a whiskey bottle, which he thumped on the table, next to the ashtray. He found a glass, poured two inches of amber liquid, then tossed it back. A second shot followed. He kept the half-full glass in one hand as he dragged a chair around to face Holger.

A plastic tumbler rolled into my foot. I bent to retrieve it, set it beside the bottle. Without a word, Holger picked up the bottle, filled the tumbler. I slid the drinking glass toward me, smelled the pungent odor of Scotch. The smooth heat slid down my throat. I ran my tongue over my lips, sweeping in the peaty flavor of single malt. A famous whiskey, one distilled only a few kilometers from the Global 500 crash site. Like a lost soul, I'd come full circle from the first disaster to the unimaginable horror soon to follow.

I brushed my fingers over my forehead. Blood had dried in the cut, forming a scab. I left it alone. I turned my leg to see the three-inch furrow across the meat of my calf. New blood oozed from the wound. I swallowed the bitter dregs of my failure and tried not to make a sound as I swabbed my leg with the other kind of alcohol.

Van Hoof swirled the liquid in his glass, staring only at it. Methodically, he reported what had happened in Meissen, what we'd done, what we'd concluded about Krüger's twelfth-night program. After he finished, the only sound was the plink of water from the faucet, dripping into the metal sink.

My nostrils burned from the smell of the alcohol. My wound was wetly red and stung. I felt Holger looking at me and I raised my eyes to meet his gaze. "The problem was with the undercover intelligence," I said.

Van Hoof's voice was a growl. "Are we back to that?" He glared at me. "Holger knows his agents. Gorm passed on everything he could safely obtain. He's not responsible for our failure."

"I don't blame Gorm," I said. "But all of the Gorm information—in particular the list of places where Stefan might be imprisoned—all of that was carefully calculated so I would walk into a trap. It was coming straight from Krüger."

Holger addressed van Hoof. "Kathryn's right. He wanted to guarantee we would not attempt to rescue Stefan."

The Belgian said, "You think Krüger discovered Gorm?"

"That conclusion is inescapable now," Holger replied, his voice weary. "Clearly, by mid-December, Krüger was using

Gorm to pass false information. Certainly the items intended to lure Stefan on board Global 500. After that flight exploded, Gorm had to realize what had happened. But before he could let me know, Krüger intervened. He extracted our recognition codes from Gorm, then killed him. Krüger used Gorm's channels to mislead us. He did it so well, I was not certain until now."

I was distracted by the astringent inflaming my leg and only a part of my conscious mind followed the conversation that continued between Holger and van Hoof. I'd figured out earlier that Krüger had used—and executed—Gorm. He'd carefully calibrated the leakage of information to bolster Holger's conviction that Gorm was still functioning effectively.

I bandaged my wound and found my clothes, stacked on the floor at one end of the counter. I removed the coat I'd worn to Meissen, then carefully pulled my jeans on under the skirt before I discarded it, too. The warmth of the Scotch relaxed me and while I put on my socks and tied my boots, pieces of information slowly rearranged themselves in my brain, as though someone were moving tiles around in a mosaic, making me see all the facts in a new way.

A phrase that Krüger had used about Stefan came back to me: *Those who have vowed to punish him for his crimes*. Those words had a religious fervor. Krüger had to appease whoever had taken that vow. He couldn't be finished with his brother, not yet.

My nerve ends came alive. Silently, I inhaled and exhaled quick breaths through my mouth. I didn't have any evidence to back up my theory. I couldn't marshal facts that would convince Holger on an intellectual level. But then, it wasn't Holger's intellect I needed to address.

"Krüger did it so well." I repeated a phrase I'd heard Holger speak, my voice matter-of-fact despite my excitement. "He's studied us for years, learned how each of us thinks. Made himself an expert at our manipulation. He enmeshed us in an elaborate charade to make us think he'd defect to the U.S.A. Now he's calculated precisely how to lead us to the conclusion that he's en route to Libya."

"Of course he's on his way there," van Hoof said. "What amazes me is that he didn't go to Tripoli last November. He should have left as soon as the international press started re-printing that news photo with him in it. Absconding then would have been the prudent thing to do."

"Prudent, yes." I leaned toward van Hoof, wanting to make him pay attention to this exchange between me and Holger. "But if he behaved that rationally, he wouldn't be in Berlin now."

"You think he's here?" Holger's tone was skeptical. "Hardly the most direct route to Libya."

My eyes still on van Hoof, I said, "I'm certain Krüger's here."

Holger sniffed. "Your 'certainty' has no grounding in fact. Coming to Berlin would pose unacceptable hazards to him."

"Except," I said slowly, "we know that escaping to safety is not Krüger's only goal. If it were, he'd have continued to mislead you about his true intentions. He wouldn't have let us discover that he'd eliminated Gorm. And he wouldn't have pro-voked the German police into pursuing him."

Holger had grown still and he was watching me intently. "You're saying he has another, competing goal?"

"The man must destroy Stefan." I paused, then spoke di-rectly to van Hoof in the intimate tones of scholarly comrades. "History offers examples of similar behavior. Especially recent history."

I had van Hoof's full attention now. I pressed on. "You're thinking of Hitler, right?" I was betting that, like all old sol-diers, van Hoof knew how the Führer had sabotaged the German war effort by diverting resources to exterminate the Jews.

Van Hoof's expression was thoughtful. "Krüger might well be in Berlin."

"Definitely," I said. "He promised Stefan's enemies that Stefan would be punished. He knows they won't be pleased if he fails to keep that promise. So he's got that incentive, fear of Libyan displeasure." I was leaning halfway across the table now, so close I could see the alert interest in the Belgian's eyes. "But what's driving him is his obsessive hatred of Stefan. Krüger's like an alcoholic drinking himself to death. He can't stop. He put his entire terrorist program in jeopardy, trying to eliminate Stefan. He's got to be here, ready to try again."

Holger's eyes went from me to van Hoof, then back again to me. He was erect, spine stiff, a chess player trying to anticipate my next move. "What is the point of speculating this way?" he asked. "If Krüger is still obsessed with Stefan, what of it? How could we find him in all of Berlin?"

I didn't speak, just let the silence build while I waited.

Van Hoof didn't disappoint me. He said, "I know precisely where to find him." The words were carefully chosen. But the pace was too fast, the tone too triumphant. He'd taken the bait.

Holger knew it, too. The lines at both corners of his eyes tightened, then relaxed. As close as he might come to a wince.

"Krüger is with the Libyans at their office near Potsdamer Platz." Van Hoof made a thoughtful murmur through closed lips, but he cut it off too abruptly to have it sound like authentic rumination. "I have an excellent plan for getting into that building."

"You can't succeed," Holger objected. "Not without more people."

"Is that true?" I asked van Hoof, sure of the answer.

"No. A large force isn't necessary." Van Hoof looked at me, the ceiling, the floor, before he continued. "You, me, Holger. And Hilly-Anne and Danièle will return soon. They'll want to help, I'm sure of that. The five of us could do it."

"Preposterous," Holger said, as I'd expected him to. "It

would be an impossible job for only five people."

I said, "But not for GSG-9." Germany's crack antiterrorist squad carried the innocuous name Grenz Schutz Gruppe, Border Protection Unit. But Unit Nine had made its bones with the Bader-Meinhoff gang, then sealed its reputation in a hostage rescue at Mogadishu that numbered no hostages among the casualties. "We'd have needed help from GSG-9 to assault any one of those places where Krüger was supposed to be holding Stefan. You surely alerted the unit to that possibility. Your German counterpart must have a team standing by in Berlin right now."

"Of course he does." Stefan hobbled into the light and braced himself against the counter. His right leg was bandaged from mid-calf to mid-thigh, splinted to stiffness. "GSG-9 can mount an assault at a moment's notice."

Holger gave him a tired glance. "You think the Germans will go in there because Hans has a hunch about Krüger?"

"They will if you tell them to," Stefan said.

Holger shook his head. "You heard. There is no proof. None." Frustration drove his pitch higher. And in that thin voice, I heard an echo of the struggle between the two sides of his nature, between the Father and the Major, between faith and intellect.

I put my hand on his arm, the sweater rough against my fingertips. "Tell the Germans you have an informant. Tell them I say Krüger has a plan to blow up twelve planes and that right now he is hiding in that building."

Holger said, "But you don't know—"

I tightened my grip on his arm. "I'm wanted in connection with Global 500. You've got me, you've interrogated me and this is what I've given you." I relaxed my hand. "It doesn't matter if you believe it. Do this for me. If GSG-9 can catch Krüger, we can save the passengers on those twelve airliners. I don't have any other way out of this mess. And what have you got to lose?"

I watched his face. Something came into those attentive eyes, something softer. "You," he said. "I will have to turn you over to the German police."

The words were final, the slamming of my prison door. And I realized that Holger had guessed where I was leading. Perhaps he, too, had considered the option of using me to activate GSG-9. Pondered it, then rejected it, because of the outcome for me. An outcome I hadn't thought of. One I couldn't face. What if I *was* wrong about Krüger? Maybe he wasn't with the Libyans in their office. And if he wasn't, then getting myself out of jail again would be an impossible task. I tried to speak, but couldn't.

Stefan did it for me. "Absolutely not."

Holger turned to him. "Once I tell them I have her, I will have no choice but to surrender her to them."

Stefan opened his mouth, then shut it again. The defeated expression on his face told me that Holger was right.

How certain was I that Krüger had gone to the Libyans? It was no more than a guess. But in the end, all the best strategies begin with excellent guesswork. From somewhere in the back of my mind, I recalled another fragment from the poem that Erika had quoted to me: ". . . the moment one definitely commits oneself, then providence moves, too." Boldness. Genius. Power. Magic. Begin it now.

"I'll surrender later," I said. "There's no time for that now. They have to get Krüger before midnight."

"You'll turn yourself in?" Holger asked.

I moved my chin down, a halfhearted nod.

Now his hand covered mine. "Your word."

Keep the faith. Show me you truly believe. Let your conviction carry us both forward. My throat was so tight I could only mumble. "My word."

He squeezed my hand, then stood and went to the phone.

But that instant of soul-to-soul rapport didn't change what I had to do. "We can't wait for them," I said to van Hoof.

Van Hoof rose without speaking and went directly to the locker where he kept his supplies. The key grated against the padlock.

Stefan lowered himself into the chair beside mine, the white tape across his nose in contrast with the reddish blue of his battered face. "Your handling of Holger was masterful," he said.

"Maybe." I shrugged. "Here I am, offered up once again as the prize."

"You'll be a minor trophy once Krüger is in custody."

"If they get him," I said. "If he's in there."

"The odds are good. Hans identified that target originally because it had connections to Reinhardt. And you explained it well. He's exhausted his other options, pursuing me. We know his plan, his destination, everything. He's in a box, no way out."

"And waiting for you to come." I rubbed my hand over my scalp. "He wants that. He hopes you'll turn up for the final showdown."

"I would. But I'm in no shape for hand-to-hand combat." He reached across the table.

I put my hands in my lap. I'd loved Stefan for a dozen years. Yet he'd kept crucial information secret from me. I'd paid dearly for my ignorance. Nothing would be right between us until I understood why he'd done that. Why he'd trusted me so little.

His hand lay between us on the table, the gauze on his wrist white against the browned skin.

I ignored it.

He said, "You think I should have told you about Reinhardt?"

"Hell, yes. Everything, right from the start."

He drew his hand back and reached for his cigarettes. "If you'd known he'd been in the Stasi, that he'd suddenly come back to life—what would you have done?"

"Were you afraid I'd stop sleeping with you? You think the

FBI would've liked me better if you were my *former* lover?"

"You think I feared you'd kick me out of your bed? Far easier to live with that than what has happened now. I knew that when you learned the truth, you would end up where you are now. Caught in one scheme after another to capture Reinhardt."

"That's the choice I wanted," I said. "Before he did this to you and to me. You shouldn't have kept it to yourself. Shouldn't have tried to do it alone. Leaving me to sit on the sidelines of your war. Bearing the consequences. But with no way to alter them."

He clicked the lighter, but didn't put the flame to his cigarette. "Reinhardt should hear us now. He would be proud of what he has achieved."

hen Holger was back. "The Germans will move immediately," he said. "GSG-9 will have that building surrounded by
eleven." He answered my unspoken question. "Your surrender
is set for eight o'clock tomorrow morning at police headquarters."

"Good," I said, standing. "Are you ready?" I asked van
Hoof.

"All set," he said.

"You can't go there," Holger said.

My down jacket was on top of my pile of clothes. I pulled
it on and grabbed a set of keys from the counter. "Unit Nine is
famous for catching terrorists. But not for bringing them in
alive." The only drawback to using GSG-9 was their preference
for summary execution. I added, "I'm not going to carry a gun
and join the assault group. But I have to be there. I have to
make sure Reinhardt Krüger stays alive long enough to give us
that information."

"And I will not allow her to do this without me," van Hoof
said. "Krüger has taken too much. Each time I think I have
nothing more to lose, he surprises me."

Erika. I felt an answering pang.

He cleared his throat. "I have to see this through."

"I need you there," I told him. "But I'm running the show."

"Fine," he said. "You lead. But let's do it. We're taking the Jetta?"

I tossed him the keys. He picked up a loaded knapsack.

Stefan turned his head, and I saw something pass between him and Holger. Then Holger said, "I will also go."

"Why not?" Van Hoof spoke from the doorway, his voice rough. "But remember, she's in charge." He knew as well as I did why Holger was tagging along. The Father-Major didn't trust him. Neither did I. The man was a wild card. But I needed his expertise.

When he opened the door, I saw the white van pull up outside. Good. Our sentries were back on duty. For a second I thought again of Erika. I swallowed hard, crossed the room to stand in the doorway to my father's cubicle. Bert had his back to me, counting out his score. Intent on Bert's hands, my father bent over the cribbage board. He didn't look up. The hair on the crown of his head was rumpled, sticking out at an angle. I yearned to move closer, smooth that cowlick down. Instead, I stepped quietly away from the door and headed after van Hoof.

Stefan blocked my path. "Casey . . ."

"You surprise me," I said. "I thought you'd try to stop me from going to that building."

"Since I cannot go, you must. If Reinhardt is there, if he's expecting me, then you may be able to take advantage of that expectation. In a way that GSG-9 cannot." He waited a beat, then said, "Be careful."

"If anything happens . . ." I couldn't finish the sentence. I swallowed. "You'll look after my father?"

"Of course." He touched my shoulder with his fingertips. "Go now. Nothing remains secret in Berlin. Not for an hour."

Intelligence leaks. In this once-divided country, Germans formed and re-formed their alliances as smoothly as shapeshifters.

I looked into his hazel eyes then, saw the struggle going on inside him. I said, "Don't worry about me." Might as well have added, Don't love me, don't care, don't stand in the center of my life, blocking my way. Let me go on alone to do what I have to do.

He gave me the steady scrutiny that meant he was reading my mind. "A good commander doesn't give an order he cannot enforce." And then he stepped aside.

"Come on," I said to Holger. "We have to be in place before GSG-9 arrives." I didn't look back.

Outside, van Hoof stood next to the Jetta. He held up the car keys. "I know the route."

"You navigate then." I took the keys and motioned him into the passenger's seat. I wanted to drive. I wanted to feel that I was in control of something. Even if it was only the speed at which I traveled.

The steering wheel was icy beneath my fingers. The chill air racheted my tense muscles tighter, and my wounded leg throbbed, a dull ache I couldn't ignore. I forced myself upright, as if my father were there, reminding me not to crouch over the wheel. The defroster was useless with three of us in the car. Van Hoof wiped steam from the glass as he described the situation we'd be facing. He was breathing through his mouth, and whiskey fumes floated above the odor of sweat, generated not from heat but from fear. My fear, most of all. The prospect of facing Krüger again terrified me. I wanted to leave his capture to people trained to execute it. But too much hung in the balance. I couldn't stand back, risk the wrong outcome.

"What you want," said van Hoof, "is to make sure he doesn't get out of there before the assault."

"You are only to observe the GSG-9 action." Holger spoke from the rear seat, his voice disembodied. "He's supposed to be lying low. Why would he suddenly take off in the next few minutes?"

The hairs on the back of my neck prickled. Anything that can go wrong will go wrong. Krüger escaping, oh-so-wrong. I said, "We can't afford to take that chance."

Van Hoof broke in, explaining. The Libyans were located off Stresemannstrasse, four hundred meters west of the site of the immense new Checkpoint Charlie Business Center, in a converted warehouse. There were only three ways by which Krüger could exit the building.

I made the assignments. Holger would cover the roof, van Hoof the rear exit. I'd watch the front door.

Van Hoof shook his head. "The roof is tricky. I've been up on the adjacent building to check it out. Makes more sense if I take the roof."

"I don't like it," Holger said.

Van Hoof twisted in his seat. "You have a better idea?"

"Stay together, maximize our strength." He wanted to keep van Hoof on a short leash.

"Sure," van Hoof said. "All of us on the roof, we see Krüger skip out the back. Before one of us reaches the street, he's disappeared." He grunted. "You know we have to split up."

"No argument from me," I said. "You take the roof, then, like you said."

"If he comes your way," van Hoof said to me, "don't try to stop him. You can't do it alone. And you don't want to drive him back inside. Use the walkie-talkie to signal us. We three can converge on him and hold him for GSG-9. If that doesn't work, at least we'll be able to point them in the right direction."

"Sounds good." I was lying. It was no plan at all. But I went along with him, to keep him going along with me. The two of us united, dragging Holger into action.

The Father-Major's disapproval hung behind me like a dark cloud as I drove. Van Hoof had me bypass the downtown and got me onto Potsdamer Strasse, headed north toward the Tiergarten.

I parked the car on a side street and van Hoof led us on foot to within a block of the Libyan building. Leaving Holger to cover us, van Hoof guided me to the nearest intersection. We synchronized watches—10:38—and I repeated the code we'd agreed upon. Then I slipped around the corner and into a recessed doorway. Across the street and twenty-five yards to my right was the front entrance to the building where I prayed GSG-9 would capture Reinhardt Krüger alive.

The cobblestones were wet-looking under the sallow streetlights. A foot above the door I was watching, a bare bulb shone from under a pie-plate shade. No other lamps were visible elsewhere on the block of two- and three-story buildings.

My fingers found the walkie-talkie in my jacket pocket. I glanced down to check that the light was glowing red. The door behind me was topped by a square of glass, faintly illuminated by a low-wattage bulb in the room beyond it. By its light I saw a cramped aisle stretching out in a straight line. Racked magazines lined the left side. A counter sat on the right, behind which was a wall of shelves filled with containers. I smelled cherry-flavored pipe tobacco, and beneath it, the harsher odor of unblended Latakia.

I turned my wrist to see the luminous dial of my watch. Ten-forty. Only twenty more minutes. What if Krüger weren't in there after all? Then sometime after midnight, twelve bombs would go off. And I'd go to jail. Would anyone listen while I tried to explain how hard I'd worked to disarm those bombs? And what would become of my father?

Second thoughts. None of them any help to me now. Krüger had to be in there. And he wasn't going to escape. Not this time.

Tires hissed on pavement. An engine rumbled closer. I crouched and pressed against the door.

A Mercedes slid past on the cross street. The rooftop "Taxi" marker was unlit. So were the headlights. Inside, the dashboard lamp cast a greenish glow on Hilly-Anne's chin. Danièle looked directly at me, but if she saw me huddled there, she gave no sign.

Part of van Hoof's *other* plan. While I'd been talking with Stefan, he'd arranged something with the girl gang. In another five minutes they'd be up on that roof with him. And then what? I checked my watch again. Ten forty-two.

The light above the entrance to the Libyan building went out. Then the door swung open. A cigarette glowed in the gap. The red coal sailed through the air, landing in the street with a shower of sparks. A man emerged, stood on the threshold. He was immobile for at least thirty seconds. Then he stepped back inside.

I heard the jingle of fine chain. A snuffling sound. The click of toenails on cement. A dog skittered outside, strained against the leash, then squatted at the edge of the sidewalk. A female German shepherd.

A bundled figure followed the dog outside. The door slammed shut. The dog pulled against the leash, dragging her companion in my direction. I crouched down again, trying to blend with the wood in the lower half of the door. The man holding the leash yanked it sharply. He said something harsh in German. I didn't need to understand the words. I knew their meaning from the tone. *Do what I say, bitch. Your life is in my hands.*

The blood in my veins seemed to lose its heat, turn to ice, stop moving. The chill paralyzed me.

Krüger. Departing seventeen minutes before the scheduled raid.

Someone had warned him. Nothing else would have brought him out in public. Strolling toward the Tiergarten, like any late-night dog-walker. Good cover. Not likely GSG-9 had cordoned off the area yet. And if the commandos were nearby, they wouldn't expose their position. Not to confront a civilian moving providentially out of the line of fire.

Krüger was about to disappear.

My thumb found the push-to-talk button on the walkie-talkie. All I had to do was click three times to alert van Hoof and the Father-Major. Three clicks would tell them that I'd spotted Krüger. Tell them to come to me. But before I could depress the button, a muffled boom sounded from inside the former warehouse. I heard the thumping blast, then the shatter of glass as the force blew the skylights upward from the roof.

The assault. But it was too early for GSG-9! And I knew Teutonic precision. They'd never have jumped the gun.

Another grenade exploded. An attack, for sure. Van Hoof and his team, going in from the roof. Right now, on their own, a kamikaze action. He didn't believe Krüger was in there. But he hadn't voiced his doubt. Agreed instead with everything I'd said. Used me to reach his own savage goal.

The dog moaned, a piercing whimper of distress. She pressed her body against the sidewalk. Krüger yanked at the leash, cursing. He got her moving again toward the corner, faster after they turned right, the two of them hurrying away from me.

Automatic weapons rattled inside the building. I smelled tear gas. I shoved in the button and put my lips against the walkie-talkie. "Holger," I said. "Krüger's on foot, headed your way. You can cut him off." I released the button.

Holger's voice. "Pinned down." The crackle of static. Then nothing.

Helpless, I watched Krüger's back vanish into the night.

29

The front door of the Libyan building flew open. A hunched figure staggered out, hands to his face, fighting the gas.

A siren wailed in the distance. The German cops coming in loud.

I bent low and ran across the intersection. Behind me came the sounds of small-arms fire, screams, explosions. I smelled gunpowder and my eyes smarted.

But nobody tried to stop me. I jogged along the empty street. It narrowed to an alleyway. I stopped to listen. All I heard was a distant siren. A few blocks to my left was the Landwehrkanal. If I continued straight, I'd come to Potsdamer Strasse. A right turn there would lead back into the Tiergarten. A man with a dog—what could be a more reasonable destination than a large urban forest? I started running.

The maze of streets and alleys dumped me out near Potsdamer Platz, construction booming where the Wall had once stood. Building cranes spiked above half-finished structures, the security lights reflecting off the cloud cover to illuminate the uninhabitable skeletons. The scene had an eerie brightness, as if the East Berlin border guards had left their searchlights behind to shine on this prime real estate, created from the former no-man's-land. Night-owl tourists clustered outside the entrance to the Info-Box, a three-decker red cube perched on stilts to offer a panoramic view of the chaos in front of me.

I looked around frantically. But for what? Not a policeman. I couldn't ask for help from a German cop. Language was my enemy now; I was a wanted woman. I longed for the cell phone I'd abandoned in D.C. I could call Stefan, have him tell the cops where to find Krüger. I felt in my pockets for a coin while I searched the area for a pay phone.

At that moment I spotted him. The dog was sniffing at something on the sidewalk a half block away. Krüger yanked at the leash again. He pulled the dog around the cluster of people and into the crosswalk, headed again toward the forest.

My breath burned in my throat. I had to keep moving. I couldn't stop to summon help. I had to know where Krüger was going.

We were northbound again. Tangled branches wove a frieze, guarding the approach to the Brandenburg Gate like the briars outside Sleeping Beauty's castle. I saw the soot-stained Doric columns, topped by the ubiquitous construction cranes. A lone biker pumped through the open gate, his knapsack bouncing against his back. Beyond that intersection was another dark patch of woods. I stopped where the treeline gave way to the Platz der Republik. A hundred feet from me, Krüger and his dog made a right turn, heading toward the deserted Reichstag building, waiting still for the leisurely parliamentary transfer from Bonn.

I stood there, struggling to get enough oxygen. Krüger and his dog hadn't gone into the Tiergarten after all. Instead, they were crossing the stony desert in front of the parliament building. As I watched, they turned the far corner, out of sight.

Behind the Reichstag building was a stunted finger of land formed by a sweeping bend in the Spree. Krüger had gone out onto that peninsula, a place from which he couldn't exit without me seeing him.

I pulled out my walkie-talkie and called Holger. I turned up the volume knob to full strength. But all I picked up was static. Nothing identifiable as words. I sent my message anyway. *Krüger's at Platz der Republik. Come and get him.*

As I worked the radio, I kept watch in the direction that Krüger had taken. A bird rose from the building's facade and headed toward me. Directly above, it hovered for a moment, wings beating rapidly, head turned into the breeze coming off the river. Then it shot away, a kestrel falcon searching for easier prey. Nothing else moved. All I saw under the yellow glow of the security lights was the Reichstag.

And all I heard was the distant sound of revelry. Somewhere far away, someone playing an accordion. Oompah music.

The sound made me think of Antwerp. The harbor cruise. The boat.

And then I got it. This section of the Spree had once been part of the East-West boundary. But now it was an open waterway and an escape route for Krüger. I'd underestimated his ability to make things happen. He'd had a fallback plan. He'd gotten word that GSG-9 was moving in and he'd put his plan into motion. How much time did I have to stop him?

Maybe he was gone.

Forget caution. I burst out of the woods and cut diagonally across the deserted space toward the far corner of the Reichstag building. The wound on my leg opened, an angry throb as blood soaked through the covering pad. I ignored the pain, straining hard, pushing to get around the Reichstag to the brink of the riverbank.

Where I found Reinhardt Krüger and his dog, standing together on a struggling patch of grass.

"I was hoping one of you would show up to wish me farewell," he said.

No lucky pursuit after all. The man had laid a trail for me. One I'd followed eagerly, as he'd known I would. I toughened my voice. "I have no intention of telling you good-bye. The police are on their way. Your best bet is to surrender at once."

"I'll be long gone before you can summon any police to this location." He moved his right hand so that I could see the pistol in it. "And surrendering to you doesn't suit me at all."

The dog whined and rubbed her body against his leg.

Krüger said, "But if you are not so eager to part company with me, perhaps we can find a mutually agreeable way to extend our time together."

"You've got to call off your goons." My voice was too high, too much like begging. I sucked in more air. "I know they're going to blow up twelve planes. You stop them, you'll have a much brighter future."

"I have no future with your people." He chuckled, an ugly, mirthless sound. "And after tomorrow, neither will you. Nor my little brother."

I felt as though a hand was squeezing my heart. "Any evidence implicating me and Stefan in those bombings—they'll know you planted it."

He checked his watch. "I doubt that by this time tomorrow, anyone will be so exacting about proof."

He was betting on a lynch-mob reaction. A safe bet.

He bent over and patted the dog on her snout. "Don't you think my Blondie looks like her namesake?"

He was crazy. A match for Hitler, the master of that other Blondie. "Are you going to do what he did?" I couldn't keep the bitterness out of my voice. "Test your poison on your dog first?"

"I'm not going to the grave, as he was. And I'm not a monster who'd destroy a fine animal." He patted the dog again. "No, Blondie is my most faithful ally, the only one I trust." He glanced toward the river.

I saw no other people, only the unreal yellow glow from the Reichstag's security lights. Krüger stood between two white crosses, memorials to those who'd attempted the river crossing from East Berlin during the Cold War—and hadn't made it. I moved my foot, trying to figure out how to spring.

He gestured toward the Spree. "My boat will be here soon. Within the hour I'll be en route to Tripoli. But I have a problem. Help me solve it, and I'll give you six of the flight numbers you claim you want."

Six out of twelve. A chance to save a half-dozen planeloads of people. Wouldn't come cheaply. Wary, I asked, "Your price?"

"My friends in Libya will be unhappy about the loss of their comrades this evening. But if I bring them the one responsible . . ."

The weight of his offer was crushing. "You need a scapegoat."

"Your presence would save me some personal unpleasantness. And I'm certain that with you there, eventually my brother will show up, too. Worth halving the effort I'd planned for tomorrow." Krüger glanced at his watch. "In less than one hour, the first bomb will explode. We can send the message that will stop that one. And the next five."

"What, you think I'd deal twice with a liar like you?"

"If you want what I'm offering badly enough," he said. "And you might consider this: I will benefit if it becomes known you arranged such a compassionate reprieve. In the short term, it will make you more useful to us."

Holger had argued that Krüger wanted to exploit my knowledge and connections on behalf of Libya. If the targeted planes were grounded before the bombs killed anyone, it would look as if I had influence over Qadhafi. That would make me a more effective negotiator. The international press would get no hint that I was Krüger's prisoner. "An illusion," I said. "As you said, useful only in the short term."

He shrugged. "Eventually you'll be punished for your crimes against the Muslim world."

My death was the only guaranteed outcome. He could be lying about everything else. But if he wasn't? Offering me a chance to trade my one life for hundreds of others. Surprising, how often people ponder how they'd handle such a choice. What do you do? they ask one another. Wondering, What would *I* do?

"I'll go with you," I said. Telling myself I wasn't all that noble. If I could get six flight numbers, maybe I could get six more. And get away. If I didn't, Stefan would come. Save us both. Not letting myself think about how unlikely all the happy outcomes were.

From the direction of the river I heard the faint drone of an inboard engine, coming closer. Krüger jammed the pistol into his belt. Then he wrapped the dog's chain around his forearm, shortening the leash so that the dog could move only a few feet out in front of him. "Go on," he said to me.

Stiff-legged, I took a step toward the riverbank. And then another. The dog came up beside me, on my left, panting as she tugged forward. Krüger followed, directly behind me.

The channel was lined with cut stones, each maybe two feet square, sloping steeply downward at a seventy-five-degree angle toward the flat water. The vessel I'd heard was now floating only an arm's length from the rocks, a powerboat like those used to patrol the river in the old days. We'd have to slide down the damp stones, splash across the last few feet to the bow, clamber on board.

Then I saw the stumpy man at the wheel in the open cockpit, his face hidden as he held the boat steady, nose pointed toward us. Standing beside him was a tall blond woman, her braided hair twisted into a crown on top of her head. Her legs wide, her rifle carefully positioned in the portside gun mounting.

The barrel swung a few inches. She sighted directly at my chest.

I was blocking Krüger's view. And Brunhild's shot.

"Down," I shouted at Krüger.

Startled, the dog leaped forward. I plunged to my right, dropping out of the line of fire. I went down with my arms flailing, grabbing at Krüger, trying to pull him with me.

I couldn't let the Israelis kill him. Not now, when I was so close to getting at least half of the lifesaving information.

I caught a handful of pant leg. He jerked back, then kicked out. The toe of his boot crashed against my skull. I sprawled on top of Blondie.

The rifle cracked three times.

Blondie howled again. I felt liquid warmth spreading over my leg. The dog was whining through her nose. I thought at first she must have been shot. I smelled urine. I started to roll off her. She slid toward the edge of the embankment, dragged there by the leash. Her toenails scraped against the stones. I grasped her leather collar. The chain extended from it, pulled taut over the edge. Krüger had disappeared.

The dog made a harsh, choking noise. I grabbed at the chain to relieve the pressure on her windpipe, then peered over the edge.

Krüger was sprawled on the rock face, legs moving jerkily as he struggled for a foothold. Only the dog's leash kept him from sliding down into the murky water. The chain was tight around his left forearm.

"Help me," he said, extending his right hand. His glasses had vanished and his face was twisted with effort, the flesh tight over the bones. In that moment he looked exactly like Stefan.

I had no thought of saving anyone but Krüger. Not myself. Not the innocent victims of his terror. Only him. Brother of the man I would never stop loving.

Flat on my belly, holding the chain in my left hand, I reached down with my right to grab his wrist.

The rifle cracked a fourth time. The dog howled, shoved her nose into my ribs.

Krüger's face contorted in the rictus of death. A taunting, evil grin. Then his fingers relaxed. The metal links jingled as they uncoiled from around his forearm. The chain came free. And his body slid silently over the stones and into the black water below.

The motor roared. The boat flashed up the river, a spray of water fanning out behind. The dog whined. Where Krüger had slipped beneath the surface, I saw only a ripple of wake from the departing boat.

Blondie whimpered, tried to shove herself deeper beneath me. I sat up, let her climb into my lap. I stroked her head. "Okay, girl," I said. But it wasn't. Krüger gone. And with him, our last hope of finding those bombs.

A van pulled up on the far side of the Platz. A squad of commandos dressed in black fanned out from it, setting up a perimeter. Not so foolhardy they'd run toward an international criminal cradling a vicious dog.

Didn't know it was only me, Casey, unarmed and exhausted, sick with the grief of failure. And Blondie, the guard dog who peed herself when she heard gunfire. What a pair.

A figure separated from the others. A very tall man, coming toward me. Hobbling along with a stick. I got to my knees. My vision blurred. Blondie licked my ear and the wave of dizziness passed. I dragged myself upright, the leash wrapped around my hand, and watched Stefan approach.

Then he stood before me, face drawn by pain.

Blondie strained against the leash, growling. Tough girl when she faced a wounded man. I pulled her close. "How'd you get here?" I asked Stefan.

"Got the doctor to bring me as far as the Libyan hideout," he said. "He's there now with Hilly-Anne. Danièle is okay."

"Van Hoof?"

"On his way to the hospital. Probably lose an arm. Claims he took out ten Libyans. Number seems low, given all the bodies." He sighed. "Did you kill Reinhardt?"

"I couldn't have," I said, realizing the truth for the first time. "I wanted him to die. But I couldn't kill him. Your brother." I reached out to touch his face. "The Israelis did it. Came in place of whoever he'd called to rescue him."

"Someone sold him out." Stefan was silent for a moment. Then he said, "He didn't tell you which planes?"

"No." The single syllable was as bleak as my future. My head throbbed. I was dizzy again. I swayed toward Stefan.

He ignored the dog, wrapped his free arm around me. He pressed his cheek against the top of my head. And in that moment of warmth and compassion, I forgave him everything. How could he have acted differently with Reinhardt Krüger for a brother?

Blood ties bind like no others.

The dog moaned. I slackened my hold on the leash and rubbed her neck. Had to hurt, there beneath the cruelly tight leather strap. Blondie. The only thing I'd gotten from Krüger. His ally, the only one he'd trusted with his secrets.

"Here they come," Stefan said.

Four men crossed the pavement toward us. German law enforcement, coming to take me to prison. Blondie saw them, too. She whimpered. I ran a finger under her collar. A special handmade affair. Different from the utilitarian choke chain I'd seen hanging outside Krüger's cabin door the first time we'd met. No, this was special-made. Special purpose. Very special indeed, I realized.

Carefully, I bent down and unbuckled it.

Four sets of black boots surrounded us. Blondie tried to crawl under me. With the fingers of my left hand I gripped the folds of loose fur on her neck. I had the collar in my right. I stood up too fast.

"Here's the answer." I shoved the leather strap toward the husky German closest to me. His edges started to blur and I hurried to say what I had to. "The flight numbers. On the back side. Burned in."

That was all I managed before I passed out.

30

Harry waved a hand toward the wall of windows. Beyond them, a U.S. Air Force jet sat on the tarmac. "I did my part." He shook his head, gestured toward the dog beside me. "But you, Casey. *She's* what you meant by a high-ranking official from the former East Bloc?"

Blondie pressed tighter against my leg and moaned to signal how distressed she was by Harry's tone of voice.

"She can't fly commercial," I said. "Not caged up in a cargo bay all the way across the Atlantic. On a military flight, she can have her own seat up front."

"At least she's a *German* shepherd." Harry stretched a hand toward Blondie's hindquarters and began rubbing her haunch. She twitched, but stood still for it. He added, "You'll have to teach her English if you're going to keep her."

"I'm keeping her," I said. "We've bonded. You know my weakness for good-looking refugees from a former Socialist society."

Harry switched from rubbing to scratching and a rich, doggy odor filled the air between us, along with a rumble of canine pleasure. "I guess she deserves to go to the U.S. in style. Since she saved so many lives today."

"Is it over?"

"The FBI's coordinating most of the police work. I know

they picked up a guy at Heathrow trying to board a United flight to Frankfurt. Had a few unusual items sewn into his clothing. Think he planned to leave half his Semtex on that plane, then catch a TWA flight back to London and repeat the process. Both airliners were scheduled to go on to the U.S. He had timers set so that the bombs would explode over the Atlantic."

As Harry was finishing the sentence, Mike Buchanan joined us. He needed a shave. He and Harry had been airborne for an hour when they got the word about Krüger. They could have gone back to Andrews Air Force Base, but Buchanan chose instead to continue on to Templehof Airport. Holger Sorensen met them when they landed at six o'clock in the morning. By eight, when I showed up with my father and Blondie, no one from police headquarters was interested any longer in my surrender. And Harry was able to talk Buchanan into giving me and my entourage a ride home. Now, we were in a restricted access lounge at Templehof, waiting to board.

I said to Buchanan, "Krüger told me his first bomb would go off at midnight."

"So far, nothing's exploded. We're grounding all equipment scheduled for use on the listed flights. Checking out every square inch before we let them back into service. That should do it, knock on wood."

" 'Knock on wood'?" I repeated. "Efrem Zimbalist Junior never used that expression."

Buchanan said, "I'm counterintelligence, remember? I don't do terrorists."

"You aren't so hot on your traitors either." I lowered myself to Blondie's level. "Bite him," I ordered her.

She licked my face instead. I definitely had to work on her English.

"You've blown my efficiency report. Never figured you for the heroic type." Buchanan glowered. "But I don't advise giving your girlfriend the details."

"My girlfriend?"

"That Lurid woman, whatever she calls herself? Been trying to get in to talk to you for the last hour. Seems to think you're hot to give her an exclusive interview."

"Perfect," I said. "Let her sit there till she decomposes. Don't tell her a thing."

"Standard operating procedure. Time you learned that, Collins." His features slid into the customary smirk. "And you better do something about that hair. I hear the task force leadership doesn't care for the butch look."

My hand started toward my scalp. I stopped the self-conscious gesture. "You've got to get over this obsession with appearances," I told him. I stood then, checking around for Stefan. He and my father had gone outside to examine the *Luftbruckendenkmal*, the monument to the British and American airmen who had lost their lives in 1948 during the Berlin airlift.

Holger caught my eye from a corner of the lounge. He waved, beckoning me over. I handed Blondie's leash to Harry and went to join the Father-Major.

"I must tell you the good news about Hans," he said.

"They saved his arm?"

He shook his head, his expression momentarily somber. "That wasn't possible." Then he smiled. "His daughter made a sound."

"After all these years in a coma?"

"They've been trying to contact him since midnight. The message got routed to me an hour ago."

"Since midnight? Midnight was when she did this?"

"A few minutes before eleven o'clock, actually." His smile grew huge with satisfaction.

I couldn't keep the skepticism out of my voice. "She starts talking right when her father is doing his Angel of Death number?"

"Something of a coincidence." He took a breath and I knew what was coming.

"Don't," I said.

He ignored me. "In mysterious ways." Then his expression grew serious again. "I owe you an apology," he began.

"No," I said.

"I should have realized sooner that the Gorm information was no longer reliable."

"But you're not like that. Always expecting deception. Your faith in the rest of us is your greatest strength." I swallowed. "Erika knew that." We stood there together in a silent moment of requiem. For a half second I thought I smelled the lemony scent of her shampoo.

I rubbed my hand over my too-short hair. At least it was mostly blond again. "She say anything intelligible? Van Hoof's daughter?"

"She said, '*Saka-saka*.' "

"Guess we can't expect miracles."

"Ah, you weren't aware that the girl was born in the Congo." He grinned. "Hans and Bert are quite excited. Seems one of her first phrases when she was learning to talk was *saka-saka*. Means 'manioc leaves,' or something like that. Vegetable you steam like spinach, Bert says. Supposed to be served with those overspiced African stews."

Saka-saka. Pili-pili. My mouth remembered the latter's fiery power. I glanced around. "Bert couldn't make it?"

Holger shook his head. "Didn't want to leave Hans alone. But if you ever get back to Belgium, he says you should stop in for a beer. Or six."

Bert. No better than I was at saying good-bye. I'd miss him. And his cooking. I remembered my friendless arrival in Antwerp and the comforting warmth of his *waterzooi*. I felt a pang that wasn't hunger.

Harry broke in. "We're boarding in another five minutes."

I looked over the room but I didn't spot my father. "I better round up my dad."

"And Stefan," Harry said. "He *is* coming with you?"

"With me," Holger said. Someone behind me asked him a question in German and he stepped away to answer it.

"Stefan'll go to Denmark first," I told Harry. "He'll visit me after he has knee surgery."

"Surgery?" Harry echoed. "His injury's that serious, he'll have to look for another line of work. I take it he'll be moving in with you?"

A month ago, I'd have jubilantly said you bet! I'd forgiven Stefan for not telling me about his half brother, but I realized now that he had other secrets. Love-blind, I'd let myself forget that all spies are sullied by the dirty work that they do. Stefan had been reinventing himself for twenty years, counterfeiting his identity, working his sleight of hand. His reticence was incurable. Could I live with a man who hid so much of himself from me?

"I don't know how it'll work out," I answered Harry. "He and I have to talk."

Harry snickered. "I can just see the pair of you, *really talking* about your relationship." He stressed the two words as if they were in quotes.

"We talk," I protested.

"All the time, I bet," he said derisively. "Probably can't shut him up long enough to get your two cents in."

"Bite him, too," I said to Blondie. I spotted my father then with Stefan at his side. The two of them crossed the lounge to us.

Harry shook Stefan's hand, then my father's. "Mr. Collins," he said. "Casey was telling me you flew SB-D's in World War Two."

"Show-off," I muttered. I'd told him my father'd flown for the Navy in the Pacific theater. Harry, my pal in intelligence, had identified the type of aircraft all on his own.

"You interested in flying?" my father asked him.

Harry winked at me, then put his free hand on my father's

elbow. "Come over and look at the bird that'll be taking us home."

"Like to fly, do you?" my father said as they moved toward the windows, Blondie in the lead.

Harry grunted.

"Me and another old codger have our own plane. Not too new, mind you, but it flies. You come on out to Oregon, I'll take you up."

I heard Harry say, "That'd be great."

I turned to Stefan. "Did he offer to take you up, too?" When he nodded, I sighed. "I'll have to get his license revoked. He's going to hate me."

"We'll work it out," Stefan said.

I tilted my head to look at him. Unshaven. Unwashed. Unmatched. The room suddenly seemed full of people I loved. Plus a dog. And at least one ghost.

"You think you'll be able to join me soon?"

He smiled. "In a month or so, if all goes as Holger predicts." He pulled me close.

My chest pressed against his. I smelled French tobacco and the musky odor of his sweat. He had secrets, yes. But he loved me. I knew that in my bones. We *would* talk, I vowed. We'd work it out.

His cheek was rough against mine as he put his mouth near my ear. "This hairstyle is extremely attractive," he murmured. "*Bardzo ladna.*" Very pretty, in Polish.

I pulled away so I could study his expression. The hazel eyes glowed with sincerity. And something else.

"You like it this short?" I asked.

"*Oczywiscie!*" Absolutely. "It gives me many intriguing ideas." His breath tickled my ear, sending a zing of pleasure south.

"Tell me about them."

"*Pózniej,*" he whispered. The Slavic pronunciation slurred

the word, elongating it into a promise that was erotic and unconditional.

"Later," I agreed. And heard the answering promise in my own voice.